WITHOUT A SOUL TO MOVE

Without a Soul to Move
William Dewey

Lawrence and Gibson

LAWRENCE AND GIBSON
Brougham Street
Wellington
New Zealand
http://www.lawrenceandgibson.com

ISBN 978-0-473-13451-8

Cover photo by Jennifer Callaway

for my father

1. HOWARD CRANE PICKS UP THE PHONE

In the last days of a Denver winter in 2003, when snow still fell and the nation was contemplating a new war, a man named Howie walked into a book store to use the courtesy phone. He took off his white tent-shaped hat and set it down on the counter, and with trembling fingers he dialed the first number. His sister answered on the fifth ring. She sounded sleepy.

But this is not just about Howie.

In that same city in the same era, there were undoubtedly thousands struggling through some sort of sorrows. Among the most public of those struggles was Adam Lister's, the details of which were chronicled in Denver's weekly independent newspaper, the *Westword*. Much of what follows was gleaned from that story, and from the Denver Post article that preceded it. What is significant is that Adam was bereaved, as Howie was heartbroken.

The third figure that interests me is a nearly anonymous figure named Wayne Talbot, who was then new to the city. While not quite in the same circle of friends as Howie and Adam, he was not entirely unknown to them, having been present at several of the same parties as they, but always on the periphery. Wayne thought of himself as invisible, or, more precisely, imperceptible: not just incapable of being seen, but of being heard, felt, or even smelled. He wondered what his existence meant to the people he was interacting with, and wondered whether he would be missed if he was gone. In the process of healing, Wayne's path would eventually cross Adam's and Howie's.

In the meantime, Howie was still standing in a quiet book store ten minutes before closing, holding a phone in his quivering hand. He had to say something.

"Susan, this is Howie. Listen, I'm calling from a courtesy phone, so I'll have to keep this short. I just wanted to let everyone know that I'm all right."

"Jesus, Howie. Where are you?"

"I'm okay. I'm at the book store. I'm working again now. I got a job today."

"You're working at a book store?"

"No, I'm not working at a book store. Listen, I'm just using the courtesy phone here. I got a job at Johnny Rockets. It's a hamburger place across the street."

"A hamburg—"

"Don't worry. It's not like McDonald's or anything like that. I get to sing and dance."

"Jesus, Howie," his sister said.

Howie was a small man whose body was taking its first wobbling steps toward middle-age; his thick, sandy hair was flecked with gray, and the flesh around his eyes was creased. That night he was still in the uniform he wore to work, white cotton pants and shirt like a 50's soda jerk, with a tent-shaped hat to match. When his sister said his name, he picked his hat up from the counter and twisted it in his hands. He balanced the phone on his shoulder.

"Howie," his sister repeated. "It's late. Can we call you back in the morning?"

He looked around the book store, then at the wooden post in front of him. "I can't give you my home phone number now," he said. "I'll call again in a couple of days. Listen, now that I'm off the clock, I can tell you, Steve Biggs is the biggest a-hole in the world. If it hadn't been for him, I never would have had to..." Howie groaned. "He just said some things that...ahhh. I just—"

"I know, Howie."

"Anyway, I don't want to talk about that right now. I'll call back in a couple of days. For now, I just wanted to let everyone know that I'm okay."

"Okay."

Howie listened to his sister breathe.

"You going to be okay, Howie?"

"Yeah," he said. "I'll be okay. I'll call again in a couple of days."

Howie hung up the phone and unfurled his hat. It stayed wrinkled. He set it back on his head and walked away from the phone. Then he stopped, turned, and went back. He smoothed out the hat as best he could, set it next to the phone, and picked up the handset. Without quite understanding that he had dialed her number, he heard Adrienne's voice.

"Um, hello Adrienne," he said.

When she had answered the phone, she had sounded tired, but after hearing his voice, she shouted his name. "Howie!"

He gripped the handset and closed his eyes.

"Where are you?"

"Adrienne, listen," he said, but after that his voice stumbled. He sobbed and said her name again.

"Howie." Her soft voice hinted at concern, as from a troubled mother.

"I wanted to call to let everyone know that I'm okay," Howie said, crying. "I'm working again. I got a job at Johnny Rockets."

"Johnny Rockets? The diner place?"

"I'll call again soon to give you my home number. I need to go now, okay?"

"Howie," she said, and he leaned against the wooden post, waiting. After a moment, in a soft voice, she said, "Take care of yourself."

He nodded, and he hung up the phone before he remembered that she couldn't see him. His eyes were filling with tears and he tried to soak them up with the corners of his hat. The book store was busy, but even busy it didn't get much louder than a birthday party at a library. Howie left through one of the front doors, and outside he turned left and walked in the door just a few feet down, right back into

the book store. He balanced the hat on his head and walked back to the phone. He dialed Steve Biggs' number. After several rings, somebody said, in a sleepy voice,
"Hello?"

"Fuck you!" Howie yelled, and he slammed down the handset on the receiver hard as he could without damaging it.

2. WAYNE TALBOT SENDS A LETTER

To understand these men—Howie, Wayne, and Adam—it is important to consider how they were seen by those whose lives intersected theirs. Wayne's case, in particular, was linked almost inextricably to the life of another, a man named Burke. That winter Burke was about twenty-two or twenty-three, separated by only a few years from his time as a high school wrestler, a pastime he had embraced by the end less than half-heartedly, but which had left him with a solid build and an industrious metabolism, such that his frequent and impassioned nights of alcohol abuse left little trace on his body. His slate-colored eyes were still bright, the skin still tight around his face. When not otherwise occupied, his mouth tended to revert to an easy smile, and his shaggy hair hung over his face with the same sort of languor that characterized his speech.

On the night that Howie was making his phone calls, Burke was coming home from his own uninspiring job, and before going up to his apartment, he stopped in the lobby to check his mail. The first two pieces in his box were for the previous tenant, the third was a coupon book addressed to *Resident*, the fourth had his name spelled wrong, and the fifth was his cellular phone bill. Once inside his apartment, he threw the coupons away with the ex-tenant's mail, tossed the bill onto his coffee table, and took a second look at the envelope that had *Burk Russo* hand-written on the front. There was no return address, and the postmark was local. He stuck his finger beneath the flap and tore open the edge of the envelope. Inside were two pieces of college-ruled notebook paper with the tattered left-hand borders of a spiral binding. Burke picked the tatters off as he read.

"Dear Burk," the letter began. He didn't recognize the handwriting, and he couldn't imagine anyone in Denver who would send him a letter. He turned to the bottom sheet and tried to decipher the signature. The last name might have been Talbot, but Burke didn't think he knew anybody with the last name Talbot.

He needed something to eat. He set the letter down on the table and went into his kitchen. The fridge was bare save for an empty cardboard case that had once held a six-pack of Sunshine Wheat, and all that was left in the freezer were a few burritos and a bag of chicken breasts that had been glued together with ice. While he unwrapped the burrito and put it on a paper towel, he kept saying the name "Talbot," trying to pair it with a name that might resemble the tight scrawl of the first half of the signature. "Talbot, Talbot, Talbot," he said, like a mantra, and after putting the burrito in the microwave, he returned to the table and looked again at the signature. *Vaughn,* he wondered. *Vaughn Talbot? Or is that an R?* The rest of the letter was written in neat, precise letters. He scanned it for a clue.

Halfway into the second paragraph, a series of staccato beeps from the kitchen announced the end of the cooking process. Burke ignored them. He set the first page down and said, "Jesus Christ," and he kept reading. By the time he finished the second page, his appetite had dwindled, and his apartment seemed suddenly dark. He leaned over and turned on the lamp at the end of his couch. That he was still not sure of the author's identity even after finishing a letter so laden with personal sentiments bothered him some, but surely somebody as close to him as the letter suggested would have known how to spell his name correctly.

It almost felt like a joke. There was a sincerity in the words he had just read that could not be feigned by anybody he knew; but neither could he imagine anybody who would write them to him honestly.

"Talbot," he said again, and a vision came to him of a little yellow sticker on the back of a *Wired* magazine. He had woken up at seven o' clock in the morning still slightly drunk at an unfamiliar place, on a short unfamiliar couch beneath a blanket that smelled of stale farts, and since his senses had been so obliterated the night before, they took everything in with a renewed diligence now. He had stood up from the couch, swayed and moaned, then wandered into the light cast by the high windows near the kitchen. On a table near the couch was a stack of mail. Burke remembered looking at the *Wired* magazine, reading its address label, and thinking, "Oh. So that's Wayne's last name. Talbot," then asking himself, "What the hell am I doing at Wayne's?"

And as far as Burke could recall, that was the last he had seen of Wayne Talbot. He leaned forward on his own couch now and reread the signature on the second sheet of notebook paper. It certainly could belong to Wayne, and the content of the letter seemed to corroborate Burke's earlier impressions of the guy. "God damn," he said.

3. Adam Lister orders a drink

Burke's girlfriend, Abby, was working that night at a bar on Thirteenth Street called Gabor's, and about three hours into her shift, Adam Lister came through the door and sat down at one of the long burgundy booths in the corner. He was a tall, slim man, but as he was sitting now, slumped over the table, he looked slight, ready to crumble into dust. Beneath the creases and furrows of his face, he might have been attractive, but his evident anguish rendered any affection on Abby's part more maternal than amorous.

She did her best to bring a smile to her face that was warm without being condescending, and she walked to Adam's table and said, "Hey there."

Adam looked up, his eyes haunted and his mouth slack. If he recognized her, he gave no indication. "I'm just going to have a glass of Glenmorangie, neat. And could I get a glass of ice water, too?"

Abby hesitated, wanted to say something, but could only nod. She walked back to the bar and gave Adam's order to Shelley. Shelley looked over Abby's shoulder toward Adam's table. "Ohhh," she said in a hushed voice. "I know that guy!"

"Yeah," Abby said. "I know him too. I mean, my brother knows him."

Shelley turned around and got the Scotch and its glass. "His parents just died," she said as she poured. "Did you know that?"

"Yes," said Abby. "I did."

"I think his mom had a heart attack, and his dad died right after," Shelley said. She handed Abby the whisky and started to fill another glass with ice water. "Like, he was so heartbroken, he couldn't bear to live."

Not having been involved in the tragedy, and given anyway to flights of romance, Shelley was bound to bungle the details. Adam's father, Abby's brother had told her, had died first, after a long struggle with cancer; the heart attack had claimed his widow four days later, the day of the service. Still, the details mattered less than their consequences: Adam Lister was miserable, and he was bringing his misery into a den of depressants. It occurred to Abby to wonder, as she set his drinks down in front of him, how many other self-medicators she was filling the prescriptions for each night. However many there may be, the severity of Adam's tragedy had to be, if not unique, certainly extreme.

Adam was not looking at her, but at the spirit she had just delivered, and for a moment she hovered, hugging the empty drink tray to her chest. "How are you doing?" she finally asked.

Adam's body jerked, and he said, "Fine," but there was caring enough in her tone to suggest that she had not posed the question idly, and he looked up at her with his head cocked slightly to the side.

"I'm Abby," she said. "Maynard's sister?"

Adam nodded slightly.

"Maynard told me about what happened. I'm—" But what could she say? Her words were useless. For all its potentially destructive power, alcohol would do more for him now than anything that might come from her lips. "I'm so sorry," she said in a soft voice, and she felt foolish.

"Okay," Adam said.

"Don't worry about the drink," Abby added, still murmuring, "it's on me," because that almost seemed like the proper thing to do, but then she wondered if she was tacitly encouraging some sort of self-destruction, and she wanted to take it back.

"No," he said, and she sighed. She forced herself to pull her eyes up from her feet and was thrilled to see a smile on Adam's face, or something closely enough resembling a smile to clear away her doubts. He handed her a twenty and said, "I don't need any change. Just, keep an eye on me tonight."

Abby took the bill slowly. Adam shooed her away with a gesture that was almost playful. Her reservations drifted away. She could begin thinking of him as she thought of any other customer, and right now she had plenty of those to keep her occupied.

Abby's passion was for theater, but that passion did not prevent her from taking her temporary vocation seriously. In the back of the bar, around the pool tables, she saw no harm in responding, if coyly, to the banal one-liners that the players offered. By smiling and resting her hand on a customer's bicep for a few seconds, she could on most nights guarantee herself a generous tip. Even this kind of minor emotional prostitution she considered a form of acting. If she could not be on stage or before a camera, she could at least practice her craft, taking on the role of an available, not-too-bright piece of ass. Somehow tonight, though, the act was losing its magic. Whenever she walked demurely away from the pool tables, she would catch sight of Adam and realize that he had been giving his own kind of performance. To allay her worry, he would meet her eyes and smile, but when he didn't think she was looking, his mouth would fall into the most miserable of frowns and his eyes would go blank. He looked like a man preparing to follow the ones he loved to their graves.

4. Howie meets up with Fisk

In another corner of the city, in a different kind of bar, a friend of Howie's sat at a counter beside an espresso machine, his notebook open before him, a pen revolving around the axis of his index finger. This was Fisk, who had since college been involved with Howie in the convoluted relationship of bandmates. Fisk's lean, wiry body was topped by a head that seemed almost too big, an illusion fueled by the large expanse of forehead and the bolts of dark hair that sprung from it as if to challenge gravity. His face was narrow, and his eyes rested in small caverns beneath a sharply angled brow.

In contrast to the misery of his peers, Fisk's life was going pretty well, and that troubled him. He was of the mind that great art could be engendered only by great tragedy, and was afraid that his songwriting would suffer for his recent good fortune. He wrestled with the problem, that night as most nights, at the coffee shop where he worked. Of the twenty or so tables in that shop, only three were occupied, and for the moment the patrons occupying them had all they needed. Fisk appreciated nights like these. Some of his co-workers lauded the busy hours because, they said, it helped pass the time; some preferred the constant influx of customers for the extra income it provided. Fisk found both observations tiresome. He lived a spartan existence, and the acquisition of fifteen or twenty dollars more in tips on a given night would not substantially change his lifestyle, not enough to make worthwhile the loss of time the gratuity depended on.

But that night, when he looked up from his journal to search the ceiling for the right word to rhyme with *gutter* and saw, instead, Howie walking through the front door, Fisk suddenly found himself wishing that the coffee shop was filled to capacity with fickle customers, and more waiting out on the sidewalks, and the phone ringing, and Jess asking if he could cover some of her tables because she wasn't feeling too hot. What he wanted, really, was an excuse not to have to give Howie his undivided attention.

Tonight, there wasn't even enough of a crowd to camouflage Fisk for the few seconds it would take to stash his notebook and pretend to be studying an order pad. Howie had spotted him instantly, and he was heading straight for the bar. Fisk put his pen down, looked up at Howie, and smiled.

"Hey, Fisk," Howie said. He gave a small wave, just a slight move of his wrist, with his arm still at his side. Howie's face lately seemed trapped in a perpetual frown, the weight of it pulling his flesh down, sagging around the jaw.

"Howie, what's up man?" Fisk said. He stood up to give Howie a one-armed hug, clapping him on the back. "Have a seat."

Howie managed a smile, likely more genuine than Fisk's, despite its melancholy twinge. He sat down on the stool next to Fisk's.

"Hey," Fisk said. "I've got to go check on my tables. You need anything? Italian soda or something?"

Howie shook his head. "Water's fine. But don't worry about it. Whenever you're done." His eyes shifted from his lap to the counter, toward Fisk's notebook. Fisk closed the notebook and put it in his back pocket.

"All right, man," Fisk said. "I'll just be a minute." He stopped by each of the three occupied tables and made as much idle chatter as he could without seeming obsequious, and when one girl asked if she could get another soy cambric, he almost wanted to kiss her. Back at the bar, on the opposite side from where Howie sat, reading the newspaper now, Fisk set up the milk to steam and asked, "So how're you doing, man? You get all that job shit straightened out?"

Howie closed the newspaper with a sigh. "Well, I didn't go back to Neuartig, if that's what you mean. I told Steve Biggs—"

Fisk held his finger up and turned to retrieve the frothing soy milk. "Hold on a second, Howie," he said. He poured the milk over a tea bag, added water, and stirred it thoroughly. When he carried it to the table he moved slowly, taking a deep breath with each step. By the time he got back to the bar, he was ready, and loath to waste any more time.

"We got a new bassist," he told Howie. He leaned back against the bar, next to Howie, with his arms folded over his chest. Howie looked at Fisk, and Fisk looked at a flyer on the wall. On the flyer he projected Howie's face, the shocked and wounded expression of his perpetually limpid eyes.

"I've only been gone for a couple weeks," Howie whimpered. "I told you I had to figure some things out."

"I know, Howie. It's just, shit." Fisk reached over the bar and grabbed his cigarettes from their spot next to the cash register. He put one in his mouth and lit it, then said, "We had gigs, man. We had shit planned, and you just disappeared. You kind of fucked us over for that party at the Warners' place." Fisk sat down and pulled an ashtray down from the end of the bar. He still couldn't look at Howie. "Stewart's little brother used to play with the jazz band in high school, and he picked up the songs real quick... Shit, man." He was having a harder time of this than he had expected he would. Last week, when they were invited to play the Mardis Gras show that Jarvis Chesterton was planning, Fisk was afraid he was going to have to say no, and he had been so pissed off at Howie. Then Stewart had suggested bringing Perry on, and it all seemed like it might work out. "I'm sorry, Howie. We didn't know what your plans were, and Perry just got real into it. He learned all

all the songs really quick. We didn't know when you were coming back."

"Well tell him I'm back. God."

Fisk kept flicking the butt of the cigarette with his thumb whenever it wasn't in his mouth. "Sorry, man. He's into it." It would have been nice to have Howie play the Mardis Gras show, but Howie was acting flakey lately. Even before his disappearance he had been acting flakey. Add to that the certain drama that firing Perry would lead to, and suddenly Howie wasn't even a practical option. Perry was at least dependable, and malleable. Plus, his presence kept Stewart happier.

"Fisk," Howie said, and when Fisk finally looked at him again, his eyes were tearing up. Howie shook his head violently from side to side, then pressed the heel of his right hand against his eye. "Oh, God," he said.

"Howie, come on."

"Jazz band!" Howie shouted, dropping his hand. "He was in the goddamn jazz band? Remember when the Unnaturalists used to play country blues? Real country!"

Fisk frowned. He had always hated Howie's obsession with the classification of things. The guy insisted on sticking some arbitrary label on every goddamn song. Why couldn't he let the music define itself?

Meaning it less this time, Fisk said, "I'm sorry, Howie. You just disappeared. We didn't know what to do." He pushed his stool back and stood up. He took the ash tray with him. "I've got to get back to work. You should come see us, at least. See how Perry's doing. We're playing a Mardis Gras show at the Bluebird." And without waiting to see how Howie would respond, Fisk walked around the counter and into the kitchen, where he would hang out and talk to the new dishwasher for as long as he had to until Howie decided to leave.

5. How Wayne was missed

The concise response of the Unnaturalists' guitarist, Stewart Baldwin, to the Howie situation could be delivered in the blunt couplet *Fuck him.* There was no real animosity driving that attitude—Stewart was actually pretty fond of Howie—but Fisk was fretting about the band, and Stewart happened to know a bassist. His blood relationship to that bassist meant nothing to Stewart; Perry was simply the only bassist he knew aside from Howie, and so Perry was the only potential solution he could offer. Had he already been in a band with Perry, and had Perry been the one who freaked out and wandered off, Stewart might have nominated Howie to replace him. It was pragmatism, not politics.

To others, Stewart's indifference could come off as insensitivity. He was aware of that, but he couldn't bring himself to care about it, and so he tried to surround himself with people who appreciated his willful oblivion, who saw it as a token of his laid-back nature. Carissa, the girl climbing the steps beside him now, was one of those. Burke Russo was another. Stewart planned to spend the evening getting drunk with the two of them.

He opened the door at the end of the hallway and they walked down to Burke's apartment. Stewart pounded on the door with the side of his fist.

"People might be trying to sleep in here," Carissa whispered.

It couldn't have been much later than ten or eleven, but Stewart didn't feel like arguing with her. He just smiled at her, and when Burke pulled the door open, Stewart squeezed past him and headed for the kitchen. Along the way, he turned on the lamp by the couch, and then hit the light switch on the kitchen wall. Over his shoulder he called, "What, were you just sitting in the dark here? Dude!"

"I'm glad you guys showed up," Burke said. "I'm...I don't know. There's this—"

From the kitchen, Stewart heard the door swing shut. He opened a beer, took a long drink, and began to transfer the rest from the box to the fridge. He paused to step around the corner and toss a can to Burke. It sailed past him and landed on the floor next to his TV.

"I got this letter," Burke said.

"A letter?" Stewart walked out to the main room and sat down in Burke's recliner.

Burke and Carissa were sitting on the couch, Burke holding a few sheets of paper in front of him, and Carissa looking over his forearm at them. Without looking up, she asked, "Did you get a beer for me, Stew?"

Stewart hesitated with the can inches from his lips. He smiled. "Here you go, babe. I brought this one for you." Half the can was gone already, but she'd appreciate the gesture. He handed it to her, and went back into the kitchen for another.

"Who sent you a letter?" he asked Burke.

"Wayne."

Stewart came into the room and sat down in Burke's shitty old recliner. He popped the foot rest out, took a swig, and asked, "Wayne who?"

"Wayne Talbot."

Stewart looked at the floor for a moment, then at his beer, then at Burke. "Is that the guy—no. Wait...who is that?"

"He's a skinny guy. Brown hair."

"Oh." Stewart took a drink. He shifted his balls through his pants. Skinny guy with brown hair. "Is he that new dishwasher at Paris?"

"No," Burke said. He held the letter up like he was about to read it out loud, then he paused. "I think you're thinking of Travis. Wayne's the guy—"

"Wait!" Stewart said. "Is he the black guy?"

"Black guy? What black guy? No, Wayne's..."

Burke trailed off, like even he didn't know what he was talking about. Stewart took a drink of beer and gave it some thought. *Wayne.* It was a common enough name, but he didn't think he had ever known anybody who actually had it. Or, "Hey, wait, okay," he said. "Yeah." He sat forward. "He's the computer geek kid, right?"

Burke seemed uncertain. He searched the room, and in searching saw the beer Stewart had tossed at him earlier. He bent to pick it up.

"Yeah," Stewart said. "He was the guy at Adam Lister's party that was talking about viruses all night, right?"

"That's him," Carissa said. "He's friends with Toby Warner, I think."

Stewart grinned. "That was a fucked up party. Remember when Davie tried to pick a fight with those goth kids? He was yelling and shoving them around, and none of them would do anything?" He laughed and took another drink. "What the hell were those kids doing there, that's what I want to know."

"Toby Warner's little brother invited them," Carissa said. "I'm pretty sure."

"Fuck," Stewart said. His eyes rolled back slightly so he could recall the images without the current setting distracting him. "I got wasted, too, that night. Davie and I started lighting ether fires in Adam's fucking driveway—"

"Yeah," Carissa said. "You were trying to show off for Jess."

He looked down suddenly, called to attention more by Carissa's tone than her words, which he hadn't quite processed anyway. "What?"

"That was the night you tried making out with Jess De-Kirk on the porch swing, in front of everyone else. Her brothers wanted to kick your ass."

Oh, yeah. Huge episodes of that night had disappeared from Stewart's memory entirely, but he remembered how he kept putting his hand on Jess DeKirk's leg, and how she kept picking it up and setting it on his lap and asking, *Don't you have a girlfriend?* He cleared his throat and drank some more beer, then looked back over at Burke.

"So what's the deal with this Wayne guy?"

Burke flattened the letter on his lap. "I don't know, man. It's kind of fucked up."

"Fucked up like how? Is it a love letter?"

"I think he's going to kill himself."

Carissa set her beer down on the table in front of them. She looked at Stewart, who was looking at Burke, trying to figure out if he was kidding. Everything about him, from the dullness in his eyes to the slumping of his shoulders, suggested that he was not. "Fuck, dude," Stewart said. He had to get another beer.

While he was walking from the recliner to the fridge, Carissa asked Burke, "Are you joking?" and Burke said, "No," then, "Check this out. This is what he wrote:

" 'Dear Burk'—oh, yeah," Burke looked up from the letter just as Stewart was sitting down again. "He spelled my name wrong, too. No *E*." He shrugged, cleared his throat, and continued reading, " 'I almost started this letter off saying "I hope you're not upset," but really I guess that's not the case. I hope you are. That's kind of the whole point. This is weird, I know. Sorry. Bear with me.' "

Burke was going to read the whole thing word-for-word, and there were, like, two pages. Stewart figured it'd be better if he just told them what it was about. Quicker, anyway. But he guessed Burke thought it was important to read it, so oh well. He sat back and took a drink.

Here's the thing, over Christmas, I spent a lot of time alone. I spent Christmas Day by myself, plus all the time leading up to it, and I had a lot of time to think about how my life has turned out, and how different it is from how I ever would have thought it would be even six months ago.

At the guy's description of his Christmas, Carissa whimpered slightly, an exhalation which Stewart understood was likely unconscious and in accordance anyway with her sympathetic nature. They had spent Christmas together, Stewart and Carissa, first at her parents' place, and then at his, and Stewart's little brother had told everyone he was donating all his gifts to the Salvation Army, because that was what the holiday was about, as far as he was concerned, and Carissa had cried and hugged his little brother. Now she looked like she might cry here, in Burke's apartment, and they were all just supposed to be chilling out, having a good time.

Transferring his beer to his left hand, Stewart reached out with his right to squeeze Carissa's knee. He kept the hand there even as Burke kept reading and Carissa's face kept melting. She was a good looking girl, he knew that, and when her face went into that sad look, it wrecked him. Her eyes were so big, so brown they were almost black, and now that they were all glistening, it was like you could dive in and swim in them.

Also, I was thinking about It's a Wonderful Life. *I must have seen a commercial for it or something. I've never actually seen the movie. But something made me think about it, and it just seemed like an incredible opportunity, to see your life without you in it, to see whether anything you do matters, and who would miss you if you were gone. After dwelling on it all afternoon in my dark, stuffy basement apartment, I kind of decided that, no, it wouldn't. If I jumped off a bridge, nobody's life would really change, not for the worse.*

"Oh, God!" Carissa said, and she put her hand to her mouth.

Burke nodded slightly, but he kept his attention focused on the letter, and he continued reading.

But I could never be sure. That's the issue. If I killed myself tomorrow, I wouldn't have a Guardian Angel or whatever to take me back and show me how people were reacting. And I wouldn't get a second chance.

So I need to ask you a big favor. For the past week, I've been holed up in an old hotel downtown. I don't figure anybody's really noticed my absence yet, but I plan to stay here for a while. What you need to do is nothing, really. I just want you to go around and listen to what people are saying. Don't let on that you've heard from me. Actually, you shouldn't bring me up at all. That's a big part of it, just seeing if I come up in conversation, and how long it takes before I do.

You're the—

Burke's voice caught, and he stopped reading. He took one hand off the letter to take a drink of beer. Stewart was a little relieved when the break came. "That's fucking awful, dude."

"It gets worse," Burke said. "This is the part that kills me. 'You're the closest friend I've got here' is what he wrote next.

"Before tonight, I had no idea he was even gone."

"What else does he have to say?" Carissa asked, and in leaning closer to the letter she pulled her leg away. Stewart's hand dropped. He pulled back into the recliner and drank, wondering why she was sitting on the couch next to Burke, and he was here.

Burke's eyes wandered to the bottom of the second page. "He just asks me to keep an ear out, and listen to what people are saying about him. And he says I shouldn't tell anybody about this letter." Burke tittered, and it sounded stupid in Stewart's ears, although he supposed Burke was probably fucked up over all this shit.

"Have you guys ever seen *It's a Wonderful Life?*" Burke asked.

Stewart was pretty sure he hadn't, but he knew what it was, at least. "*Yes, Virginia, there is a Santa Claus,*" he said, and he thought he might get a knowing chuckle out of that, but Burke and Carissa only stared at him. Burke looked puzzled, Carissa annoyed. Stewart wished there were more people here.

"That's *Miracle on 34th Street,*" Carissa said.

"Oh." Stewart had never watched any of those movies, and the tone of snobbery he detected in Carissa's correction bothered him; his mother was a devout, by-the-book Christian, and when he was growing up the holiday was about pink and purple candles and Bible passages, never about TV specials. So, so what if he was detached from the popular culture of the past fifty years? Carissa couldn't hold that against him.

"Anyway," Burke said, "I guess Wayne watched *Wonderful Life* over Christmas, and now he wants me to be his spy, or his angel, or whatever."

"Do you think he wanted us to track him down?" Carissa asked.

She said it like she hoped Burke would say yes. Stewart stood up and headed for the kitchen. He asked if anybody wanted another beer, but they didn't even respond.

"I don't think so," Burke said, to Carissa. "I was supposed to be the only one who knew about this, remember?"

Stewart came back and sat down. "I don't get it," he said. "Why you?"

"Apparently he thinks he and Burke are best friends," Carissa said, finally turning to look at him. But as if that useless news brief justified ignoring him otherwise, she immediately turned back to Burke. "You don't think of yourselves as close friends, right?"

Burke shook his head. "Acquaintances, maybe." He chewed his lip and creased his brow, and finally he said, "A few months ago, a bunch of people and I came back to my place after a show, and I think Wayne was here. I'm sure he was. That was the first night I ever really talked to the guy. I was pretty drunk, and I had snorted a bunch of Ecstasy. The state I was in, I thought he was fascinating, and I must have said as much to him. He's been over here a couple times since then, and he comes into Abo's a lot while I'm working. He'll just stop by and ask what I'm up to, and then we'll stand around and talk for a little bit, and I end up making some excuse to go."

Carissa's eyes were all misty. "God, that is so sad," she said.

The way Stewart saw it, if Burke had stayed away from Ecstasy, none of this would have happened. It was a pretty faggy drug. "And from those few encounters," he asked, "the guy has gotten the impression that you two are best buds?"

Burke sipped his beer and considered the question. He shrugged. "I called him one night after I had gotten in a big fight with Abby, just cause I wanted to go out and get obliterated, and I didn't want to be by myself. I think it was when you guys were in Tucson, and—I don't know. I just couldn't get a hold of anyone else. Turns out, though, Wayne doesn't drink. But he went to The Park with me, and he paid for half my drinks, until I was completely useless. Next morning, I woke up on his couch. He took me out and bought me breakfast, and I thanked him profusely, told him how much I appreciated having somebody who'd listen to me. That was a few weeks before Christmas."

Stewart imagined the scenario, imagined how similar it might have been if he had gotten in a fight with Carissa and Burke was out of town. "Then you made up with Abby," he said, "and now everything's fine..." Stewart trailed off and looked at Burke again, really studied him, and all the shit he always ragged on Burke about—the high-lighted hair and the tight-fitting Rayon shirts—all seemed suddenly less harmless. "You know, I was just kidding before when I said that about the love letter, but now—" Stewart cocked his eyebrows, "You think maybe he's gay? And you maybe sent him some wrong symbols or something?"

"He's not gay," Carissa said.

Stewart wasn't so sure. He didn't remember the guy too well, but it answered a lot of questions. "How would you know?" he asked.

Carissa had picked up her beer again and was holding it in her lap, but she made no indication of wanting to drink it. "That night at Adam's party," she said. "Wayne was hitting on some girl, and they ended up making out."

28

"What girl?"

"Just some girl."

"I don't remember that."

"That's cause you were outside lighting fires in the driveway," she said. "Or making out with Jess."

Stewart sunk deeper into the recliner. His beer was getting low, and it was starting to seem less and less likely that they'd be going out later.

Carissa turned to Burke and asked, "When you were poring your heart out about Abby, did Wayne reciprocate at all?"

"I'm not sure." Burke said. He hadn't finished his beer yet. "I was pretty much just babbling by the end of the night. I don't remember what I told him, much less what he might of told me."

"How much do you know about him?" she asked.

Stewart wondered if he should go for a fourth beer.

"I really don't know much at all," Burke said. "He moved here about a year ago, I think, and he lives—"

"Where'd he move from?"

Burked frowned. "Don't know," he said. "He's a web programmer, I'm pretty sure."

Stewart stood up and moved over to the couch, to sit on the armrest and put his arm around Carissa's delicate shoulders. To Burke he said, "He said he'd call you, right?"

"Yeah," Burke said. "I guess I'm just supposed to wait until he does."

That was what it looked like to Stewart. He pulled Carissa's beer gently up from between her thighs and took a sip.

"Don't you have his phone number?" Carissa asked.

"I did," Burke said. He patted his pockets absently and looked around the room. "I don't know what I did with it. Maybe Toby Warner gave it to me." He turned to Carissa. "You said he was friends with Toby, didn't you?"

"Yeah," she said. "At least, I think he is. That's who he came to that party with, anyway."

"We should call Toby," he said.

"Tonight?" Stewart said. "It's kind of late. Why don't you just ask him at work? When you work together next?"

Burke looked at the Coca-Cola clock on his wall, the battery of which had died months ago and whose hands were locked at about 10:42, gathering dust. "Yeah, I guess you're right," he said.

"You should drink up," Stewart said, gesturing with Carissa's beer toward Burke's. "No reason to let this thing ruin our night, huh?"

Carissa snorted and shrugged off Stewart's arm. She stood up and walked down the hall to Burke's bathroom. Burke took a drink. Stewart stared after his girlfriend with a bit of remorse. Something about the way she was acting made him think he wouldn't be getting laid tonight. "Shit, dude," he said to Burke. He slid down the armrest to collapse in the couch.

6. ADAM GETS CARRIED AWAY

Where Stewart had gone into the night with a celebratory mind, and gradually gotten pulled down by the tedium of his friends, Adam had begun feeling morose and was now building to a frenetic peak. With each beer Stewart finished, the night looked a little less promising; with each drink of whisky Adam took, his future brightened.

For the past several nights, Adam had been sitting at home alone in his house talking to the ghosts of his parents, looking at old photographs, and listening to music from when he used to be happy. He had gotten to a point where it became clear that he had to leave, to go outside and be once again in the company of people who were still living. He understood, too, that there was more at stake now, that his life would never be the same as it once was, but he still wasn't sure quite what his next step was supposed to be. The world was rife with injustice, with death meted out arbitrarily, or, when it wasn't arbitrary, then dealt first to those who most deserved life and far too late to the petty and small and useless.

When the girl—a girl whom he had known once, somehow, in the life he used to live—had brought him his first drink, he still believed that he was impotent in regards to that fickleness of death. It was only now, three drinks later, as he was coming to understand his own potential, that he realized he had harbored those suspicions of powerlessness.

He let fall two drops of water into his whisky from his straw, and then swirled the glass to spread the drops through. His father was not here to drink with him, and his mother was not here to make fun of their ceremonies, but Adam raised his glass anyway, and he took a drink. When his parents were living, their lives had been marked always by celebration. Even after the cancer, they would find cause to celebrate, blessed by the outpourings of love that were a direct reaction to all the good they had done.

The well-meaning platitudes of neighbors and community leaders could not comfort Adam. Nothing comforted him, nothing answered the questions that kept coming. He hated that none of this was his fault, that there was no way to go back in his memory and say, "Ah, if I had only...", and imagine his parents back to life. Had it been his fault—had he been drunk and driven his parents into an oncoming semi truck and killed them, for example—he would have loathed himself, no doubt, and that loathing might cripple him for months. But with time he was sure he could overcome such a personal failure, maybe even use it to his advantage. He could have learned from the wretched mistake, turned the moral lapse into a crutch to lift him up, making his character once more fit and able.

But, this! He could do nothing! You could not fight cancer with good intentions; you could not overcome a heart attack with tenacity.

"How are we doing over here?"

How, yes? There had to be some way. He had to fight back. Maybe he could not strike directly at the cancer, but could he, perhaps, strike at a world that allowed cancer to exist?

"Adam?"

The girl was back. Adam blinked, realized he had been staring into the flame of the candle at the center of the table, and his eyes were drying out. He looked up at the girl. "Sorry," he said. "I was...thinking." His whisky was gone. That must be why the girl had come by. He attempted a smile and held the glass out to her. "Yes, please. I'll have another."

"Okay," she said. She took the glass, but she didn't leave immediately. Her face was clouded, and she seemed uncertain. Adam cemented his smile, and she nodded and left. How many glasses was that? It didn't matter. She had distracted him from something; his mind had been on the verge of a tremendous discovery, and he had to scramble back to it. He pulled another twenty from his pocket, the last one he had brought with him, because the he who had planned this night hours ago had foreseen the possibility of losing track of his finances and had limited his budget accordingly. That was a hundred dollars gone, and if he wanted to spend more he would have to stumble home first.

Anyway, there was no need to spend more. There was no need to spend even this last twenty, but he had already sent the girl away. He might as well finish this next drink and let the drink lead him back to that mental brink, to the dawn of understanding.

Yes, he had been thinking of the cancer that had claimed his father's life, that had taken, indirectly, the life of his mother as well, by making her fret for years over the fate of her husband, by taxing her heart, by making demands of her that her body could not meet indefinitely. By the time his father had finally succumbed, his mother was too weak anymore to continue living, even though continuing no longer meant the same struggle that had characterized her life for so long.

That was what mattered. She *had* struggled, and in her struggle she had shown the cancer that she was unafraid, or, if not unafraid, then unwilling despite her fear to let the cancer do what it would. That was what the ghosts had been trying to communicate to him: the struggle. The cancer that had consumed his parents was not limited to a few rogue cells; the cancer was everywhere. It surrounded Adam still, and threatened at every turn to smother him, him and everyone he loved.

The struggle was what mattered. There were others who struggled; Adam had grown up reading of their exploits, and even if he was only seeking diversion, did he not also take from those tales a certain satisfaction at the thought that wrongs could be righted? In Gotham City, in Metropolis, even in New York, powerful men and women saved lives and gave hope to thousands of others too weak to fight for themselves.

Adam took a long drink of whisky. He thought about all the mornings he had spent idly drinking his coffee and skimming the newspaper, reading of brutal crimes and responding with nothing more than a slight shake of his head, and it shamed him to know that he had taken so long to be moved. Only when the cancer that plagued the entire world touched his personal life did he understand its dread impact. He lurched to his feet. The cancer was here, in this bar, now. The girl who had been helping Adam was fighting it, he could see it across the room. Here it took the form of two men, low-lifes, "*Hoodlums*," his dad would've called them with a wry smile. The men, such as they were, wore baseball caps and polo shirts with upturned collars, and they stood around a pool table holding cues and talking in loud voices, but, make no mistake, they were the cancer.

They had the girl pressed up against a wall, grinning their wicked grins, fingering their pool cues like phalluses. Yes, Adam had known this girl, the sister of a friend he had once had, and she would play the midwife. Here in this dim bar on a cold January night, Adam would leave the womb and shake off the amniotic fluid of his past, a past of ignorance and cowardice. With a roar, he was born anew, and the first of the girl's attackers was hurled across the room into a rack of pool cues. The other was looking at Adam now, pleading, afraid, and Adam relished his fear. He shoved the man backwards onto the red felt of the table, and his hands were fists, instruments of divine fury. It was glorious. He hated only that it had taken so long to come to this, that he had not been able to seize the cancer when it was devouring his father, to feel it trembling beneath his hands, afraid, as it had for so long made others afraid.

Adam strangled the cancer, pummeled it, ravaged it, and he reveled in its powerlessness.

Cold, gentle fingers touched his arm, and Adam turned and faced the object of his rescue. Tears hung from her eyes, but she would live. "You're safe now," Adam said. He put his hand on her shoulder, nodded stiffly, and walked outside into the cold.

7. Adrienne and Howie at the Park

On a scale of happiness, where one was the perfect soul-crushing suffering of a woman who has lost her entire family to a holocaust, and ten was the unadulterated bliss rarely achieved without the assistance of some narcotic or true love, Adrienne Warner would probably have been sitting comfortable at about eight. She laughed much more frequently than she cried, and the closest she had come to catastrophe in her life so far was the flood in her parents' basement six years ago that had ruined roughly half her wardrobe and drowned her guinea pig, Owen.

If she had to guess, Adrienne would have put Maynard, her boyfriend, at nine, and Howie at four. The suspicion that Maynard was an entire measure more happy than she was created a font of considerable guilt, because she was pretty sure that their shared love was the primary reason for his nine, and sometimes she wished she could muster up the tiny bit of increased satisfaction it would take to bring equilibrium to their relationship. Part, no doubt, of her inability to match Maynard was the corresponding suspicion that Howie's four was caused by his unrequited love for her, which turned that font of guilt into a torrent. Since the root cause of her inability to requite Howie's love was her love for Maynard, her love for Maynard was, indirectly, a cause of her guilt concerning Howie's misery, and for feeling guilty about loving Maynard, her guilt concerning Maynard's happiness was compounded, so that keeping her contentment balanced directly at that eight demanded constant energy.

It hadn't always been so difficult. When she first met Howie, she and Maynard had only been together for a few months. She had told Howie she had a boyfriend immediately after he asked her out, and at the time such candidness seemed an adequate safeguard; any greater precautions would have robbed her of a certain degree of autonomy. But, in the intervening year and a half, as Maynard had shifted in her estimation from decent prospect to Most Wonderful Boyfriend Ever, Howie, too, had shifted, from innocuous charmer to hopeless leech.

No, she reflected, that wasn't fair. Howie was hopeless, at least in his love for her, but she could not dismiss him so easily: if he was still hanging around her, it was due as much to her refusal to shut him out as it was to his own clinginess. The truth was that she enjoyed spending time with him, when he wasn't wretchedly avowing his insatiable love for her. When he could forget about the base physical attraction long enough to talk to her like she was a person and not a goddess, he could be engaging and funny. He could entertain her, and he could make her think, and at those moments, when he was at his best, she loved being with Howie.

But lately, for the past several weeks, he had not been at his best. He had been dejected, self-absorbed, and tiresome, and in the meantime things kept getting better with Maynard, and their future kept looking brighter. To be around Howie then was like having a hangover thrust at you in the midst of a rollicking binge. Had he been like this when she first met him, after the Unnaturalists show at Herman's Hideaway in that bleak fall of 2001, she would have had no problem dismissing him from her life completely, as perhaps she should have when he first confessed his feelings to her last fall. By agreeing to continue spending time with him, even with the re-stated caveat that she was perfectly happy with Maynard and that no romance could ever come of it, she had given Howie tacit license to nurture his affection for her.

Now, that affection was fully developed, a foolish and awkward adolescent, with no trace of the adorability it had commanded in its infancy, and she was ashamed of it. Ashamed, too, of the part she had played in its upbringing. If she had this past year and a half to live over again, she would have aborted Howie's infatuation the moment it took seed. But to abandon it now wasn't merely a distasteful notion; it was literally unimaginable. When he called and asked if they could meet, she wouldn't even consider the possibility of telling him, "Nope, sorry," but would go along out of a sense of duty.

The obligation led her, today, to Washington Park, to a park bench beside a frozen lake, with Howie at her side. What was once a verdant, healthy place that brought to her life a certain contented calm was now barren and crusted with ice, and she was still here, hunched into a ball hugging herself to keep warm, and shivering.

Howie exhaled sharply and coughed. "You know where they're playing? They're playing the Bluebird. The Bluebird!"

Adrienne did not have to ask whom Howie meant, because for the past hour he had been talking about nothing else. To some extent, she was relieved at how upset he was about the band, even as she suspected, somewhat egotistically, that his rift with Fisk was less a source of misery in and of itself and more a consequence of the misery caused by his heartache over her; she was relieved because his obsessing over the band provided an excuse not to talk about the situation she felt she responsibly ought to be bringing up on her own.

"Fisk never got gigs at places like the Bluebird when I was in the band," Howie said. "Never."

Adrienne forced her cold, stiff lips into a smile and patted Howie's hand. "It's just a coincidence, Howie. It didn't happen *because* you left the band." As soon as the words were out, she knew they were the wrong ones.

"I didn't leave the band," Howie whimpered. "Fisk just replaced me."

"After you took off for two weeks," she pointed out. "Nobody knew what happened to you. We were worried. Fisk was, too, I'm sure."

Howie nodded. He pulled his hand out of the pocket of his pea coat long enough to wipe it beneath his nose. "I'm sorry, Adrienne."

A few flakes of snow were making a tentative descent around them, and Adrienne felt one brush past her cheek. She wiped at the spot where it had touched, and in a soft voice she said, "You don't have to apologize to me, Howie."

"Stewart's brother is only nineteen years old," Howie said. "Nineteen!"

Adrienne turned her gaze back toward the lake. "What are you going to do?" she asked.

"Do?"

"I mean, how long are you going to stay at Johnny Rockets?"

"Oh. I'm not really sure."

"Are you looking for another job?"

Howie shivered. In a small, weak voice he told her, "Don't worry about me. I'll be okay."

"Don't worry about you!" she repeated. Worry was all she did about Howie anymore. While she might have given up on the prospect of ever seeing him as happy as he had been when they first met, she hoped at least to see him emotionally sound. His dismissive command not to worry, then, set off a spark against her smoldering resentment, and she reeled on him, her voice raising with each word spoken. "You quit your job, Howie! You trashed your apartment and just took off! I didn't know when I'd ever see you again. And now that you've finally resurfaced, you're working for minimum wage at a fucking hamburger joint! Where do you get off telling me not to worry?"

The warm sting of tears came to her eyes, and before she could reign them in, Howie was crying himself at the sight of them. "I'm sorry," he said in a trembling voice, and moved to pity Adrienne reached out to him. He put his arms around her waist, buried his face in her coat, and wept, saying repeatedly, "I'm sorry, Adrienne. I'm so sorry."

Adrienne coaxed Howie to his feet and walked with him halfway around the lake to her car. He hugged her again after she opened his door, then dropped his arms and looked at the wet pavement. "It's not minimum wage, though," he said so softly that she had to cock her head towards him. She bent her knees slightly to try to look at Howie's hanging face, and he said, "The base pay is two-thirteen an hour, but mostly I'll be working for tips. It's a lot better than minimum wage."

8. WAYNE'S BASEMENT APARTMENT

Later that night, and colder, Carissa Snow found herself in the back seat of Burke's car ruminating on her connection to the man whose house they were planning to visit. Beside her sat Toby Warner, whom she had known for years by name and sight, but never in any more profound way. Many of his friends and many of hers had gone to high school together, and their paths tended to cross regularly enough to warrant warm smiles and several minutes of conversation. It was on Carissa's suggestion that Burke had talked to Toby to try to learn more about Wayne Talbot, but all they had learned was that there wasn't much to learn, at least not from anyone they knew.

Earlier in the evening, Burke and Carissa had met in the parking lot of Abo's, the pizza shop where he and Toby worked, and they went inside to talk to Toby. Toby was by himself behind the counter, tall and gangly, with thick, curly hair and a week's worth of beard, his tee-shirt dusted with flour. He was leaning over the counter at the far end, engaged in conversation with a girl Carissa knew but was slow to recognize. Abrasive death metal blared from the speakers, so Burke had had to shout when he said Toby's name, and as he did, Carissa realized the girl at the end of the counter was Jessica DeKirk. She had a round, happy face that fostered in Carissa an immediate, illogical resentment.

When Burke asked how well Toby knew Wayne, Toby shrugged. "Were you the one who invited him to that party at Adam Lister's?" Burke asked.

Toby nodded and said, "Well, Jess invited him, really."

Jess looked up. She came around the corner to stand beside Carissa.

"We just gave him a ride that night," Toby added. "It was only the second time I had met him."

"Why?" Jess asked. "What's up?"

And Burke had told them about the letter. He told them he was thinking about going over to Wayne's apartment to see if he was around. Jess had gotten all excited and said she wanted to go along. Toby had asked them to wait until his shift was over and he'd join them.

Since Stewart was working, and Abby was at one of her brother's parties, it was just this odd group of four. Jess had called, "Shotgun!" and got in the front. Carissa, watching her numbly, had climbed into the back next to Toby, who sat with his knees folded up at a sharp angle pushing into the back of Burke's seat. They were spared the awkward silence by Jess's prattling to Burke about a club she had gone to a couple nights ago. Listening to her, Carissa considered for the first time that Jess might have been as responsible as Stewart for his lapse that night at Adam's party. She wasn't sure whether that was a comfort.

For Carissa, sleeping with Wayne had been an act of spite—an extreme one, and one motivated as much by alcohol as a broken heart—but not one of affection. Granted, Stewart had been drunk that night, too, when he started groping Jess DeKirk on the porch swing. Had that been the only time Stewart had made her feel inadequate, she might have been inclined toward forgiveness. She might not have left him there in disgust and gone in to do snakebites with the girls in the kitchen. Wayne, then, might never have been used the way she used him. At the time, that thought hadn't even occurred to her. Even the next morning, when she was hungover and bed-ridden with self-loathing, she thought a lot about Stewart and about the future of their relationship, but she did not think much about Wayne. She assumed that all men appreciated cheap, meaningless sex, and since Wayne was gone from the back seat of her car by the time she woke up, she had no reason to believe he was any different.

Before she saw Stewart again, Carissa had made up her mind not to tell him about Wayne, or tell anybody. It was enough for her to know that she had it in her to move on from Stewart, and to have fun without him, even if it took five shots of mixed liquor to do it.

And just as her transgression had been settling into the dust of her memories, the letter showed up. Carissa couldn't decide if it made her feel better that Burke was the one Wayne chose to contact. It certainly would have wracked her conscience to learn that her neglect had driven a man to such despair, but at the same time, such a letter could have been a testament to her capacity to elicit love, a capacity she wasn't sure if she still maintained.

So when she heard from Abby that Burke was planning to visit Wayne's apartment, she had told Burke she wanted to be there. Two days had passed since the letter had showed up, and Wayne had not called or written in the meantime. Burke's worry was not, Carissa figured, an entirely selfless worry: he didn't know Wayne well enough to care about him personally. What he was concerned about was the effect Wayne's death would have on him.

Carissa, for her part, wasn't sure how seriously to take the letter. The experiment, such as it was, struck her as the byproduct of a morbid self-absorption. Surely he was more interested in knowing what the world was like in his absence than in actually leaving it. And if he did discover just how little impact his life had, he would probably just choose to move away from Denver. But suicide? It seemed a little drastic.

If Burke had asked her that afternoon why she wanted to go to Wayne's apartment, she would have answered without hesitation, "Curiosity," and that was at least partly true. She wondered about Wayne, and she wanted to see how he lived. Mostly, she wanted to see if there was any sign among his domestic remains that his night with her, at that party, had meant something.

"Here it is," Burke said, pulling to a stop. They had wandered down a few wrong streets, it looked like, but he had finally found it. Carissa stepped out of the car immediately, eager to distance herself from Jess. The street was dark, and she saw nothing that looked like an apartment building. On the opposite side of the street was a long row big rectangular things with cheap nylon signs marking them as tire warehouses or stamp factories. Facing those, beyond the curb Burke had parked against, was a pitted sidewalk and a series of office buildings. Burke stepped out from the driver's seat and began walking toward a small house at the end of the block. The street number was painted in white on a green canopy over the front door, and on the frozen front lawn was a wooden sign that said *Porter &* *Wambeke, Attorneys.* Facing them from one of the windows was an orange-and-black CLOSED sign.

"He lives in a law office?" Carissa asked.

"He lives in the basement," Burke said. He led them around the back to a short flight of concrete steps. "That was what woke me up that time I passed out here. They were rolling around in their office chairs upstairs, and the phone kept ringing."

They walked down the steps and Burke tested the door knob. "It's locked," he said.

Jess reached past him and tried twisting it herself.

"It's locked," Burke said again. "Wait here. I'm going to check if I can pry open the windows."

Carissa watched him go, debating whether to urge a less destructive path, but she wanted to get inside as much as Burke did. When they had talked about it earlier, she had only given passing thought to the illegality of the whole plan. Maybe Jess or Toby would try to talk them out of it. She looked at them and offered a weak smile. Toby nodded. Jess shivered and stomped on the concrete. Carissa looked up the stairs again.

"So how well do you know this guy, Cariss?" Jess asked.

Carissa hesitated. "I don't, really. I mean, I met him at that party..." She flushed and looked down at her shoes.

Perhaps Jess would take that flush as censure of her own behavior, or perhaps she would try to figure out if it meant something else.

"Toby and I met him a little before that," Jess said. "We were at the Bug Jar, and he started talking to Toby. I guess he had just moved here." She shrugged. "I thought he was kind of cute."

Toby shuffled his feet and straightened his spine. He thrust his chest out slightly.

"Was he?" Carissa asked. "I don't remember. I don't know if I could pick him out in a crowd." Only after saying it did she realize it. Her memory was so clouded with booze and time that she could hardly recollect his face. It boosted her ego a bit to hear Jess say he was cute. Of course, she reflected, Jess apparently thought Stewart was cute, too. Trying to be objective as possible, Carissa decided that Jess was at least as pretty as she was. She had a beautiful complexion, and her hair was nice, long and straight, wrapped up in a bun on the back of her head. Back at Abo's, Carissa had noticed a slight paunch on her, but now that she was wrapped up in her winter clothes, you couldn't tell. Her breasts were bigger than Carissa's, though, and she had no doubt that Stewart had noticed that.

"Back up a second," Toby said. He pushed Jess away, not too gently, and stooped down to the door mat that they had all to some degree been standing on. Carissa moved her foot. Toby lifted a corner of the mat.

"Nice try," Jess said, wrapping her arms around herself. There was nothing beneath the mat.

Carissa looked around. Near Toby's shoulder was a light sconce with no bulb. Carissa stood on her tip-toes and with her right hand lifted the shell from the sconce, a cube of glass trimmed with brass. With her left, she felt around the base, and when her fingers brushed over a key, she grinned.

"You been here before?" Jess asked when Carissa pulled the key out. Carissa dropped the shell. The glass shattered.

"Shit," she said. She kicked the broken glass into the corner, then placed the shell—minus three panes of glass—back on the sconce. Jess was grinning at her. "My fingers are cold," she said. "And, no. If I had been here before, I would have gotten the key before Burke went to break in."

"I was just kidding. Chill out."

"We should tell Burke we found a key," Toby said. From inside there came a crash and a muffled swear.

Carissa squeezed between Toby and Jess and unlocked the door. Inside, the only light came from a window near the kitchen, from which a screen hung, swinging. Carissa could just make out the shape of Burke leaning against a counter, rubbing his leg. Somebody turned on the lights.

"Fuck," Burke said.

"What happened?" Jess asked. She walked past Carissa to Burke. Toby closed the door and followed her.

The apartment was big, bigger than the kind of apartments most of Carissa's friends had, and the things inside were nice. The carpeting was like office carpeting, just flat and gray, but there was a pretty Persian rug in the middle of the room. A few framed prints adorned the off-white walls, a Dalí, the *Chat Noir*, and a picture of the Golden Gate Bridge.

"I landed in the sink," Burke said. "I knew this window led to the kitchen, but I thought I'd be able to hop down onto the counter. Fuck."

"What did you do to your leg?" Jess asked. She reached out gingerly toward the spot Burke was nursing.

Carissa stood next to a cluttered table near the door. It was still cold in here. The heat had probably been turned off for weeks.

"Twisted my ankle or something," Burke said. "It's fine." He put his foot down and walked gamely into the main room. "How did you guys get in?"

"Carissa found a key," Toby said.

"Yeah," Jess giggled. "And she broke Wayne's light sconce."

"He'd be flattered," Burke said. In the corner of the room was a computer desk without a chair. The only chair was at the table that Carissa was looking at. She pulled it up and sat down.

"How long has Wayne been in Denver?" she asked.

"I don't know," Burke said. "Half a year, maybe?"

It looked like he hadn't thrown anything away since he moved into the place. The table was thick with old magazines and loose paperwork.

In the kitchen Jess and Toby were talking in low voices. It sounded like they were fighting with one another.

"His home page is Hotmail," Burke called out from the computer. "It's got his address in here. Anybody have any guesses at his password?"

Nobody did. Carissa read some of the paperwork. They looked like business contracts or something. Among them, she found a bank statement. It looked like Wayne did well for himself, which confirmed her suspicion that his vague suicide proposals were half-hearted. Sorting through all these personal documents brought on a new wave of guilt, but her intentions had to count for something, didn't they? Of course what she was doing was wrong, even criminal, but it was with an eye toward the greater good. Nobody else here seemed to have a problem with it.

"What are you doing, Toby?"

Carissa looked up. Toby was stooping, looking at a book shelf next to the kitchen, and Jess stood next to him with her arms crossed.

"I'm checking out his movies," Toby said. "That's the first thing I do whenever I go into a new apartment. Movies and CDs. You can tell a lot about a person by looking at what he likes."

"I can't get into his e-mail," Burke said.

Carissa sifted through the things on the table. One was an old flyer for a show at the Bug Jar, with Jess's name and phone number on the back in a loopy handwriting. Maybe Carissa wasn't Wayne's only fling.

"Jesus, there's a lot of porn on here," Burke said. "Every page in his browser history is a porn site."

"His movie collection blows," Toby said.

"You liked *When Harry Met Sally*," Jess said.

"No I don't! God!"

Near the top of the pile on the far edge of the table was a balled up plastic bag from Gart Sports. As Carissa was unwrapping it to see the name of the store, a receipt fell out and fluttered to her lap. She picked it up and read it.

"Oh," she said, and she called out softly to Burke. "You should come see this."

Jess and Toby started arguing about *Empire Records*.

Burke looked over at Carissa from the computer. In the pale light of the monitor, she noticed the circles underneath his eyes and wondered seriously for the first time what kind of toll the role of Wayne Talbot's Best Friend was taking on him. "What is it?"

Carissa pushed her chair out and stood up. She walked over to Burke and handed him the scrap of paper. "It's a receipt," she said. The item description read S&W 686 357 MAGNUM REV, and she was pretty sure she knew what that was.

"The date on this is one day earlier than the postmark on the letter he sent me," Burke said. On Wayne's monitor there was an image of two blonde girls, naked, one with her finger inside the other. Over at the bookshelf, Toby was saying something about "predictable Hollywood bullshit." Carissa wiped the tears from her cheeks before Burke could notice them.

9. ADAM'S NIGHT OUT

The earliest accounts of Adam Lister's adventures on the streets of Denver came to me second- or third-hand. Many such accounts surfaced in the months after the *Westword* story was published, but this one struck me as more believable than most, if only for its banality. I heard this from an acquaintance of mine who said his brother had introduced him to a guy named Nic, who was one of the city's legendary drinkers. Nic liked to tell people about a late night, after the bars had closed, walking home with a friend of like temperament and intemperance. It was the friend, Eddie, who had to stop on the way to relieve himself. He had been prepared to do it much earlier, right outside the bar on a conveniently parked Aston Martin, but Nic had convinced him to hold it in.

"You wanna break your parole for pissing on somebody's car, man?" Nic asked him. Eddie told him he was a pussy. They stumbled into an alley they assumed was deserted and Eddie braced himself with a shaky hand against the brick wall. He unzipped and started to piss. Nic saw something in the shadows move. It was a homeless man, he was sure, and it didn't even dawn on him to feel frightened, but when he swayed closer to it and tried to focus his eyes, he thought he could see horns.

"Shit, man," he said. "What the fuck is that?"

The prospect that they might encounter the devil crouched next a dumpster did not seem immediately implausible to Nic, and for a moment his fears of running into the police and ruining Eddie's parole seemed petty.

Then the figure rose, wobbling slightly as it did, and Nic saw that what he had taken for horns were, in fact, the pointed ears on the familiar cowl of Batman. In the center of the man's chest was a golden oval, and inside that, the bat.

"Holy shit, man," he said, hitting Eddie's shoulder. "Check it out, it's fucking Batman!"

Eddie looked up and squinted. He leaned back and trickled urine onto his pants. Batman straightened up and towered over them.

"Go home," he said. His voice was pretty fucking scary.

"This is fucking awesome!" Nic said. "Are you real, man?"

Batman shouldered past them, keeping to the shadows, but when he got to the mouth of the alley he paused. There was another group of late-night revelers coming down the opposite side of the street.

"Batman!" Eddie said. "Batman!"

Batman turned back toward them. Eddie was leaning against the wall, smiling, with his fly undone and his penis hanging out, dribbling. "Batman!"

"Is this like a bet or something?" Nic asked. He reached out to touch the symbol on Batman's chest. "That costume is awesome, man. It's just like the movie one—"

Batman shoved his hand away.

"Hey," Eddie said. "Don't fuck with Nic, dude." He shoved Batman, and although his motor skills were suffering, he caught Batman sufficiently off guard to upset his balance. Batman stumbled, then righted himself and spun around to face Eddie.

"Eddie," Nic tried to whisper, "don't be a dick. This's fucking Batman"

"Fucking Batman," Eddie said. He was looking at his shoes, but he tried to shove Batman again. Batman grabbed his wrist and threw him against the dumpster. He fell in a heap beside his own puddle of urine.

Nic came up behind Batman and shook his head at Eddie. "Batman's gonna kick your ass, man. Stop being a dick."

Batman was looking out toward the street, where the crowd across the street had stopped, trying to figure out what they had heard.

"You're really into this, aren't you?" Nic asked. Eddie sat up and wiped off his sleeve. "That costume is fucking tight."

"You broke my wrist, you crazy fucker," Eddie said sulkily.

"You deserved it," Nic said. "That's what you get for acting like an asshole."

Then Batman was running. Nic tried to run after him, but Eddie started whining and calling his name, and he hesitated. He looked back at Eddie and when he turned around again it was too late. Batman had gone.

10. HOWIE'S MARDIS GRAS ADVENTURE

Some of my readers, I expect, will be unwilling to accept the testimony of drunks in regard to Batman sightings. The testimony of drunks in regard to their own drunkenness, however, is usually swallowed eagerly. We take such testimonies not just as an account of the facts, but as an affirmation of the drunkenness that brought those facts about. The stories are prefaced with an index of the alcohol consumption leading up to them, and since the drunkenness plays such a crucial role in the stories, their veracity is foregone. Howie's stories were generally like that. The one that began with his sister coming to visit him at his new and temporary home began, also, with Howie sober. He had been sober for several days, and was capable of gauging his sister's reaction to his state with nothing clouding his objectivity other than the inborn conviction that his sister disapproved of every aspect of his life. Her eyes traveled over the room, over the concrete floor and the sleeping bag pressed into the corner, over the grimy windows and stark walls, and Howie knew by the way those eyes trembled that he had succeeded again in falling short of her standards.

"Fisk's cousin is letting me stay here for a little while," he said. "I couldn't keep the apartment. I didn't know how soon I'd find a job. I didn't know whether I could pay rent."

"You could have stayed with us for a few days," she said. "But this..." She shook her head. "Howie, this is disgraceful."

"Jonathan never would have let me stay with you."

"You could have stayed for a few days."

"I was out of work for two weeks."

Howie did love his sister, but she could be cold. Her perception of him was colored by a sororitorial affection that demanded its concern be tempered by total control; she excused her nagging by couching it in professions of love, with little consideration for whether her advice was consistent. "Stop wasting your money," she might tell him. "You need to think ahead, save, plan for the worst." And, later, "Why don't you get a car? Every other human being has a car except you, Howie."

And now,

"You can't stay here," she said. "You can't stay at Johnny Rockets. What are you going to do?"

Why did it bother her so much that he didn't own a car, anyway? He never asked her for rides unless they were both going to the same place. The city was already choked with loud, hissing, honking, farting cars and trucks and motorcycles, and driving only made Howie nervous anyway, and what was the point? Why was the car you drove so important to your identity?

"Howie."

Howie looked up, met her eyes, and winced. "I couldn't find another job anywhere," he said. He sat down on his sleeping bag and leaned against the wall. His shirt stuck. He could feel it. When he pulled away, it would try to cling to the wall, and if Susan saw that, she would judge him, judge his living quarters, judge its sticky walls. She would notice his shirt sticking if he moved, so he had to stay as he was, leaning back against the wall and trying to make it seem comfortable.

Susan stood in the doorway holding her purse in front of her with both hands so it dangled between her legs, and she looked around with those trembling eyes, and no way would she sit down. Not in here.

"Howie," she said, and the name was her whole sentence. Whenever she said "Howie" the way she was saying it now, she meant, *Howard Allen Crane, I am disappointed in you. You have so much talent, so much to offer the world, and what do you do? Nothing. You do nothing. You're thirty-three years old and you're still single and you make no attempt to meet women, and at this rate who knows if you'll ever have kids, and mom would be so disappointed if she saw you right now, sitting on that old disintegrating sleeping bag leaning against a cracked, mildew-coated wall and you haven't showered in three days and you haven't been to the dentist in two years and how much longer do you expect to live eating peanutbutter-and-honey sandwiches for every meal, and you're thirty-three years old working at a goddamn hamburger joint earning two dollars an hour and you don't even own a car! Howard Allen Crane, how do you live with yourself?*

And Howie pulled his knees up to his chest, with his back still pressed against the wall, and he sniffled and said, "Susan."

Susan sighed his name, then turned her head to look out the front door. Howie took advantage of her distraction to peel himself away from the wall, and he scrambled to his feet noisily, hoping that all the sounds would bleed together somehow. Either he had convinced her by the inflection in his voice that he could take care of himself, or she was so disgusted by his apathy that she no longer wanted to try dealing with him, because when she turned back to face him, she sighed again and said only, "Let's go," and led him outside to her car.

They had nothing to say to one another on the ride to Susan's house and their intimacy prevented them from the awkward compulsion to say something anyway, which Howie supposed was its own sort of blessing. His mind was occupied with the imagination of what was to come this evening, at a party at Maynard's house, in what would be Howie's first substantial social outing since his breakdown.

At Susan's house he shaved and bathed and sprayed himself with some of Jonathan's cologne. He had brought his black suit, the only one he hadn't sold, and he wore a silver silk shirt with no tie. Looking himself over in the mirror, picturing Maynard in one of his baggy sweaters and his unpleated Dockers, Howie struggled to comprehend how Adrienne could stay with Maynard for as long as she had.

He walked from Susan and Jonathan's to Maynard's, where he was greeted warmly by Maynard's sister—she was an actress, or at least she hoped to become one, and so it made sense that she would be the one to greet him, to *act*, as it were, like it was great that he had come, and that she was so happy to see him again and relieved that he was okay, and really, Howie, you shouldn't disappear like that, you had us all worried—and he gave her his coat and told her, in response to her final question, "Just ginger ale, please."

The house was teeming with faces. Everywhere Howie looked he saw faces he hadn't seen in weeks. Maynard stood near the stereo holding a short fat glass of something pink, wearing a baggy navy blue sweater and unpleated Dockers. His feet were bare, and, Christ, he hadn't even shaved. It looked like he was trying to grow a beard. Friends of similar miens surrounded him, laughing at his jokes, clapping him on the shoulder, no doubt talking about all the women they had screwed.

The proper thing to do would be to go talk to Maynard and thank him for inviting Howie to the party, to do that first, to show Adrienne that he, Howie, was a decent person, that he cared about etiquette, even if nobody else in the world did anymore. But where was Adrienne? There were a lot of people in that little room. Maybe she had gone somewhere else, to another room, to get away from everything. Maybe she had had enough of Maynard's crude jokes and his loud laugh and she needed a little solitude.

But, no. There she sat, by the fireplace, talking to Jarvis, her hair done up in elaborate curls, but her face plain, untainted by make-up. Her dress was black and low-cut, her arms bare. Howie took a step toward her, and her left hand moved up to brush a lock of hair away from her eyes, and Howie's heart swelled. Then he stopped. Something glittered. On the finger just next to the pinky, Adrienne wore a ring, a gold band and a modest, ice-colored stone.

Maynard's laugh was suddenly louder. Adrienne looked up at Howie and smiled, but her eyes didn't smile. Her eyes started to fill with tears, and the fingers of her right hand flitted over the ring.

"Here you go, Howie," Maynard's sister said. She had appeared at his elbow, holding a glass. "Sorry it took me so long."

Howie took her hand, the one not holding the ginger ale, and pulled her away, toward the kitchen. "Do you have any whisky?" he asked. "I'd really like to have some whisky."

Maynard's sister set the glass down on the counter. She frowned, and Howie wanted to yell.

"I thought you just wanted ginger ale," she said.

He wanted to yell.

"Well, yeah, at first," he said, in a steady, reasonable voice. "But now I'd really like to have some whisky. Do you have any whisky?"

"Sure," she said. It struck Howie suddenly that he didn't even know her name. She was pretty—not like Adrienne, and short, a bit on the fat side, but pretty—and maybe she wasn't acting when she greeted Howie so warmly. How old was she? Twenty-four? Twenty-five? Twenty-six? Thirty? No, not thirty. She was young, and maybe she really did like Howie. He felt like crying.

She took a bottle of Jameson's from a cupboard and unscrewed the cap. "Do you want it with the ginger ale?"

"Can I just have the bottle?"

She looked into his eyes, and her hand trembled. "I don't know if that's a good idea."

"Please? I'm really thirsty." His hand moved toward the bottle.

"Are you feeling okay, Howie?"

"Sure. Sure I'm feeling okay." Maybe he should kiss her. If he kissed her, she might let him have the bottle. Did she know how madly he loved Adrienne? How completely, stupidly, nauseously in love he was with the woman who was going to marry her brother?

"Howie, don't cry."

His hand fell to his side. She put the cap back on and set the bottle on the counter.

"I'm sorry," he said, crying. "I'm so sorry."

"What's wrong, Howie?"

He felt her arms circling him uncertainly, and his body crumbled. "I'm sorry," he said. She patted his back and he said, "My head hurts. Do you have any Advil?"

She let go and opened a drawer beside Howie's hip. A clear plastic bottle with a yellow and brown label rested at the front of the drawer.

"I'm allergic to aspirin," Howie said when she reached for the bottle. "Do you have any ibuprofen?"

"Let me go check the bathroom," she said. "Wait here, all right?"

Howie nodded, and as soon as Maynard's sister was out of the room, he grabbed the bottle of Jameson's and left the house.

He ran for a few blocks and turned into an alley. His hands were numb. He took a long drink from the bottle. His coat was back at Maynard's house. It didn't matter how well he dressed—his chin was weak. Maynard had a very strong chin, with a definite jaw line. Howie's face was droopy. Why would any woman pick him over Maynard, the way his face sagged, and his chin just melted into his neck, no matter how well he dressed?

He shivered.

Even the weather was against him, biting his ears and stinging his face. Of course it would be the coldest night ever, and his coat and scarf and gloves would be back at Maynard's house, and tonight when everybody else had left, the coat would still be there, on the bed where Maynard and Adrienne would be screwing for hours, right on the coat. She would moan, and Maynard would fuck her harder and harder, right on top of Howie's coat. When they were done, she would have little anchor imprints on her nude back from the buttons on the coat, and Maynard would roll off her and wipe his penis on Howie's scarf.

Howie shuddered, and he uncapped the Jameson's again. He had hoped the alcohol would warm him up, but his hands still stung, and his ears felt like they were bleeding. Sometime while drinking, he had sat down against a dumpster, and when he tried to stand up, he fell. His hands were too slow to catch himself. He landed on his teeth and chin. Fingers held up to the lips came back without blood, and he pulled the bottle to his chest and stumbled away, hugging himself, pursing and unpursing his lips to stretch his mouth and keep it from freezing.

Out of the alley and across the street, into the next alley, Howie decided he needed to go inside or he would freeze to death. How would Adrienne feel then, when they discovered his body, stiff and unfeeling, with frozen tears clinging to his cheeks? Even Maynard might be a little sorry!

Howie tripped on a groove in the concrete and fell again, but his hands managed to take the brunt of the fall this time. The bottle rolled out from underneath him, miraculously unbroken. And Howie, scraped and shivering, on his knees, following the bottle with his eyes, saw next to it the wide studded tire of a pick-up truck. The body of the truck was a good foot-and-a-half from the ground, and the driver's side door was solid white while the rest was painted with streaks of blue and green and yellow and purple, and the dented tail gate had *Boy Toy* written on it in faux graffiti print, and surely anybody who owned a truck like that wouldn't mind if Howie sneaked into his house, through the doggy door, and onto the cold red linoleum kitchen floor, to sleep and to warm his body.

Howie's teeth were chattering. The kitchen was dark, and not much warmer than outside. He was on his hands and knees, and his hands were flecked with blood. Blood! Funny, then, that they didn't hurt. Still, the responsible thing to do would be to wash the wounds, to clean out the grit and filth from the alley. An infection could be disastrous. How would Adrienne react to seeing him with a prosthetic hand? Would her pity give birth to profound admiration, or would she merely shudder in revulsion when he reached out to hug her?

The problem was that doggy door. He hadn't thought much of it when he came in, but looking back at the rubber flap now, the question of what kind of dog would require such a large opening struck him like a physical blow, would have bowled him over had he not already been, and he shook his head and decided to crawl right back out into the cold.

After that brief respite indoors, the spite of that February air was even bitterer. His hands throbbed and his nose felt like the tip of a frozen French fry, and why the hell had he left that bottle of Jameson's back there next to the truck? Maybe he should go back and get it.

Howie crawled on his hands and knees across the brittle lawn to the alley, and when he reached the truck it occurred to him that the owner probably only drove it on rare occasions. He probably never kept anything of value in that truck, so what sense would it make to lock the door, especially back here in the private alley mere yards away from his bedroom window? Howie grabbed the bottle from beside the truck's wheel and stood up to test the door. Sure enough, it opened, and he crawled inside and curled into a fetal ball. He sucked down another shot of whisky and tried not to think about how warm it was back at Maynard's house, and how much warmer it would be in bed with Adrienne, to hold her, and to be held by her, and to feel the beat of her heart through her bare breast, and how many carats was that diamond, anyway? What a plain, traditional ring it was, slim gold band with a diamond in the center. Was that the best Maynard could do?

The truck was preferable to the house only in that Howie didn't have to worry about some huge mongrel dog here in the truck, but it was still inhumanly cold. If he could only turn the heater on, he might be okay. He breathed into his hands and smelled whisky, and he figured, heck, maybe the keys were above the sun visor. People still did that, right? With a truck this garish, might not the owner leave the keys inside out of a subconscious urge to see the thing stolen, to get it the hell out of there—

There they were. If Howie could just get his fingers loosened up a bit and make them work... Christ! The air was cold! The truck's vents were blowing cold air! Howie pressed buttons and turned knobs until all pointed to something red, and even that didn't make a difference. He rubbed his hands together and directed the vents toward the floor. He hugged himself.

"Stupid Denver," Howie said. "Stupid winter," but the cab was growing warmer. Before long, it was almost balmy. He moved the vents again, and now the air from them was like a zephyr, and he could almost forget how wretched it had been without.

Why was he still in Denver, anyway? It didn't make sense to stay here after all the crap he had been through. Fisk and Stewart and Davie were playing a show next week without him, with Stewart's goddamn little brother, and Adrienne obviously didn't give a damn about him, and Susan... Susan!

Screw it. Fisk and Stewart and Davie and Stewart's little brother were going to play a Mardi Gras show at the goddamn Bluebird, well, screw them. A Mardi Gras Party in Denver! There was no reason for Howie to stay here. Why not New Orleans? He could go to New Orleans, and he could celebrate Mardi Gras there for real, and he could find a new band, and he could be playing shows out in New Orleans while Fisk and all his Fiskish assholes were sitting around in Denver wasting their lives.

The crunching-metal sound of the pick-up truck scraping against a dumpster pulled Howie out of his reverie. He blinked and looked around and shook himself. This could be dangerous if he wasn't paying close attention. He freed one hand from the steering wheel to take another drink of whisky, then he put the uncapped bottle between his legs and shifted into second gear.

The truck was squirrelly on the icy streets. Howie had a tough time getting the hang of it, but by the time he reached the entrance ramp for I-70 it was beginning to feel all right. Really, starting and stopping were the only hard parts. Once he got out on the interstate it would be all straight and no traffic. All he had to do was stay awake and stay between the lines and just go straight.

Had they noticed yet that he was gone? Maynard's sister might have said something, but who would care? Adrienne hadn't even acknowledged his presence, and now it was three o' clock in the morning and Maynard was probably already passed out drunk, snoring next to her, and she would be awake next to him, twisting the ring on her finger and wondering about her life. Howie wouldn't even write from New Orleans. She would just have to wonder.

Or, no. He would send her a postcard on her birthday, real plain and bland, with a terse, impersonal message that would remind her how little he cared about her, and this was all just a formality, sending a postcard on her birthday, because he remembered things like that, even if they didn't mean anything to him. And then, when he finished recording his first CD, he would send her a copy, and the first thing she would do is open it and turn to the THANK YOU section of the liner notes to see if her name was listed, and she would twist the ring on her finger and think about how *fat* Maynard had gotten, and how he never did anything anymore, just drank beer with his friends. In about ten or fifteen years, Howie would come back to Denver, just for a visit. He would have kept in touch with Susan, and he would tell her how well things were going for him. But she and Jonathan would be struggling, trying to put their kids through college and both still working full-time, and she would have to ask him for help. The best, though, would come later, after he had seen to Susan, when he went to visit Maynard and Adrienne. To Maynard he would just be a hazy memory, a semi-familiar face that alcohol had drowned in the intervening years, but to Adrienne...Oh, how she had missed him! He had stayed in shape, not like Maynard, and age only made him look more distinguished, with traces of gray in his hair and handsome crow's feet like JFK's when he smiled. All the drugs and booze and sexual misadventures of Maynard's youth would have rendered him impotent or sterile, and there would be no children, no reason for Adrienne to stay in this loveless, pathetic marriage, and Howie would have forgiven her. That was what made Howie remarkable: for all he had suffered, his love for Adrienne was still strong, not some fleeting fantasy, and she would mean as much to him in ten or fifteen years as she ever did, and he would give her a second chance, and she would abandon Maynard to go back with Howie to Louisiana and live this life, the life she was meant to live, with him, forever.

The truck convulsed. Howie straightened his back and blinked. He was far outside Denver, and the darkness of the night was dwindling. Somewhere in the east the sun was contemplating the next day, and the truck bucked and Howie took his foot off the gas and looked around. Eastern Colorado, flat and uninspiring, stretched out for miles in every direction, and the truck coughed and shuddered.

The needle of the gas gauge had gone past the E, resting now impotently on its side, and Howie thought about how foolish it had been of him to drive drunk, to take somebody else's car and not even check to see if it had enough gas to get to New Orleans. He coasted to a stop on the shoulder of the interstate and hot air blew into his face. The goddamn truck was uncomfortable. The heat was oppressive, too much for Howie, too much for any rational man. He opened the door and spilled out onto the cold asphalt. He climbed into the bed of the truck and took off his suit coat and balled it up underneath his head. What he dreamed about can only be imagined, since he himself had forgotten it by the time the highway patrolman woke him up hours later, when the sun was up and the sky was blue and the day was full of promise.

11. A NIGHT AT THE OLD HOTEL

Howie Crane was, when he was arrested on the side of the interstate at the age of thirty-three, already a seasoned drinker. For Wayne Talbot, drinking as a pastime had up until the last few weeks never much appealed to him, so when he embraced it as a method of self-destruction, he was not as practiced at it as he might have been. He had become accustomed to a life without alcohol as, living in a basement apartment for half a year, he had become accustomed to a life without light. If that latter deprivation had had any effect on his psyche, he was not consciously aware of it. There were, after all, plenty of other legitimate reasons for his misery, and to boil it down to a simple longing for the sun would have been to cheapen it. Still, having light—knowing that some sort of external change accompanied the sweeping of the hands on his three-hundred-dollar watch—couldn't have hurt.

These, however, were not the sorts of considerations that usually occurred to Wayne Talbot. He was a pragmatic young man, and he had labored most of his life under the notion that he could control the flow of his emotions on his own. Weather, time, changes in the government—these were all things that went on regardless of how he lived his life, and so he had never bothered to devote much thought to them.

His ambivalence toward daylight was such that, when he woke up at a few minutes after four on a Friday afternoon, he loathed himself not at all for sleeping through the day, but only set his mind to trying to calculate the volume of alcohol he had poured into himself in the last twenty-four hours. One pale shaft of light made its way past the edge of the heavy curtains, but the curtains themselves absorbed enough of the fading sun to cast a gray pall over the room, and by that pall Wayne could see his right hand splayed out inches from his eyes, and beyond that he could see underneath the bed. The bed wasn't boxed in underneath, like so many beds in newer hotels, and he appreciated the view such openness afforded him. He wondered why some hotels bothered to box in the undersides of the beds at all, and supposed it had something to do with the cleaning staff, tired of getting down on their hands and knees day after day to retrieve travelers' jetsam.

Wayne imagined how the maid would respond to his corpse. The first response would be horror, then pity, but ultimately, the maid must fall into the antagonistic mood typical of all who worked in the customer service industry. She would see Wayne as just one more inconsiderate asshole she had to clean up after. Once the coroner zipped him up and toted him away, the maid would be left scrubbing at the spot on the carpet where he had vomited up all the alcohol he had just forced down his throat to give himself the courage to pull the trigger.

With the same suddenness that the thought motivating him had entered his head, Wayne lurched up and staggered to the bathroom. Most of last nights' vodka made it into the bowl, cut with yellow bile and a handful of half-digested white cheddar Wheatables. And wiping the corners of his lips, Wayne sat on the floor with his back against the bath tub, giving his stomach time to decide whether it was finished. His eyes were closed, and a thin sheen of sweat graced his cheeks and his forehead.

He didn't spend much time anymore trying to figure out where he had gone wrong. When he had first gotten to Denver, it seemed like everything was going to be fine. He was only twenty-four years old and expected to be earning a salary in the neighborhood of sixty-thousand working from home. Proposals kept coming in from small businesses all over the country, followed quickly by checks for such sums that he could pay for rent and food, invest enough to ensure a comfortable retirement, and still have enough to spend on himself. The miserliness and workoholism that had ruined his personal relationships through his entire college career in Berkeley finally seemed to be paying off.

One aspect of moving that so appealed to Wayne was the chance to start over, to be in a new place where nobody had developed any preconceptions about him, and he didn't have to suffer being known as "that computer geek kid," or "that weird guy with the corduroy pants." In Denver, Wayne could establish himself as he saw himself, and with time others would see him the same way.

Maybe the problem was that he wasn't sure how he did see himself. Before long, he found himself falling into the same old patterns. For the first few months, he hardly left his apartment, and when he did leave, it was usually just to get groceries at the King Soopers two blocks away. The apartment itself might have been a poor choice, too. The appeal of it had been its size and seclusions, and he had envisioned grand parties there, with no one to complain if it was too loud. Things might have been different if he had instead settled in an apartment building full of people his own age, people he could pass in the hallways and nod to, and make small talk with at the mail boxes. As it was, the beauty of his apartment was wasted; what did it matter if he could host grand parties, if he didn't have anybody to invite to them?

So he decided, after those early lonely nights, that if he wanted to meet people he was going to have to make a conscious effort to do so. He started going to coffee shops and sitting for hours at a time, making a deliberate attempt to show off the cover of whatever book he had brought along, inviting conversation with every bit of vocabulary his body language commanded. Nobody talked to him. He didn't know how this was supposed to happen. He would berate himself endlessly as he sat staring at the words in his book, not even remembering to make a show of turning the pages every once in a while. Invariably he would leave without having amassed the nerve necessary to converse with a stranger.

On one of those nights, he had gone to the cash register and seen a little pink flyer for some kind of art show at a place called the Bug Jar. It said there would be films showing, and since Wayne considered himself a bit of a film buff, he decided to go.

At the show, among scores of people dressed in tight clothes, with black-frame glasses and unwashed hair, Wayne had felt out of place and, when the discussions he overheard centered around local musicians and artists, unforgivably ignorant. But it was there that he decided to stop worrying about his status as a recent transplant and finally embraced it. "Actually, I just moved here from California," he told people over and over again, and then confessed to never having heard of whatever subject was being entertained. His sociability that night had secured him an invitation to a party later in the week, and for a while things seemed to be looking up. There were a couple of random sexual encounters, completely foreign to him, and with girls who didn't really appeal to him, but it felt good to have such intimate contact with anybody after so much time alone. From somebody at the party, Wayne heard about a rap group that was playing later in the week, and he went to that, too.

That was the night, more than the party, where everything started to change. For the first time in his life, Wayne felt like he belonged to a group, if only fleetingly. He sat around a table at the bar, sandwiched between people who looked him in the eyes and talked to him. They had drinks with him, and when they left the show, they invited him *by name.*

Wayne didn't know whose apartment they were stumbling toward, and while they were stumbling there he wasn't sure whose weight he was supporting, but when they had been there for a couple hours, and he ended up in the living room talking to Burke, he felt for the first time that he had made a real human connection. All of Burke's friends were cool, all funny and intelligent, and Wayne enjoyed spending time with each of them, but it later became clear that he was at the periphery of their circle rather than in it. He became comfortable going out in Denver, and there was a short list of people he could even call to find out when things were happening, but Burke was the only person who ever treated him like anything more than a passing acquaintance.

Burke was also the only person who ever called Wayne. The entire time he was in Denver, he never got a phone call from any of the people he met. When he called others, he was greeted warmly enough, but he always got the feeling that if he didn't reach out, he would return to being alone.

That feeling reached its nadir during the holidays. Wayne had an uncle and an aunt in Colorado Springs whom he could have called, and chances were that they would have felt sufficiently guilty to take him in. He envisioned the entire day, with his aunt getting drunk and talking about what a wonderful person his mother had been, and his uncle sitting in the corner frowning, trying to figure out how the hell they were related. It was the only prospect less appealing than being alone.

Wayne pulled himself up by the toilet and leaned forward against the sink. Drinking was a habit he had spurned through college but he had come to utilize here as a means of cementing new relationships. These crippling hangovers, which had been his only company of late, had the tendency to set his mind wandering. It was under their influence, at his apartment one month earlier, that he had come up with the idea to disappear. The convincing took a bit longer and the preparation a couple days longer still, but he had been in this hotel for about two weeks now, by his estimate. He hadn't brought a calendar with him.

He ran some cold water over a plush wash cloth and shuffled out into the main room. It was still dark, getting darker. Custom suggested he ought to get something to eat, but he was in no hurry. He lay down on the ornate bed and draped the wash cloth over his face.

Burke had no doubt gotten the letter by now. There had been a moment, halfway through the writing of his letter, when guilt assailed him for dumping everything on Burke's shoulders, but Burke would understand, if anybody would. After all, Burke had done the same thing with Wayne a couple months earlier, when he was having trouble with Angie, or Abby. Burke had been a mess that night, and among all his friends in Denver, he had reached out to Wayne. Wayne understood that this did not necessarily mean that Burke felt closer to him than he did to some of his older friends, but unlike most of his other friends, Wayne had no prejudices about Abby, or Angie, or whatever, and that kind of objectivity was what Burke needed.

Obviously, when Wayne offered what comfort he could to Burke, he wasn't doing so with the expectation that Burke would one day pay him back with a like display of friendship. It was simply that, when it came down to this, Burke was the only one Wayne could trust. Without Burke, he wouldn't have bothered with the whole *Wonderful Life* exercise. He would just have left his body for his landlord to find.

By now, enough time had passed for Burke to gauge the reaction of their friends to Wayne's absence. Together, they would be able to determine if his life was worth living.

12. Adam's next night out

"A Dark Knight's Dark Night" appeared as the cover story in Denver's independent weekly paper, the *Westword*, in the late autumn of 2003. It was no longer news then, but the article was a more in-depth rendering of the events that had been covered earlier in the year and then forgotten about. With everything else going on in the world that spring, even the story of a costumed vigilante was hardly considered compelling enough for a major news break. Adam's picture did make the front page of the *Denver Post* on the day after he was discovered, but below the fold, in the left-hand corner, and with only two scant paragraphs and an invitation for the reader to turn to another page somewhere deep inside.

The *Westword* piece was illustrated with a rough portrait of a figure that looked something like Batman, composed of image scraps cut and pasted together in the semblance of a second-grader's art collage. The sub-header, in a similarly crude font, read, "What made a local small business owner go Batty?"

The piece was mostly biographical, limited to what led up to the police report and with only the laziest conjecture as to what actually happened that night. Much was made of Adam's relationship with his parents, and of their success in the non-profit world. There were a few great quotes from some early 90's news stories, feel-good pieces, with a young Adam talking about how lucky he was to have spent his childhood giving away toys with his parents to less fortunate families.

Over the course of the years, that budding philanthropist became the troubled man in an abandoned parking lot on 28th street, struggling into a Batman costume within the confines of his car. I like to think he had at least toyed with the notion of creating his own superhero identity, but ultimately found the project too daunting. The first options that occurred to him would have been bland derivatives like Mighty Man or Captain Power, and the more he tried to come up something unique, the more intricate the corresponding costume had to be.

The allure of Batman was that Adam didn't have to waste time designing a costume, or even, thanks to sundry sellers on eBay, manufacturing one. And since what he was attempting had never been done before in this world (a world which, he might have argued, demanded heroics more than the robot- and clone- and malevolent alien-populated worlds of Marvel and DC did), he was not obligated to demonstrate any true innovation. If Stan Lee had created a character called Batman in the sixties and had him running around fighting crime, he obviously would have been labeled a plagiarist, but Stan Lee was limited only by his pencil and his imagination, and motivated, moreover, by profit. It would be unfair to expect Adam, with more practical concerns, to demonstrate the same sort of flair.

Accepting that Adam actually did have a confrontation with Nic and Eddie on his first night out, we must accept, too, how disappointed he would have been by it, at least initially. The man he hurled into a dumpster was no master crimelord, not even a petty crook, and in battling him, Adam was only wasting time, distracting himself from the war. But, was the man innocent? It was on that notion that Adam paused, and carefully considering that notion, Adam could curb his disappointment. The man he had attacked was a public menace, without question, and it seemed perfectly likely that he might have, in past circumstances, turned his aggression on somebody weak and helpless. Certainly, his friend's remark about parole suggested that

Adam might not have been the first to face his malignancy. His injury that night might just change the way he comported himself with strangers on the street in the future. He would know Batman was out there, watching. Heartened, Adam, as I imagine him, would have adjusted his cowl, flexed his leather-decked hands, and headed back out to carry on the fight.

One question the *Westword* story did attempt to address was that of Adam's venue. It is not insignificant, the reporter suggested, that Adam ended up on the corner of 29th and Arapahoe, in the heart of Denver's Five Points neighborhood. In Denver's recent history, and especially in the years of Adam's youth when he had devoted so much of his time studying the exploits of superheroes on his living room floor, Five Points had an unsavory reputation. It was imagined by the white children of wealthy parents to be a haven for crime and gang violence, imagery that was rooted in the playground gossip of Bloods and Crips and hookers, fueling nightmares for Adam and his peers, and making the existence of costumed crimefighters seem not only reasonable, but necessary.

Although it had its barren spots, with big square buildings and mostly empty parking lots, where comfort and aesthetics had been neglected in deference to industrialization, the streets Adam was patrolling that night were not swarming with miscreants. They were not swarming with any life. He alone cast moving shadows by the rows of street lights. Those, too, bothered him, being too frequent to create any useful caches of darkness from which to strike. In the comic books, Batman hung around on roof tops and swung down to crime scenes with long ropes anchored somewhere off-panel. Adam understood the importance of surprise in confronting evil, and he saw the benefit, too, in exploiting gravity to turn himself into a weapon, tackling criminals at terminal velocity, using them to cushion his fall, so that nothing was left to do except bind them with the very rope he had employed in his flight from the building top.

However, although those maneuvers might look impressive in a static series of boxes, they were impractical for the streets. The physics involved in swinging from the talon of a gargoyle toward a violent rapist were far too complicated to calculate in the time needed, and the risk of injury outweighed any possible advantages. The alternative was to rely on stealth, to conceal himself in shadows until an opportunity to do good afforded itself. But concealing himself was what he had been doing when he was discovered by Nic and Eddie, and the mere fact that he had been discovered made the prospect of hiding less appealing. It seemed to reduce him to the same level as the breed he was meant to combat.

Stripped of the power to make a properly dramatic entrance, when Adam finally stumbled on an opportunity to protect the innocent, he could do little more than step forward and announce his presence in a menacing voice.

There is no telling how precisely Adam viewed the scene that he approached. What the *Westword* described as a frustrated designated driver trying to coax his inebriated younger sister back home, Adam seemed to witness as the abuse by a pimp of his defiant employee. He saw a young man dressed in sweat pants and a hooded sweatshirt beneath an oversized Broncos jacket grabbing a girl by her elbow, and he saw that girl struggling to pull free, kicking her pimp in the leg.

The young man grabbed her by the hair and told her to get in the fucking car. She twisted around to bite his hand, and he yanked his hand away and swore. Adam was already moving toward them, to the idling car pulled up crookedly to the sidewalk and the cloud of carbon monoxide hovering in the cold air around them.

"Let her go," he said, because he had already been forming the words before the girl had broken free. She had backed away and was screaming slurred obscenities at her brother, but when Adam spoke, she fell quiet.

Adam hesitated. He cleared his throat. "She doesn't want to go with you," he told the young man in the most authoritative voice he could manage, no doubt disappointed by the tremor forced on his speech by the frigid air. "Get in your car and leave."

The young man Adam had taken for a pimp was too awed to be angry. His sister overcame her shock almost instantly. "Yeah," she said. "Fuck *you*, Waffles." She stumbled over to Adam and put her hand on his arm. "Get in your fucking car and leave. This is fucking Batman, you prick."

If Adam's interference had stalled the young man's anger, the girl's insult was enough to rev it back up. "Damn, Tally. Stop fucking around."

"Leave her alone," Adam said. He put his hands on his hips and thrust his chest out slightly.

"Look, man," Waffles said. "I don't want to fuck with you, but this isn't none of your business. Why don't you go find some bad guys to beat up or something, and let me take care of my—"

"Fuck off, Waffles," the girl said. She hugged Adam's arm and looked up at him. "Fuck him up, Batman."

Waffles reached for the girl, and Adam shoved him backwards.

"Fuck him up!" the girl screamed.

Waffles shoved Adam. "Watch it, man," he said. "She's fucking drunk," but Adam had lost interest in talking. He lunged forward with an animal growl and grabbed Waffles by the throat, then threw him into the side of the car.

"Jesus—"

Adam punched him in the stomach, and he crumbled.

"Holy shit," the girl said. She had lost her balance when Adam pulled away from her, and now she was sitting on her ass on the cold ground. Adam looked down at her. "Are you okay?" he asked gruffly.

"You crazy motherfucker," Waffles said. "I'm going to fuck you up."

Adam spun around as the guy was climbing into his car. He took hold of the guy's hood and yanked him back, letting him fall to the pavement.

From across the street came an angry voice. Adam looked up and saw two more men coming toward him. One of them was calling to the girl, by name, asking what the hell was going on. The girl giggled.

"Waffles," said the other, as they got closer. "You okay, bro?"

These two were bigger than their friend, but not too big. Adam's muscles tensed. One of the men held back, his eyes shifting uncertainly from Adam to his prostrate friend. The other ran forward and shoved Adam, but Adam had anticipated the attack. He moved back only enough to throw off the guy's momentum, then stepped in and delivered an uppercut with his right arm. His fist glanced off the man's cheek, and the man shoved him again.

"Shit," said the girl from somewhere behind him. He almost stumbled. Beyond the periphery of his mask he could see Waffles making his way to his feet. Then somebody kicked his own legs out from underneath him. He fell on his back, rolled to his side and tried to get up. The one called Waffles ran forward and kicked Adam in the ribs, and the other, who had hesitated when they first approached, kicked him in the head. Adam saw bright flashes of light, and he forgot for a moment about trying to stand. They kept kicking, all three of them now, and then one grabbed his cape and yanked him to his knees. The girl was still sitting in a heap on the cracked asphalt, still giggling. Waffles delivered a quick succession of punches to his belly, and whoever had his cape wrapped it once around his neck and squeezed. Adam swung out and hit Waffles in the testicles, something heavy hit the back of his skull, and he fell.

13. Howie and Jarvis and the girls in the back of Jarvis's car

The owner of the truck Howie had stolen was not interested in pressing charges, so when Howie was picked up from the drunk tank the day after his arrest, he was as free as a man can be whose heart is chained to a woman. He had called Adrienne from the jail, but it was Jarvis Chesterton who picked him up. Jarvis had been a friend of Howie's for years, their relationship drifting easily between the business of show promotion and the camaraderie of drinking. His dark hair was cut short, crowning a broad face with a U-shaped jaw, a face almost cold in its impassivity. The coldness was belied by a hearty and easily provoked laughter. When Adrienne called him the morning after the party, Jarvis had been nursing his own hangover and was convinced in that hazy state that he was hearing the beginning of a joke whose punch line, he hoped, would include an invitation out for more drinks. He had chuckled, and then at the other end of the phone Adrienne was silent. After a moment, she had told Jarvis, "I'm really worried," and he understood that this was actually happening.

Once he had time to consider the implications of what Howie had done, Jarvis felt a swell of pride for the little guy. To Jarvis, Howie's stunt demonstrated that he was finally coming to terms with the idea that Adrienne was beyond his reach. The response to that epiphany was not only logical, but awesome in the literal sense of the world.

Adrienne had posted Howie's bail, but she could not break her plans for dinner with Maynard and his parents to drive all the way to Burlington and bring Howie home. Jarvis told Adrienne it would be healthier for Howie if he went, anyway, and his going would save them from having to break the news to Howie's colossal bitch of a sister. After picking Howie up, Jarvis drove a few blocks from the jail to a gas station and made Howie refill the tank while he went inside. He bought a bottle of green tea, a Rockstar energy drink, and a bag of sunflower seeds. Outside, between him and the car and slightly to his left, he noticed the smile of a young girl standing near a Coke machine with another girl. Jarvis smiled back, and the girl who had smiled moved toward him. Her friend hesitated.

"Are you guys headed west?" she asked. Jarvis kept walking, and the girl fell into step next to him. She was short, wearing a backpack, with straight brown hair that went down nearly to her waist. Her friend, slightly taller, with fat red cheeks and wide eyes, followed them, hugging her arms. "We're trying to get Denver," the first girl added.

"Baby, we *are* Denver," Jarvis said. He looked across the roof of the car and called Howie's name, and when Howie looked up Jarvis tossed him the Rockstar.

"What?" the girl asked.

Jarvis took a good look at the girls. They seemed young, and under most circumstances he would have balked at the idea of picking them up. But now he was thinking of Howie, and thinking that maybe a pair of girls like this was what Howie needed to keep his mind off of Adrienne. "Why do you want to get to Denver?" he asked.

"We're trying to get to a concert," the girl said. Her friend still wasn't talking. She was just looking at their car, chewing on the corner of her lip.

"Do your parents know you're hitchhiking?" asked Jarvis.

"We're eighteen," the girl said. "Well, I mean, I'm nineteen. I'm over eighteen. I mean, my parents aren't..."

"Do they know you're hitchhiking?" Jarvis asked.

The girl rolled her eyes. She turned to her friend, who shrugged and looked at the ground. The girl turned back to Jarvis, straightened her back and sucked in her cheeks. He wondered if she was trying to make herself look more mature. "We can give you gas money," she said.

Jarvis waved his hand and said, "Psh."

"We're meeting some friends in Denver for this concert," the girl said. "We couldn't leave with them because they left yesterday, and we both had to work. That means we've got a ride home for tonight. We just need to get there."

"I don't want to get pulled over down the road and find out you're runaways," Jarvis said. He liked making a game out of it. "If your parents are looking for you, Howie and I could get into a lot of trouble." Without looking away from the girl, Jarvis could tell Howie was nodding.

"Our parents said we could go so long as they didn't have to drive us."

Stupid Howie. Nodding! He would have left this luscious thing here on the curb.

"Your parents sound pretty awesome," Jarvis said. "That's Howie. I'm Jarvis. The back door's unlocked."

He got into the driver's seat. The girl got in behind him, and her friend went around to the other side of the car and took the seat behind Howie's.

"My name is Katie," the girl said.

Howie got in and frowned at Jarvis, but he turned in his seat to tell the girls, "Hi. I'm Howie."

"Beth," the other girl said in a soft voice.

Jarvis pulled the car out of the gas station and headed for the interstate. "What concert are you guys going to?"

"It's this band called Wilco," Katie said. "They're just about my favorite band ever."

"Sure," Jarvis said. "Wilco's great. Howie used to played with Wilco, did you know that?" He grinned at Howie.

"What are you talking about?" Howie asked. "Listen, we opened for Jay Farrar once. That was about the closest we ever got to playing with Wilco."

Jarvis sighed. Howie was one of the shrewdest characters Jarvis had ever known, but his was a special kind of shrewdness. He could manipulate people and situations astoundingly, but only if in doing so he was manipulating himself. There was a certain sort of charm in that, Jarvis supposed, but Howie's arbitrary integrity made it tough to convince him to bullshit, even when bullshitting was in his best interest.

Jarvis found the girl's eyes in the rearview mirror. "You know who Jay Farrar is?" he asked.

"Um, yeah. Is he in Wilco?"

Howie snorted. "No, he's not in Wilco."

"He *was*," said Jarvis.

"No," said Howie. "He was in Uncle Tupelo, but, see, when Uncle Tupelo broke up, the members split up, and they made Son Volt and Wilco. Jay—"

"Howie," Jarvis said in a low voice, "stop jerking off. Nobody gives a shit about Uncle Tupelo or Son Volt. Wilco's big. Wilco's what you should be selling."

"You're in a band?" Katie asked Howie.

Howie started to nod, caught himself, and took a long drink of his Rockstar instead of answering. The girl took his shame for modesty.

"What do you play?" she asked.

Jarvis let go of the wheel to pantomime playing a bass.

"Bass?" the girl said, and Howie almost smiled. "That's awesome! Beth plays bass, too."

Howie turned in his seat to look at the other girl. "Really? How long have you been playing?"

"Only for like two years," the girl said softly. Jarvis had to strain to hear her.

"That's so great," Howie said. "That's really great."

Jarvis wondered if these girls were alive yet when Howie had gotten his first guitar. In the interest of abetting the potential chemistry between them, he decided not to ask. Ever since Jarvis had introduced Howie to Adrienne, Howie had been in a sexual rut, and now, more than anybody he knew, Howie needed to get laid. Even if getting him there involved ignoring certain statutes, Jarvis was willing to play a role in it.

"What kind of music do you play?" Katie asked.

Howie shrugged. "It's kind of hard to put a label on, really. See, I draw inspiration from a lot of really different, disparate sources. Like, anything from Loretta Lynn to Camper Van Beethoven."

The girl nodded, but Jarvis guessed by the cloud covering her eyes that the names Howie was spewing meant nothing to her. Still, she was not ignoring him, and that had to be significant. Even if she was only a child, she was enthralled enough by Howie's status that she felt compelled to feign a certain erudition, at least enough to justify her enthusiasm. "I want to see you play some time! Do you ever play shows?"

"We...I'm having—" Howie coughed softly. "I'm not playing with the band I was playing with right now."

"Oh," the girl said. "That sucks." She waited for Howie to elaborate, but all Howie said was, "Yeah," and then nobody wanted to talk.

Jarvis looked back up at the rearview mirror, and the girl named Katie was looking at Howie. Her friend was just staring out the window to the north.

"I've been having some personal problems lately," Howie said softly. "That's why I'm not playing with the band right now."

Jesus, no. Jarvis knew where Howie was heading, knew what horrors he would be unleashing on his chances of getting laid, but he could do nothing to stop it. He imagined this was how average German citizens must have felt during the Holocaust.

"What kind of problems?" Katie asked.

"Howie," Jarvis muttered, "don't do this."

If Howie heard him, his heart overruled the counsel. "There's a girl," Howie said. "Back in Denver. I guess I probably don't need to say more than that."

"Aww," the girl said. She almost whimpered. Even her friend looked up, and for the first time her face expressed something other than glazed wonder. It was pity. Jarvis wanted to club Howie. He always pulled this game. He'd find strangers and tell them of his struggle to win Adrienne's heart, and the strangers, privy only to the selective details that Howie offered, would invariably decide that Howie deserved love, if anybody did. He could be charming in short bursts, which had sparked in the beginning some doubt even for Adrienne, doubt about her future with Maynard. The random people, men and women, whom Howie encountered at bars and coffee houses, would not witness his charm give way to petulance. They would be convinced that Adrienne must deep inside care more for Howie than this Maynard douche bag, and they would encourage Howie to hang in there. What Howie was doing, Jarvis had come to realize, was subtly offering his opinions to others, in such a way that they believed they were coming to their own conclusions when they told Howie what he most wanted to hear. These girls, with the acute emotions and romanticism of youth, would be putty in his rhetorical hands.

"When we first we met," Howie said, "we were just two people with a few common interests. She had come to one of my shows, and she was into the music, and we hung out for hours that night talking. About nothing, and everything."

Jarvis's pipe was in the glove box. He wondered if the girls would freak out if he started smoking now. He couldn't bear to listen to this again.

"She was seeing somebody at the time, and she let me know," Howie went on. "And in a way, that made it easier. It was like the burden was lifted. I didn't have to impress this girl, didn't have to put on the face that every guy puts on when he's trying to get into the girl's pants. I could be completely honest with Adrienne, and she with me, because neither of us was trying to get anything out of the other."

"Scuse me Howie," Jarvis said, reaching across Howie's lap to open the glove box. He had already loaded a bowl, oblivious to however the decision to do so on his way to the Kit Carson County Jail might have been perceived by anybody else. It was a long time to spend on the road, and absurd to imagine spending it with only as much marijuana in his system as he had smoked before leaving the house that morning. Fortunately, Howie was still turned in his seat, not paying much attention to what was going on in front of him.

"And of course," Howie said, "being in that situation, we ended up exposing facets of ourselves that nobody ever exposes to each other, strengths and weaknesses, hopes and fears—things that old couples who have devoted their lives to one another are still unearthing thirty years into their marriage."

Jarvis took his lighter from the console, clutched the steering wheel between his knees, and took a deep hit.

Howie kept going. "After a while, I realized I had fallen in love, against my better judgment and without even realizing it."

It couldn't be both, could it? If he didn't even realize it, Jarvis wondered, what better judgment could it be against?

"I told Adrienne..." Howie wrinkled his nose. He turned and noticed Jarvis. "Dude! What are you doing? I just got arrested! What if we get pulled over?"

"You just got arrested?" one of the girls asked. "Can I have a hit of that?" asked the other. It was pretty much simultaneous, as far as Jarvis could tell. He didn't know which had said what.

"Sorry, little guy," Jarvis said. "I needed that. Don't worry. I won't get pulled over." He held out his hand with the little glass pipe and the lighter to the back seat. It was the less talkative girl who took it. Jarvis had already forgotten her name. Her friend, Kate, repeated the question, "You just got arrested?"

Howie sighed.

"Dude," Jarvis said in a low voice. "Tell em why. They'll eat it up."

"I got arrested," Howie said with a sigh. "Saturday morning. I...uh...I was driving drunk."

"He doesn't drive much," Jarvis added.

"I don't drive much," Howie confirmed.

"He doesn't even own a car."

"I think they're vile. They're destroying the earth. We need cars dead."

"What were you driving then?" Kate asked. "When you were arrested?" Her friend offered her the pipe, and she shook her head, so her friend took another hit. Beth, that was her name.

"I—" Howie sunk down into his seat. He took the pipe when Beth passed it back to the front and handed it to Jarvis. "On Friday night, her boyfriend proposed to her. Well, that's when I found out about it, anyway. I don't know when he proposed. I didn't find out until I saw the ring on her finger. I was so wrecked I ran off with a bottle of whiskey, got drunk on the streets, and stole a stranger's truck to take myself away from all this."

"Oh my god," Kate said. She reached forward to put a hand on Howie's forearm. "That's so horrible."

This is where it would come. The girls would assure Howie that he and Adrienne shared something truly special, and that he should fight for it. They would justify for him his pre-established resolution to win Adrienne at any cost. Jarvis took another hit, then set the pipe down in the console.

"You've got to kick that chick to the curb, man," Beth said.

Jarvis looked up at the rearview mirror. Beth was still staring out the window. Kate was nodding. "Yeah," she said. "I mean, how long ago was it you guys met?"

Howie's eyes were glazed.

"It's been about a year and a half," Jarvis said. "I introduced them."

"And she knows how you feel about her, right?" Beth asked.

"I put it all on the line just before Christmas," Howie responded. "I told her everything."

"But she's known for longer than that," Jarvis said.

"She knew I liked her. I told her that much."

"Point is, she's had time," Beth said. She had an almost gravelly voice, and Jarvis wondered if maybe he had misjudged her age. He liked to hope he had. "She knew what she could have had, and she passed it up. That's her problem."

"Totally," Kate said. "I mean, this might seem weird, cause I know we just met, but you seem like an awesome guy. You shouldn't get so hung up on this girl."

Yes! Yes! Jarvis wanted to pump in his fist in the air and scream *Preach on, sisters!* But he kept his hands on the wheel and watched the highway. Howie had heard all this from him plenty of times. Maybe now, if Jarvis kept aloof, and the message was being delivered by two attractive enough females, Howie would listen.

"What you're doing now is giving her the best of both worlds," Beth said. "She gets to see you when she wants to; she knows you'll always be there; and then she's always got this other guy to go home to. You need to say, 'Fine. You want him, you take him. Have a nice fucking life.'"

"Yeah," Kate said. "Yeah." The girls couldn't see it, but Howie's face had completely lost the spark that had illuminated it a few minutes ago when he was talking about his earliest encounters with Adrienne. His brow was knitted, and Jarvis imagined that he was close to accepting what he was hearing, maybe picturing his life without Adrienne for the first time in months. "If you let her go, and she really cared about you, she'll come for you. You win. And if you never hear from her again, then it's all for the best, and it's good you found out when you did."

"I mean, you fucking stole a truck for her," Beth said. "I wish a guy would do something like that for me. If she can't recognize how awesome that is, she's not even worth your time."

Howie was nodding slowly. He might not have realized he was doing it, but it meant that some part of him was not only listening, but agreeing with what the girls were telling him. These girls were magic. They were fairies, or angels, here to guide Howie down the right path. That Jarvis had once hoped for them to physically couple with Howie seemed now profane. Because they were capable of so much more. He handed the pipe back and said, "I think there's probably another hit in there." Then he began fishing around in the pockets of his cargo pants, and he added, "I've got some more weed if you want to load another bowl."

"Don't worry about it," Beth said, pulling her backpack up from the floor. "I've actually got some stuff with me. I'll hook you up for giving us a ride." She opened a pocket of her pack and pulled out a film canister, and Jarvis chuckled. It comforted him to know that whatever gods were looking out for Howie's heart were also concerned with him.

"Rock and roll, eh, Howie?" Jarvis asked. Howie nodded gravely and said, "Rock and roll, Jarvis."

14. The Burden of more tomorrows

Jarvis and Howie and their two fellow travelers would make it to Denver without incident. The smoking would continue, as would the conversation, and for the two and a half hours the four were in a car together, they were privileged to that ephemeral contentment that travel will sometimes engender, and that unexpected acquaintances made in the course of travel will surely enhance.

And just as Howie's happiness in those short hours was almost a direct result of his contact with others already decidedly happy, so was Burke's angst on that same morning a result of his contact with one miserable. Wayne had called him the night before, the Saturday night that Howie had spent in the Kit Carson County Jail and Adam had spent in Denver Health. Burke was out at the Cricket on the Hill, next door to the bar where Abby worked, drinking with Abby, with Stewart, and Carissa, and Fisk, and two or three others when his phone rang. Inside, where it was warm and happy, it was also loud, and Burke didn't notice the ringing. Then Abby nudged him with her elbow and pointed to the pocket of his jacket. He pulled out his phone. The display said *Caller ID Unavailable.*

When he answered the phone, he just heard his name repeated to him in a phantom voice, and he yelled, "Who is this?"

"Burke, it's Wayne." Then hissing, then, "Are you alone?"

"Uh, hold on," Burke said. He covered the mouthpiece and told Abby, "It's Wayne," then crawled out of the booth and walked to the door. As he was leaving he heard some-body at the table say, "Who's Wayne?" Stewart shouted af-ter him, "Tell that fucker to come out with us."

"Wayne," Burke said. "Wayne, what's up, man?" He pushed open the heavy door and stepped outside into cold and silence.

"Who's there?" Wayne asked. "Who are you with?" Burke looked back at the door. "Oh, just, the usu—"

"Don't tell them it's me, okay?" Wayne said. "I don't want them to know about our...experiment."

"Um, yeah. Okay. I didn't."

"Can you meet me tomorrow?"

"Tomorrow?" That was Sunday. Burke didn't think he had anything else going on. "Yeah, I can meet you tomor-row. I'm not working."

"At ten? Do you want to get breakfast at ten?"

"Okay. Where?"

"I was thinking Pete's," Wayne said. "I know there's a risk somebody could see me there, but it seems sort of ap-propriate, you know?"

"Yeah, totally." Burke hoped his enthusiasm wasn't too exaggerated. He had no idea what the significance of Pete's was. "Where are you? You should come out with us, man. Have a drink."

"No. Not yet. I can't yet."

Burke's hand was cold and his phone was cold against his ear.

"I'll see you tomorrow at Pete's," Wayne said. "Ten o' clock."

So Burke had been compelled to set his alarm to wake him at nine thirty the next morning, and at nine thirty he pushed the snooze button. At nine forty-five Abby woke him up and asked him what time he was supposed to meet Wayne.

"Shit," he said, and he sat up in bed. He reached for his pants with his feet, and pulled them toward him with his toes.

"Do you want me to come with you?" Abby asked.

Burke shook his head. He pulled his pants on and stood up and grabbed his sweater from the floor. Behind him, Abby was looking through his dresser for something of his to wear. He walked out to his living room, where Carissa was lying on the couch and Stewart was sprawled out on the floor. Carissa's eyes were opened, and when Burke came in she sat up slowly, arching her back and stretching her arms out over her head.

Abby walked past Burke and into the kitchen. "Good morning," she said. "Anyone want coffee?"

Carissa nodded. Burke sat down at his wobbly table. "I'll have some coffee."

"Don't you have to get going?" Abby asked. She had her back to him, pouring coffee grinds into a filter.

"Pete's is only five minutes away," he said.

"Oh, yeah," Carissa said. She came to the table and sat down beside Burke. "You're meeting Wayne today, huh?"

Burke nodded.

"Have you figured out what you're going to say to him?"

Burke shrugged. "I wasn't supposed to tell anybody about the letter. I'm wondering if I should tell him that I have."

"I think you should," Abby said. She put the coffee in the filter and turned on the machine, then sat down on Burke's lap. "You can't lie to him." Burke nodded.

"I don't know," Carissa said. "You're the last person he has any hope in, and if he thinks you've betrayed him, it might be enough to push him over the edge."

Abby frowned. She put her head on Burke's shoulder. "Oh, baby, I'm so sorry you have to go through this," she said. "Carissa's right, though. It might be worse for Wayne if you're honest."

"Can you guys please shut the fuck up," Stewart called out from the living room. "Christ!"

"Tell him everyone misses him," Abby said. "I mean, tell him people have noticed he's gone, and since you're his best friend, they've been asking you about him."

"No," Carissa said. "You can't tell him you're his best friend. You can't reinforce that idea if it's not true. Tell him to come back, yes. Tell him he can't keep hiding. Just, avoid the topic of your friendship altogether, if you can. That's what I think."

Abby nodded. Burke stared off at the coffee machine, which was making noise, but achieving nothing. The coffee pot was still empty. "Babe, did you put any water in there?" he asked Abby. She lifted her head from his shoulder and looked at the coffee pot, then swore and stood up to turn it off. Burke looked at his watch. It was a little after ten. "I've got to go," he said. His shoes were next to the table with the socks he had been wearing last night, and he put them on, then walked to his door, stepping over Stewart, who without lifting his head mumbled, "Tell that guy about next weekend. Tell him to join us. He'll see an angel for fucking real." Burke opened the door and left the apartment.

Outside the sky was bright blue and cloudless, and the sun pounded Burke's eyes, but it was still bitterly cold, and he followed little puffs of his breath down the sidewalk the four blocks to Pete's. It was almost quarter after ten when he got there, and he realized with a pique of guilt that he was hoping Wayne would have given up on him and gone home, or gone to wherever it was he was going these days, but Wayne was there, sitting in a booth near the window, looking at a newspaper with a cup of coffee in front of him. Burke realized when Wayne glanced up from his newspaper that for the past few days he had been putting on Wayne's head the face of somebody else he had met near the same time. He knew who Wayne was now, surely, but his features were so common, so unremarkable, that they had failed to stay etched in his memory.

"Burke," Wayne said, folding shut the newspaper and standing up. "Hey." He gave Burke a hug, and Burke returned it awkwardly, trying now to put a name to the face that his mind had substituted for Wayne's. He sat down across the table from where Wayne had sat, and Wayne sat again. The diner was filled completely, and it was noisy, so they had to talk in loud voices.

"How are you doing, Wayne?" he asked, and without even realizing it he was putting an inflection on the question that evinced genuine concern rather than idle curiosity. It was supposed to be a perfunctory greeting, but now that he was face to face with the guy again, Burke realized that he wanted an honest answer.

"I'm not doing horribly, I guess," Wayne said. "I've had better days. But I've had worse. It's good to see you."

Burke nodded, and he brightened slightly. He remembered now where he had seen the face that his memory had told him was Wayne's. It was the face of Carissa's cousin, who had come out to visit from Kansas and was staying with Stewart and Carissa last year for a couple weeks, back when Burke was first getting to know Wayne. Now that he realized the false connection, and that he was studying Wayne's face again, the two didn't seem all that alike. Carissa's cousin had a flatter face, with dull eyes. Wayne's face was sort of pointy, and he had a pretty substantial beard going now. Burke was fairly certain that was new.

"You got my letter, right?" Wayne asked.

"Yeah, of course. That's why I'm here. I mean, I'm here because you called. But—well, when you called, I knew why you were calling. I knew what you wanted to know. And you were right. People noticed. People were asking about you."

"Yeah?"

"Yeah. We hadn't seen you in, like, weeks." How long had Wayne been gone before he sent the letter? When was the last time Burke had seen him?

"Who?" Wayne asked.

"What?"

"Who was asking about me?"

Burke realized suddenly that he wasn't sure whose lives Wayne had been hoping his absence would affect. He couldn't remember who had been with him when he had met Wayne the first time, or any of the times. So far, most of the people Burke had talked to about the letter had only the haziest recollection of who Wayne was. Could Wayne be so delusional that he imagined all these people to be close friends, as he imagined Burke was? Or had he perhaps gotten to know some few random acquaintances of Burke's like Toby Warner and Jess DeKirk, and had taken them in his ignorance to be closer to Burke than they truly were? There was something actually comforting in that question, because it could justify Burke's own ignorance, and offer some kind of hope that Wayne was not as anonymous as they both feared. Raising that question now, though, only made it more difficult to answer the one Wayne had just asked.

A waitress appeared at Burke's elbow. "I'm sorry," she said, but she had nothing to apologize for, not to Burke. "I didn't see you show up. Did you want to see a menu, or were you just going to have coffee?" She had her arm extended over the table, holding a coffee pot, hovering over his empty cup.

"Uh, yeah," Burke said. Wayne was staring at him anxiously. "I mean, just coffee." The waitress started filling the cup, and Wayne was still waiting for an answer. Having a menu would give Burke a justification for distraction. "Actually," he said, as the waitress turned to leave. "Yeah, could I get a menu, too?" He turned to Wayne. "Are you eating?"

"I wasn't—yes." Wayne smiled at the waitress. "Yes, I'll take a menu, too, please. Thank you."

The waitress told them sure, and she smiled at Burke and walked away for the menus. Burke tried to think of something to say to keep Wayne from asking about specifics.

"Last night I was out with Abby and a few of the Unnaturalists, over at Cricket on the Hill. You ever been there?"

Wayne looked at him blankly.

"A whole bunch of us were just shooting the shit, and I asked if anybody had seen you recently—"

"You asked?" One of Wayne's eyebrows went up, and his mouth fell into a frown. "You weren't supposed to ask. The whole idea was to see if anybody else noticed I was gone, without you saying anything."

Oh, yeah. Shit.

The waitress came back and gave them each a menu and told them to let her know whenever they were ready. She smiled at Burke again.

"Well, at first it was just me and Abby and Carissa and Stew," Burke said. "And Carissa asked about you, and we were all talking. That's what started it. I pretended I didn't know anything, and then Fisk and a few of his friends came by, and since we had just been talking about it, I just threw it out there. I didn't bring it up originally." Burke took a drink of coffee. He reached to the end of the table and grabbed a couple of creamers, dumping them into his coffee, just for an excuse to avoid looking Wayne in the eyes.

"Carissa?" Wayne said.

Why had he said Carissa? He wasn't even sure Wayne knew who Carissa was. Maybe it was completely unbelievable that Carissa would have asked about Wayne if she didn't know about the letter. "Carissa Snow," Burke said. He stirred his coffee for several seconds, while Wayne stared out the window in silence. He took a sip, and still Wayne didn't talk. "Stewart's girlfriend," Burke added.

Wayne turned back to face him. His brow was furrowed. "I know Carissa, yeah. Wait. I didn't—" He took a sip of coffee, then opened his menu. "I never met her boyfriend. But, yes, I know who she was. She was asking about me?"

"Last night," Burke said. "Yeah. When it was just the four of us, we were talking about who to invite over to...well, we've got this thing going on this week, and we were throwing out names, and Carissa mentioned yours, and she said she hadn't seen you in a while. I just kept silent. But then, when everyone else showed up, we all got to talking, so I asked if any of them had seen you recently. I figured it was safe that way. Sorry if I screwed anything up."

Wayne shook his head. "No. It's okay, I guess."

The waitress came back and asked if they were ready. Burke told her he had changed his mind, and Wayne mumbled, "Yeah, me too." The waitress laughed and hit Burke's shoulder and said thanks a lot, and she told them to hold on to the menus in case they changed their minds again.

"Where are you living now?" Burke asked. "You should come out with us some time this week. You know, slide back in. Get comfortable again."

Wayne chewed his lip. "This isn't enough," he told Burke. "I need more. I'm going to keep hiding out. For another week, at least. Keep listening. What's most important for me now is to know if I make a difference. It's not enough that people ask about me. I want to find out if the world we be any worse off if I wasn't in it."

"Ask me, I think you're too preoccupied with this shit," Burke said, and he realized in saying it that he was talking to himself as much as he was to Wayne, or talking to the new self that Wayne's confidence in him had given light to. For most of his life, Burke had managed to drift along free from worry. He tried to imagine himself in Wayne's situation, far away from anybody he knew or cared about, or far from anyone who knew or cared about him, and he figured he'd probably just sit around his place drinking and playing video games. It might almost be a blessing not to be bothered with social obligations. And he guessed that was what this was here, with Wayne, a social obligation of such weight that his will was being crushed by it.

Perhaps his difficulty in sympathizing with Wayne had something to do with his inability to imagine himself in a similar state. Wayne was too wrapped up with details, like a little kid staring too close at the panel of a comic book, seeing every little dot, and forgetting the image those dots made up. What did it matter what people thought of you,

Burke wondered. What difference could that make in how you lived your life? Wayne needed to meet Stewart: there was a guy completely oblivious to the notions others harbored about him, and blissful for that oblivion.

This morning, when Burke was leaving, Stewart had called out to him, and Burke had almost forgotten. But it made sense. It was what Wayne needed. "Dude," he asked, "have you ever eaten acid?"

Wayne twitched. "Have I what? *Eaten* acid? What do you mean?"

"LSD," Burke said. "There's some stuff going around town right now that's supposed to be awesome. We bought a bunch yesterday, and we figured sometime this week we'd all get together, maybe at the Unnaturalists House. Trip our balls off. You want to join us?"

Wayne's face was ashen. He shook his head. Burke remembered then that the dude didn't even drink, and figured he probably didn't do drugs either. While with most of his friends, Burke might have considered the invitation a minor gaffe, here he was afraid that it might reveal to Wayne further proof that he hardly knew him.

"I have to think about some things," Wayne said. He slid out of the booth, pulled his wallet from his pocket, and dropped a five on the table. Burke moved to get up, but Wayne waved him back. "Don't worry. I'll call you again in a few days. Stay here until I go."

Burke nodded. He wondered if Wayne wanted him to try and convince him not to leave, but he couldn't bring himself to stand up. It was easier to stay where he was, inside where it was warm, to sit and watch the faint indentation of Wayne's body disappear from the vinyl of the booth. He said he'd call in a few days. That must mean he expected to be alive still in a few days.

15. After Adam fell

What Wayne was looking for was the sort of flood of concern and well-wishing that Adam Lister's fight in the streets of Denver set in motion. Had Adam, however, been aware of his pitied celebrity, he would have resented it. The success of his mission relied on the very anonymity that haunted Wayne. Adam's charisma was so insidious that even those whom he had intended to make victims of his righteous fury could not hate him for long. Driving away from the stretch of sidewalk where Adam lay bleeding, the men who had beaten him expressed worry as much as anger. The conclusion that the dude was seriously fucked up could not be argued against even by Waffles, who was cupping a pair of throbbing balls in his hand. So when Santi, who had been most reluctant to deal any serious blows, asked the others whether they ought to call 911 from the pay phone in front of King Soopers, even Waffles could not find it in himself to dismiss the idea. The closest to protest that anyone in the car got was perhaps the silent protest of Tally, who was passed out in the back seat and would have by the next morning forgotten everything except the haziest recollection of the silhouette of Batman commanding her brother to let her go.

The police, privy only to the knowledge that "Some dude in a Batman costume got beat up," as passed onto them by the dispatcher from an anonymous source, proceeded to the scene with a reasonable measure of skepticism. Even when they discovered the subject of the phone call sitting on a curb on the side of the street, they suspected nothing out of the ordinary. Most likely, he had just come from a costume party; they had seen such things before. Revelers in outlandish outfits seemed always to be appealing targets for muggers, for reasons the two officers who stopped to talk to Adam never bothered to consider. He tried to stand when they pulled up in front of him, and he swayed, then sat again. They asked him what had happened and he shook his head. They asked his name, and when he didn't answer they gently searched him for ID. The lack of a wallet corroborated their speculation about a mugging, as did his apparent confusion and uncommunicativeness, which they attributed to a traumatic head injury. They called for an ambulance and waited with Adam for the paramedics, making only small talk, content to let a detective figure out the details later, after the victim had had time to recover.

The paramedics, when they arrived, cut away Adam's mask despite his feeble protests and wrapped a bandage around the oozing wound they found underneath it on the back of his head. There was no doubt, then, that he had suffered a concussion. After that nobody bothered trying to figure out how it had happened, not right away. Adam was taken to Denver Health, given four stitches and some pain-killers, then allowed to rest.

The hospital staff had no reason to expect that when he awoke he would still refuse to give his name and health insurance information. Were his condition coupled with Wayne Talbot's virtual facelessness, the hospital staff might well have gotten a chance to witness his refusal, and he might have languished unidentified in that room for days. But Adam Lister was a name that meant something to many people in Denver, and he was enough of a presence to be recognized by a nurse working the Saturday morning shift. She got the story of his arrival from her co-workers and peeked into his room while he slept to get a face to go with that story.

"Oh man," she said, "I know that guy."

"You know that guy?" her friend asked.

"I know him." The two walked away from the room and back to the nurse's station. "He owns a club on Colfax. He booked my little brother's band just a few months ago. Man. Wow. And this was the guy you said was dressed up like Batman?"

"Yeah," her friend said. "But he doesn't remember anything leading up to it. If you know somebody who knows him, you should call them."

The nurse sat down and called her brother. Her brother said holy shit and that's so fucking crazy, and he told the nurse that he would call Danelle Rawlings, who was Adam's business partner. He figured Danelle would have a good idea about how to get in touch with Adam's parents, and as soon as he said that out loud he remembered what he had heard about Adam's parents and he felt shitty. But he called Danelle anyway. He thought he might have a hard time convincing her that it really was Adam that his sister had seen in the hospital room, but Danelle seemed willing to take it on faith. She said "Thanks," and that she'd be down there in fifteen minutes, and Adam's rescue was assured.

16. On Howie's ignominious return

On the day after Howie came back from Burlington, and the day after he and Jarvis had hugged the girls they had picked up and said goodbye, and the girls had promised that they would call the next time they were in Denver, and Jarvis had promised that he would get Howie a show out in Burlington, and Howie had promised the girls that he would call them when it happened, and the girls had promised they would be there—on the day after all that, Howie went back into Johnny Rockets and apologized for missing work. His manager told him not to let it happen again, and he started his shift.

Working with Howie that day was a young man named Sonny Liccardo, a burly eighteen-year-old with a shaven head and a half-sleeve of tattoos on his left arm, the ink still bright. Sonny Liccardo was not too happy about the prospect of closing the restaurant with Howie. He knew everybody he worked with was a loser, and he had gotten used to that, so meeting Howie wasn't a new experience for him. Really, Howie was worse; he fell in that small pool of old people for whom whoring out at Johnny Rockets was some kind of thrill. Sure, Sonny liked the money, but he wasn't kidding himself, the job blew. Maybe it was a step up from fast food (although when the faggoty manager got on Sonny's ass about not dancing, and when Aretha Franklin came on over the speakers for the fourteenth goddamn time in his six-hour shift, Sonny tended to wonder about that, about whether it really was better than fast food), but it was still just a miserable part-time job serving shit to assholes. It was bad enough Sonny had to be working here now; he couldn't imagine being an old fucker like Howie and coming into this place and hitting the time clock five times a week—and worst of all *looking forward* to coming into this place. Every time Sonny saw that sad sack of shit, he had a brainless smile on his face, and when the song they were supposed to dance to came on, he actually walked out clapping and hopping up and down like he was into it.

But that Monday when Sonny saw him, Howie looked like shit. His face was all puffy and there was a cut above his eye like maybe he had been in a fight, and he wasn't smiling. The whole night he didn't smile, and whenever they had to dance, Howie went out and did it like his body was being dragged through the motions by a strung-out puppet master. It was pretty fucking awesome. Seeing chirpy people become miserable was one of Sonny's greatest pleasures. It was what guided his performance as Supervisor.

That night, after they locked the doors and turned the front lights out, Howie grabbed the mop from the back without a word, with the same stiff motions that had been characterizing his mood all night. This was Sonny's fourth time closing the restaurant with Howie, and the first in which he considered it might be okay to kick back and have a few beers. He went into the kitchen where Alejandro was emptying the grease traps and pulled out a five dollar bill. "Hey bro," he said, "want to go across the street and pick up a couple forties?"

Alejandro threw a meaningful glance over Sonny's shoulder and asked, "What about the new guy?"

"Yeah," Sonny said. "Grab one for him, too."

"Is he cool, man?" Alejandro asked.

"I don't know," Sonny said. "Go get the beer. I'll talk to him while you're gone. And, here, I'll take care of the grease traps."

Alejandro nodded. He freed one hand to take the five from Sonny, and then Sonny took the grease trap, and Alejandro went out the back door.

Alejandro was an old guy, too, but he was cool. Mexicans were cooler than white people, and most of Sonny's co-workers were white. There were three people his own age that Sonny thought were all right, but the managers were cunts, and anybody over thirty was a douche, except for Alejandro, and Sonny figured that was only cause Alejandro was Mexican. But this Howie guy, who knew?

"Howie," he called, shoving the grease trap in and walking back to the front of the restaurant. "You want to take a break?"

He came out from behind the counter and found Howie pushing the mop listlessly over the same spot on the floor. Howie looked up at him with tired, swollen eyes. "I've already taken my breaks," he said, but he stopped mopping.

"Yeah, so have I," Sonny said. "But, fuck, bro, I don't know about you, but I don't feel like cleaning right now." He hopped up on a bar stool and waited, tense. He was afraid Howie might say he wanted to get out of there, and then Sonny'd have to bust his ass, too, and Alejandro would just get a free half-hour for shopping for beer. But Howie shrugged, and he pushed the mop away toward the wall. He didn't even flinch when it slid down the wall and clattered to the floor.

"So what's up, bro?" Sonny said. "You're not looking so cheery today." Howie came up beside him and sat down two bar stools away. Sonny wanted to butter him up, get on his good side to make sure he wouldn't narc on him for the beer, but he didn't want to seem *too* friendly.

Howie shrugged. He set his elbows on the counter and put all his weight on them, then cradled his droopy jaw in his hands. God, he was soft. Sonny wasn't really into sports anymore, but he still lifted, and he took care of his body. This guy, Howie, he was just a soft little skin-flap of a man. Not fat, like most of their customers, but *soft*.

"Usually you're all into the dancing and stuff," Sonny said. "What's up?"

Howie sighed and his whole body trembled. His eyes began to shimmer, and it seemed for a moment like he was ready to cry. Sonny wished he hadn't sent Alejandro off for forties. No way was this Howie dude going to be down for drinking on the job. He was a total puss.

"My life is crap," Howie said. He still had his chin cupped in his hands, leaning over the bar. "I keep thinking I can change it, but everything I do just makes it crappier. Everything was so stressful before, and I thought coming here would be good for me. I thought I'd have fun. But, Jesus, now I look at myself, at this stupid uniform, and I wonder, what in God's name am I doing here?"

Sonny stiffened. Howie sounded completely revolted. "It's just a job, bro," he said.

"Yeah, but what a *degrading* job!" Howie looked over at him and his eyes were all squinty. "Listen, when I came in here for an application, that didn't even matter to me. I thought it would put me on some level higher than those people who come in here—like, yeah, I'm just flipping burgers, but maybe I know something you don't. Maybe *I'm* the one whose value system is intact."

"You don't flip—"

"But who am I kidding? I'm a monkey. Anybody who comes in here will see that. They'll see me as just another pathetic, unaccomplished twit. They won't say, 'What's a guy like that doing working at a place like this?' They'll just say, 'Why's it take so long to get a shake? Where's my nickels?'"

"I'm only working here to save some money up," Sonny said. He was going to add more, to tell Howie about his plans to start a record label, but Howie cut him off.

"That's just it! You're a kid!"

Sonny hated that shit. A kid? He was eighteen. His goatee went all the way around his mouth.

"Listen, you're the kind of person people expect to see when they come in here," Howie continued. He wasn't holding his chin anymore; he was looking at Sonny and waving his arms. "Without even thinking about it, they know this is temporary for you."

Okay. At least Howie understood that much.

"But they see me, and they just see an anonymous loser. They don't think about what else I might be moving on to, they think this *is* my goal. They think I'm shit." A few flecks of spit shot from Howie's lips, and then he snapped his mouth shut. His nose wrinkled, and the watery film gathered over his eyes again.

"Hey, hey, bro," Sonny said. "Nobody sees you like that." He clapped Howie on the back. "People look at you, and they got to wonder." He looked past Howie to the kitchen to see if Alejandro was back yet. "*I* wonder. I mean, yeah, most people working here are my age, but there've been a few older people, and most of them I just figure are dickheads. But you I always wondered about. I mean, like, what the fuck? How'd you end up here?"

"Yeah?" Howie said. He sniffled and wiped the back of his hand over his nose.

"Yeah. You seem like a cool guy."

Howie nodded.

"Where'd you work before you worked here?" Sonny asked. "Did you get laid off or something?"

"I quit my last job. It was a stupid office job, and they were all... I just said screw it. There was this one guy, he was just... I hated it. I just quit." Howie's eyes lit up a bit, and he leaned in close to Sonny and said in a conspiratorial voice, "I told the manager to fuck himself."

Sonny couldn't contain his shock.

Howie nodded solemnly. "I was having a hard...well, they were assholes. It wasn't what I wanted to be doing. There was a lot of stress outside of work, and then it carried over, and I started neglecting my music because whenever I came home from work I was too tired—"

"Wait wait wait," Sonny said. "Your music? What kind of music you do?"

Howie's head wobbled. He frowned, but something in his eyes made Sonny think he was delighted by the question. Sonny didn't care about the charade; for the first time, Howie seemed like he might have something worthwhile to offer the world.

A heavy sound came from the kitchen, jerking Howie out of his contemplation.

"Oh, hey," Sonny said, "you don't mind if we drink, do you? Alejandro went out to get some beer..."

The blood drained slowly from Howie's face. Had he not been so animated that his cheeks burned seconds earlier, Sonny might not have even noticed the paling. But he did notice, and he noticed Howie's jaw tremble as he tried to answer. Dammit. Just when Sonny was thinking the guy might be cool. "I don't mean here now," Sonny added. "I mean, we'll finish up here. It's just, sometimes we hang out here afterwards, you know? It's quiet and everything. I told Alejandro—"

Howie's jaw locked. He nodded once fiercely, and he said, "Fuck it." The way he said it, he reminded Sonny of the Polish foreign exchange student at Cherry Creek. Sonny and his friends used to encourage the kid to swear, and they'd laugh their asses off at how he would blurt the words out in a loud, insistent voice, then look nervously over his shoulders to see if he had offended anyone. Howie looked over his shoulders the same way. Then, flushing, he looked at Sonny and said, "I have a pint of Cutty Sark in my jacket, too."

"Yeah?" Sonny said. "That's cool. Maybe we can crack that open later." He didn't want to ask what Cutty Sark was. He figured they could have the beer first, and then if they still wanted more, he could have Howie go fetch the pint of whatever it was. "You know, sometimes we kick back in here after the restaurant closes, before we finish up. We just chill for a while, cause it's no hurry. We don't have customers or anything."

Alejandro came up front with a bag tucked under his arm. Alejandro was a small guy, too, but he had an awesome mustache, really thick and dark, so he looked like a bandito, even in his stupid white uniform. He nodded at Howie. "How are you, my friend?" he asked. He set the bottles down on the counter in front of Sonny and went past Howie to sit down. Sonny liked that, that he was in charge of doling out the beer. Both these guys were over twenty-one, but since Sonny was the supervisor, they waited for him to act first. He pulled a forty out—it was Coors Light, which must have been on sale, because usually Alejandro would come back with Steele Reserve, or whatever was cheapest—and twisted the cap off, then slid the bag down the counter to Howie. Howie took a bottle from the bag and handed it to Alejandro, then he pulled the last one out and slid the bag over the edge of the bar.

"I thought I was going to cut back," Howie said. "After Friday." He took a drink from the bottle. Alejandro grabbed a paper cup and poured the beer into that.

Sonny took a drink. He grinned. "You have a little case of the three-two-flu on Saturday? That why you called off?"

Howie shook his head, not like he was negating Sonny, just like he was trying to shake a memory away or something. "Look, I felt pretty bad on Saturday, yeah. But I've worked with worse hangovers than that. Lots worse. I would have come in, but—" Howie looked at Alejandro, then at Sonny. "Dang, you guys have to promise not to say anything about this, okay? I mean, to the managers?"

They nodded.

"Listen, I got arrested Friday night," Howie said. He drank again. "Or Saturday morning. I had to spend a night in lock-up." He shook his head and drank some more.

This was too fucking awesome. Sonny looked past Howie to try to get Alejandro's eye, see what he thought of all this, but Alejandro was just staring forward, drinking his beer and smacking his lips after each sip.

"What, were you driving drunk?" Sonny said, feeling a twinge of admiration. He had never had the balls to drive drunk.

Howie nodded. He took another drink, then grimaced and said, "Hey, no offense? I appreciate the offer, but I'm not too into beer. You mind if I..." He nodded toward the back.

"No," Sonny said. "No, not at all, bro. Go ahead."

Howie walked back to the coat room. Sonny scooted down a seat and tapped Alejandro on the arm. "You hear that, *ese?* Dude was driving drunk."

Alejandro took sip of beer and smacked his lips. "It is not a smart thing to drive drunk," he said, shaking his head. "Is dangerous. Some one could get hurt."

Howie came up front again in time to hear Alejandro's remark. He frowned miserably and said, "I know, Alejandro. I feel awful about it. You know, I don't even own a car? I never drive. That's the thing. I was so drunk, I didn't know what I was doing. I just thank God nothing bad happened."

He sat down between them, and now since Sonny had scooted down a seat, they were all sitting right next to each other. Howie unscrewed the cap from the bottle he had brought up and took a long pull, and then he set the bottle down. Sonny read the label. Scotch whiskey—that shit was for real. And Howie drank it just like he was drinking water.

"Who was the car that you drove?" asked Alejandro. He was refilling his cup now. Sonny had to pick up his pace.

"I don't know," Howie said. "I never found that out. It was a pick-up truck I found parked outside somebody's house, and the keys were in it."

"Oh, shit, man," Sonny said. "You mean you stole it?"

"Well, the keys were in it. I took it, but the guy who owned it, he didn't want to file the incident report with the police or anything. He just said he'd come pick it up later."

"But you stole it, right?" Sonny said. "That's awesome!"

"That's the thing," Howie said. "It was never reported as stolen. He didn't know it was gone until the police called him, see? So if it wasn't stolen, you can't say I stole it. It was just...I just took it because I was drunk and I wanted to go to New Orleans. The guy has it back by now probably."

"You have a lot of luck, my friend," Alejandro said.

"I'll drink to that," Sonny said, holding his forty bottle out. Howie clinked it with his pint, and Alejandro with his paper cup, and they drank. Sonny was feeling a little buzzed. These guys were all right. He had definitely misestimated Howie, too. That was balls, stealing a car. "Why'd you steal the car, bro?" he asked.

Howie took a drink of the scotch, then Sonny guessed he must have changed his mind about the beer, because he opened it back up and poured it into a cup like Alejandro had done. Sonny reached over the bar and grabbed a cup, too. Howie took a sip of beer, and he said, "On Friday night, I went to a party of this girl's that I like." He paused, then shook his head. "No. I can't lie. I love her. She is the most amazing creature on the planet. She's bright, she's funny, and she's into all the same kind of music as me." He took another drink, and he added, "Plus, she's beautiful."

Sonny listened, and Alejandro listened. Or, it looked like Alejandro was listening. He wasn't looking at Howie still, but it seemed like he was paying attention. He was nodding, anyway.

"But," Howie said. Sonny realized he was holding his breath. Of course, there had to be a *but*. All cool chicks had some big old *but* that fucked everything up. "She's in love with somebody else. On Friday, I found out that the guy asked her to marry him."

Alejandro shook his head and muttered something. Sonny was pretty sure it was a Spanish cuss word, but he couldn't tell which one. He needed to have Alejandro teach him those again.

"And?" Sonny said. "What? She say yes?"

"I guess so. She was wearing a ring."

"Harsh, bro." Sonny shook his head, and put his arm around Howie, just to pat him on the shoulder and say, you know, *I feel for you*, and that was it, and he pulled his hand back. Alejandro patted him on the back too.

"She meant everything to me," Howie said. "That's why I decided to leave. I couldn't imagine staying in Denver if I can't have her."

Sonny knew a few chicks like this chick Howie was talking about. He had had the number done on him, too. "How long you been together?" he asked Howie.

"We're not together."

"Shit," Sonny said, "I know that." He nodded to show Howie that he really did. The words just didn't come out right. "I mean how long you known her?"

"Almost two years," Howie said softly.

"And this other guy, how long's she been with him?"

"Almost three years." Howie took a shot of the scotch, then a sip of beer.

"And all that time, she's still hanging around with you?" Sonny said. He said it like he was skeptical, but skeptical of the situation, not of Howie. "This chick's wet for you, bro. There's no way a chick's going to let you hang around her for two years if she knows you want to get in her pants, unless she wants you to. If she wasn't into you, she'd a been like, 'Fuck off, Howie. I got a boyfriend.' Fact she didn't do that means, bro—she wants your cock."

Alejandro nodded. "She is jus waiting, man," he said. That guy could drink, too. Jesus, he really could. "It was the same with my wife when we did know—when I knew her. The first time when I knew her, she had a boy friend. He had a better job than I had and a bigger house, but she did not love him. She did not know she did not love him until she knew me."

"See?" Sonny said. "And what did you *do* about it? That's what Howie needs to be hearing about right now. Listen to this, Howie. Alejandro has a *wife* that he stole from another dude."

Alejandro nodded. Sonny looked at him and Howie looked at him. Sonny said, "Tell him, bro."

"What?"

"Tell him how you got your wife from the other guy!"

Alejandro shrugged. "I jus told her man. I said to her to leave him, and that was what she need to hear. She leave him."

"There you go," Sonny said. "He just fucking told her, and she left. You ever tell this chick you love her, Howie?"

Howie nodded. "She knows."

"Well, you got to tell her it's him or you."

"That is what she is waiting for," said Alejandro.

"That's what she needs to hear," said Sonny. "Only reason she hasn't left this faggot is you haven't convinced her that you're worth it. Right now, she's got you, and she's got this other dude, too, so why would she bother ever leaving him?"

Howie sniffed. "That's what the girls in the car said, too."

"What girls?"

"On the way back from Burlington, my buddy picked up some hitchhikers," Howie said. "I told them about Adrienne, and they said I was giving her the best of both worlds. They told me I should give up on her, since she hasn't left her boyfriend yet."

"Give up on her? The fuck?" Sonny shook his head. "No way, bro. No way. Who were these girls you picked up? How old were they?"

"Just some girls," Howie said. "I don't know. Eighteen, maybe."

"Eighteen?" Sonny shook his head. "Howie, bro, *I'm* eighteen, okay? Girls my age? They don't know shit. You can't listen to them for shit. You want advice? You got to listen to Alejandro. Alejandro's gone through the exact same shit. He knows what's going on."

Howie nodded, but he was nodding with more conviction now, like what Sonny was saying was finally being absorbed by his soggy brain. Sonny called out to Alejandro and said, "Tell Howie what he's got to do, *ese*."

Alejandro took a long drink of beer and sucked on his mustache. "I already said, man. You got to get the girl. No matter what."

17. WAYNE'S LIST OF THINGS TO LIVE FOR

Wayne, alone again in his hotel room, decided that he had devoted too much energy to philosophizing. He had never put so much strain on his imagination, and now the strain was getting to him. In his past, abstract thinking had not played a central role in his decision-making; he had always broken down the problems he faced into numbers, quantifying the pros and cons and weighing them against one another. When looking at colleges, he had only applied to Berkeley, after determining that his acceptance was inevitable and after he had calculated the cost for four years and compared that calculation to the potential value of his education there, with an estimate of the income his degree would afford him. The move to Denver had been handled with a similar precision, with Wayne's realizing that his salary was not dependent on geography, and that he could drastically improve his net worth if he moved away from the Bay Area and its prohibitive cost of living.

None of which precision should suggest that Wayne gave no consideration for the human element. Denver had gotten a higher value assigned to it when he was shopping for places to live because of fond childhood memories associated with the state of Colorado, and because of the perceived cultural benefits of choosing a capital city. But *too much* consideration for the human element, Wayne had always believed, could lead only to irrational choices, with greater potential for resultant misery. It had just happened to him, with his letter to Burke, and his abandoning of all his routines to hole himself up here in this swanky room.

He had forgotten the importance of deliberate, impassionate internal debate in coming to the best conclusions.

There was no reason, Wayne saw now, to wait and learn what his friends thought of him, and how they felt about him and how he was missed in his absence. All he had to do to make up his mind whether to end his life was determine how much his life was worth. He sat down at the desk in the room and pulled out a sheet of hotel stationery from its thin drawer. Using the straight edge of the Gideons' Bible, he drew a line down the middle of the paper. Then, at the top of the page, perpendicular to the first line and intersecting it about a three-quarters of an inch down he drew another line, giving himself a table with two columns and space at the top to title them. Above the left column he wrote REASONS TO LIVE, and above the right, REASONS NOT TO. Whichever list was longest when he finished would be the greater of the two, and Wayne would have his answer.

"I am alone," he wrote in the right-hand column.

There it was. That was the big reason. It weighed more than anything he might write below it or next to it. But,

"I am successful," he wrote on the left.

What did that mean, anyway? Successful? He made decent money, sure. He had a big apartment, and he drove a nice car. And here he was at one of Denver's nicest hotels, sitting on an antique chair before a large, heavy desk of maple. Was that success, if he had no one to share it with?

Wayne looked down at the list. He was philosophizing again. This wasn't supposed to turn into a debate over the relative merits of success versus the drawbacks of loneliness. One was a positive, the other a negative, and that was what mattered.

But what about value?

Damn.

He brushed the list to the floor and pulled out another piece of stationery. This time he titled the right-hand column REASONS TO LIVE and inside it made a narrower column. He did the same on the left, except with the title REASONS TO DIE. That made more sense. It was direct.

Underneath REASONS TO DIE he wrote, "I am alone," and in the narrow column next to it, he wrote "-10." Again he wrote "I am successful" opposite that, and then he paused. He rested the eraser on his lips and thought about all of success's perks. Finally, slowly, he wrote beside it "+3." He considered adding to the list the facets of success he had been thinking about earlier, but that didn't seem appropriate, since he had already given success a value. "But if I were truly successful," he muttered, "would I be contemplating suicide?"

He erased the first line from the right-hand column and blew the eraser dust away. "I make decent money | +1," he wrote, then, "I have a big apartment | +1," and "I drive a nice car | +1." It looked pathetic, really, and the single item on the left—with its big double-digit negative—seemed to be trembling with suppressed laughter at the weak defense the right was putting up. "I have a B.S. in Engineering and I graduated *Summa Cum Laude*," he added. That took up two lines, and he decided to rate it +4.

"I have had sex with two different women in the past month."

It seemed a little desperate, but that kind of success was new to Wayne and it had boosted his ego. His misery in California had been rooted in part to thwarted romantic advances. Any change from that had to be positive. "+3," he wrote, and he set his pencil down. This was good. He should have done this earlier.

But even though the list on the right was longer, it was still no more powerful. The living of his life was worth 10, and the taking of it the same. He was at an impasse.

Wayne couldn't remember what he had done with the gun. He took a drink from the bottle of vodka at his elbow and, drinking it, wondered when was the last time he had grimaced at the taste of alcohol. Maybe that had some positive value.

The meeting with Burke hadn't really gone like he hoped it would. Burke was a good guy, but he was no guardian angel: he could not give Wayne a glimpse into the world as it would be without him in it. That left Wayne without a clear idea of what he would do next, and now he thought back to the last thing Burke had said, about the LSD. Up to a few weeks ago, Wayne had never been drunk. He wasn't against drinking per se; he had simply never understood its appeal. The same, he supposed, could be said about drugs. He knew what caused drunkenness, as he knew, theoretically, what cause acid trips, and he had always figured that knowledge would rob the experience of fun for him, thinking about chemicals and protein-coupled receptors and serotonin subtypes, in much the same way as the act of watching movies lost its allure if you were too familiar with the actors and all the work that went into filming. Wayne was also leery of the phsyiopsychological dangers of the drug, perhaps mostly because the only information he had on the matter concerned an old man he had seen wandering the streets of Berkeley, flailing his arms and raving. As the story went, the man had manufactured his own LSD in a basement apartment and drank it at parties with whisky and green tea until he could no longer distinguish reality from the machinations of his addled mind.

This weekend, Burke wanted to *trip* with Wayne. It was flattering, in a certain light. And, the more Wayne considered it, the less intimidating the possibility of frying his brain seemed. If he did take too much and ended up like that old man in Berkeley, wandering the streets muttering obscenities to himself, might he not be happier than he was now, or at least ignorant of how unhappy he was? That almost seemed like the most appealing prospect. Frying his brain could be the goal, and after that the question of whether to live or die would be meaningless. And if he failed to destroy his mind? Well, then he would be back to where he was now, measuring the value of his life. Then, at least, he would have given himself the opportunity to

have one transcendental experience before he killed himself. He could think of no reason to tell Burke no.

18. The perusal of Adam's library

In a state of ambivalence similar to Wayne's, although under perhaps less severe circumstances, Adam Lister's friend Danelle stood in a doorway watching Adam sleep. Danelle was a short, unremarkable woman, surrendered to pudginess and not resentful of it, almost grateful for every trait of hers that went against the norm of physical perfection. Her hair was too thin, her face too flat to win the hearts of any superficial lover, and so she was able to focus the energy that her peers devoted to mating to shaping the world she lived in. For many years now, Adam had joined Danelle on this mission. Although their relationship had never been consummated as such, Danelle was closer to no one in Denver than Adam, and Adam closer only to his now-deceased father. Danelle, then, knew that Adam had not been to a party on the night he received his blow to the back of the head. When the nurse's brother called her, she hadn't heard from Adam in over twenty-four hours. She had been calling around to their mutual friends to ask if anyone knew where he had gone—his car was missing from his driveway and he hadn't been answering the phone. They had all been worried about him since that episode at Gabor's and this sudden unannounced disappearance compounded the worry.

So it had been with a certain sense of relief that Danelle went to pick him up from Denver Health. The relief did not, of course, negate the worry; Adam's hospitalization was cause for a whole new breed of worry, but at least he was alive and accounted for. Danelle gave the staff Adam's health insurance information and paid his co-pay. And since the police were unaware of any crime he had committed, Danelle was allowed to take him home as soon as the doctor signed the release.

She had been told about the Batman costume but she didn't bring that detail up on the drive home. She kept her questions vague, hoping Adam would volunteer some fact or another that would dispel her suspicions.

"The last thing I remember," he said with a Vicodin slur, "is going to sleep on Saturday night. And then, the hospital."

Danelle did her best to believe that. What doubts remained she kept to herself. The next evening, after watching Adam fall asleep in her bedroom, she called Maynard.

Maynard was one of a small circle of acquaintances whom Danelle could count on to be concerned enough about Adam's health to act, but not so concerned that he would want to shunt Adam off to a psychiatric ward. She still hoped they could avoid that step. She asked Maynard if he could meet her at Adam's place in fifteen minutes. When Maynard asked what was up, she told him she'd explain it all when they got there.

Danelle had a key to Adam's place in the city, just as Adam had a key to hers in the foothills. The trust between them was so ingrained that it no longer even seemed necessary to label it trust until now, because what Danelle was breaching had to have a name. It was an ugly thing, this chore she had given herself.

When she got to Adam's house, Maynard was waiting out front, leaning against his car and smoking. Danelle nodded hello, and Maynard asked again, "What's up?"

Danelle looked at the house. "I wanted your help," she said, "with Adam's comic books."

Maynard snubbed the cigarette out on the sole of his shoe, then followed Danelle's gaze toward Adam's front door. "He's still at your place, right?"

Danelle nodded.

"How's he doing?"

"He seems okay. Been sleeping a lot. He says he doesn't remember anything about Saturday."

"So, what," Maynard asked, "you want to bring him some of his comic books?"

"No," Danelle said. She shook her head. "I want to hide them."

"Hide them."

Danelle sighed. Braced for Maynard's resistance, she added, "I know this sounds puritanical, but I'm afraid those things have had a negative effect on him. I think he was dressed like Batman because he was trying to...I don't know. Fight crime. You know the state he's been in."

Maynard whistled.

"Maybe all this is just part of the grieving process," Danelle said. "It can't be permanent." She hoped it wasn't permanent. "I just thought it would be better if, while he's going through this, we... We try not to encourage anything. You know?"

They looked at one another. Maynard seemed skeptical.

"If you wouldn't mind," Danelle said. "I was hoping we could keep the books at your place for a while. Just, make sure nothing like this happens again."

"And what're you going to tell Adam?"

"I'll think of something."

She walked up the concrete path and Maynard fell in behind her. "This feels a little weird," Maynard said. "I feel like Tipper Gore or something."

Danelle unlocked the front door and stepped inside, guiding Maynard to the spare room in the back. "This isn't censorship," she said. "Not really. This is... it's like removing sharp objects from the reach of someone who's suicidal."

She opened the door. Rows of white boxes stared out at them. Adam and his father had built the shelves in this room especially for the storage of his comic books, hundreds of them, ones he had collected himself for years and ones his father had passed on to him to kindle his love for them. Danelle tried not to think about the bond they represented. She picked up a box and told Maynard, "What Adam's doing could potentially destroy his life. It only makes sense to try to prevent him from doing it again. Anything that might contribute to that destruction has to go."

Maynard hesitated but eventually he picked up a box and followed Danelle outside to Danelle's Pathfinder. They put the boxes in and, walking back, Danelle said, "Anyway, we're not like those comics code authority assholes, trying to ban books. I mean, we're not passing moral judgment on the things. This is about Adam, not Batman. I mean, shit, we're not going to burn them."

"I guess that makes sense," Maynard said. They picked up two more boxes. "We're not making a blanket statement against comic books. If anybody else wants to read them, that's fine by us, right."

"Sure," Danelle said. "More power to them."

"Read the shit out of them."

They left the boxes in the truck and went back for more. "Anyway," Danelle said, "the Nazis were destroying art. That's another matter entirely. They were afraid of ideas that might pose a threat to their power."

"Well," Maynard said, "but that's not what the... The Tipper Gore stuff, and the, what was it, the comics code people? They weren't afraid of comic books as a threat to power. Right?"

"No," Danelle said. "But I'm not talking about the comics code authority now. I'm talking about Nazis."

"Oh. Okay."

"Nazis burned books because they were afraid of the ideas contained in those books."

"Yes."

They kept picking up boxes. Danelle said, "In comic books, there're no big ideas. It's all just guys in tights beating the shit out of other guys in tights."

"And girls with huge breasts and tiny waists."

"Well, I don't think the girls with huge breasts had an adverse effect on Adam's mental health."

"No," Maynard said. "I'm not saying they did. I'm just going on what you were saying, about how they're not art. They're catering to the lowest common denominator."

"Yes! It's crap. Crap isn't worthy of the protections given to true art."

"Of course it isn't."

"Fucking A."

After about twenty minutes they had loaded all of Adam's boxes into the bed of the pick-up truck. Maynard leaned back against the truck and reached into his pocket for a cigarette, but Danelle told him, "We're not quite done yet."

"No?"

"No." She waved at Maynard to follow her into the house. Maynard, sighing, put his cigarettes away and followed. In the room, there was one tall traditional bookshelf not as deep as the ones built for the comic book boxes and lined with graphic novels. "I think a lot of these are just collections of stuff we've already taken out. Like *The Death of Superman,* and all those ones next to it. I know he has the original comics of those."

"Maybe we should leave that," Maynard said. "It could serve as a reminder that superheroes are mortal. It might force Adam to think twice before trying something like this again."

Danelle chewed her lip. "I guess," she said. "But, thing is, right after Superman dies, he comes back. He comes back four times or something. Or there're four versions of him. I read some of them—the collections, I mean. Adam didn't like anybody handling the originals." Saying that made Danelle feel guilty all over again in a whole different way. She pulled some of the graphic novels off the shelf. "So I guess we should take the one where he gets reincarnated, and leave one where he dies. It's the notions of invulnerability that are dangerous."

"What do you mean by dangerous?" Maynard asked.

"Just, anything so far outside the bounds of real life."

"I thought we were getting rid of the things that might inspire him. Like, all the Batman titles." He came up next to Danelle and reached for Adam's copy of *The Dark Knight Returns.* "That's a good one, actually," Danelle said. "I mean, it's more realistic than most of the stuff out in the truck. It sort of puts Batman in the real world, and shows how people might react to him. If he was real."

Maynard flipped to a page where Batman was leaping from a skyscraper towards a giant, bat-shaped glider. "You think this stuff is realistic?"

"*More* realistic," Danelle said. "I mean, he at least acknowledges that a guy who decides to dress up like a bat and beat the crap out of people has got to be crazy."

Realizing what she had just said and what it suggested about the friend who lay healing back at her apartment, Danelle's face turned red. She looked back at the book case.

"Put it that way," Maynard said, "and maybe it's worse. All that other stuff can be dismissed as fantasy, but this book—for somebody in Adam's position—this book might make him think that the idea is feasible."

Danelle nodded slowly but she didn't speak.

Maynard held on to the book. "He's got a lot of titles by the same author," he said. "Are they all like that?"

Danelle read the spine of the next book in line. "*Batman: Year One,* yeah. That one should definitely go. That's Adam's problem to a tee."

"What about *Sin City?*"

"Those aren't even superheroes," Danelle said. "They're crime novels. You can leave them."

Maynard pulled out one of the *Sin City* books and opened it up. Danelle looked over the rest of the titles. After a moment, Maynard slapped the book shut and grabbed the rest of the series. "They might not be wearing tights, but these are as bad the rest. This guy—" He held up the first book, and a bandaged ugly face leered at Danelle from the cover. "—he's fucking invincible. He's shot repeatedly, beaten, stabbed, and he keeps going. This can't put any good ideas in Adam's head."

Danelle didn't argue. She turned back to the case and grabbed a book from one of the lower shelves. "You ever read *Watchmen*?" Maynard peered over her shoulder. "It's like *Dark Knight Returns* as far as trying to imagine superheroes in the real world, but...I don't know. It's not glamorized so much, I guess is the thing. There's a character who tries to foil a bank robbery and his cape gets caught in a revolving door, and so he's helpless and the bank robbers shoot him."

"Ooh, that's good. Leave that one."

"What about the Marvel titles, Spider-man and X-men and stuff?"

Maynard hesitated. "I used to read that stuff when I was a kid," he said. "And, you know? I don't know, but it always seemed to me there was a bit more complexity in their world. Everybody had all this angst and personal foibles. It made them more interesting. When Phoenix died? Man, that was some sad shit."

Danelle started gathering Marvel books by the handful. "Yeah, but, that's the whole thing. It's like the death of Superman. Everybody dies all time in Marvel series, and they never *stay* dead. A few issues later, and, bam! It was a clone, or a robot, or some alien pretender who died, and the real character's fine."

Maynard frowned. "I guess you're right," he said. "It's like a revolving door to heaven."

"And if Adam's thinking about that..."

"And he gets it into his head that he can never die..."

"Bad Mogambo."

Maynard started grabbing the rest of the Marvel collections. When they had cleared them out he asked, "You think we've got enough?"

Danelle looked at the shelf, and then down at the load in her arms. "Yes," she said. "I guess it's the best we can do for now."

The two walked their books outside to the truck, dumped them irreverently into the back, and left Adam's house. I like to imagine that, in his bed across town, Adam's eyes opened, and his mind's eye saw the spare bedroom emptied of all its treasures except for the occasional reminder of every hero's mortality.

19. The matter of Adrienne's engagement

Adrienne had once imagined that if she could split her heart into two parts, with her passion and her intellect still devoted to Maynard and her playful bohemian side remaining for Howie, she would have. Making those two men happy would have meant the world to her, once. But lately she had begun to wonder if she really would seize that hypothetical opportunity. She wondered, mostly, if Howie was somebody she could see even half her self spending the rest of her life with.

Her mind was traveling paths like this a lot in those weeks, not solely in regard to Howie, but also to her decision to settle with Maynard (and it was *with*, she kept insisting—*with*, and not *for*). At the head of each path her mind traveled, she examined her life now, compared it to the life she was leading five years ago, and tried to imagine what it would be like in five years more, or ten, or even twenty. On the first examination, she was content: with Maynard, she had found reason for all the fickleness in her past, for all the hearts she had been accused of breaking. This, the feeling in the pit of her stomach, this bliss, and the wonder at her fortune, was what she had been holding out for, and when she looked back at the constant inebriation and the rampant promiscuity of her early twenties, she felt not the slightest hint of longing. She would never imagine trading what she had now, with Maynard, for that past.

It was those imaginations about her future that led Adrienne to trouble. Sure, she was happy now, and she would concede with minimal debate that she was happier than she had been in her entire life. How did she honestly feel, though, knowing she would never be with another man after Maynard, and how would she feel about that when she was nearing her fortieth birthday? Would the aspects of Maynard that had compelled her to fall so deeply in love with him still seem significant then? Or would he only serve as a suggestion of what excitement her life might have held?

Most of her consciousness struggled to convince Adrienne that such thoughts were the product of that part of her that still feared heartache, the part that was trying to protect her from the inevitable pain at the end. But acknowledging that prospect didn't make the gloomy thoughts easier to dismiss. Once they surfaced, she couldn't keep herself from trying to imagine how her life might be better. If her mind drifted to Howie then it was only because he was so constant and throbbing a presence in her life, not because she ever considered him as a viable alternative to Maynard. Since the very thing that set her on guard with Maynard was his avowed commitment to her, Howie's more extreme avowals could hardly cast him in a better light. He was a friend. He needed her now and she respected that, but she didn't relish her role as comforter. She looked forward to the day they returned to the platonic relationship they had enjoyed when they first knew one another. It bothered her to use the term *relationship* even in her thoughts, but it could not accurately be called much of anything else.

Howie had been back from his stint in jail for three days, and Adrienne still hadn't called to ask how he was. When he stopped by her apartment on a Tuesday morning, she realized she had been expecting it, and, guiltily, that she had been dreading it. "Can we talk?" he asked, standing on her door step, and Adrienne said, "Talk about what?" Then she let her head fall and she said, "I'm sorry. That sounds awful. Come on in."

She backed up and Howie stepped inside. She shut the door behind him. He took off his coat. There was a sheen of sweat on his forehead and his hands trembled. His lips were dry, she could tell just looking at him.

"Adrienne, I..." He swallowed. He kept shifting his weight from one foot to the other, with his jacket tucked underneath his arm. He swallowed. He looked to his left, at the chairs in her living room, then back at her. She was still standing with her hand on the door knob.

"Could I...do you think I could have a glass of water?" he asked. "Please?"

"Sure." She walked into the kitchen and took a glass from the drying rack beside the sink. As she was filling it, Howie called from his spot at the doorway,

"Listen, I've been thinking a lot since I...since Friday. I don't know what was going through my head that night—I just." He sighed and shook his head.

Adrienne came back and handed him the glass. She looked into his eyes and tried to hide her pity. This visit had to be brief. She could not let him fall apart.

He smiled weakly and took a sip of water, then ran his tongue over his lips. His hand was still trembling.

"Do you want to sit down?" she said slowly, frustrated by the silence, and in spite of her desire to rush him out of the apartment.

Howie let out a breath and turned and walked to the living room. Then he stopped and looked over his shoulder at her. She smiled but did not move. He looked from the futon to the loveseat to the overstuffed chair, then finally, hesitantly, sat down at the edge of the loveseat.

Adrienne sat down in the overstuffed chair.

"I've been doing a lot of thinking," Howie said again. His eyes met hers fleetingly, then traveled down to the armrest of the chair, where she had draped her left hand. She thought she could feel the engagement ring heat up under his gaze, and she resisted the impulse to pull it back and tuck it under her thigh.

"I guess Maynard asked the big question, huh?" he said, in that voice that was slightly more than a mumble. This was one of the few times she had heard Howie refer to her boyfriend by name.

"Yes," she said. "That was why we had the party. He announced it to everybody at midnight. But you were gone then." Then, almost unwillingly, she asked, "Where were you, Howie? Where did you go?"

"I went," Howie said, and Adrienne noticed the familiar tears forming in his eyes. She wanted to grab him and shake him. He sighed and looked out the window.

"That night was really important to me," she said softly. Some vicious imp reared up within her and asked if that was true, and she pushed it away. To Howie, she added, "I wanted you to be there."

"I wasn't there," Howie said, his voice wavering with pent-up sobs, "because I couldn't bear to be around you. I wasn't there because I love you."

He uttered the excuse like it was the same incredible revelation it had been when he first offered the words to her three months ago. Then, the proclamation had come at the bottom of a note scrawled drunkenly on the back of a cocktail napkin from the 15th Street Tavern and tucked beneath the windshield wiper of her Honda. By now, she was not only accustomed to the idea, she was tiring of it. She said nothing.

"To be in the same room as you and...him—" There, that was how she was used to Howie referring to the man she loved. *Him*, forced out of the lips like a swear. Howie shook his head. "Adrienne, I love you," he said. "I love you more than any woman I've ever known, and I can't bear to let you—"

"Howie," she interrupted. "Don't." She wouldn't look at him now, either. The hand that had been hanging languidly over the arm rest when their conversation began was now clenched, and her fingernails were digging into her palms. She felt tears welling up, but they were held at bay by her astonishment at Howie's audacity, and the resultant rage. "I understand that you love me. But I never asked for your love, and I never gave you any reason to think I would return it. I've been nothing but honest with you, and I've appreciated having you around as a friend, but I swear to God, Howie, if you start talking to me about what you're going to let me do, that's it. It's over."

She had been staring at the door as she spoke. Now she brought her gaze slowly toward him, unsurprised to see tears running down his cheeks.

"You can't possibly understand," he said.

"I'm in love with Maynard!" she insisted. "If you refuse to accept that, I can't keep you in my life."

The expression of hurt and shock on Howie's face made it clear that this wasn't the effect he had anticipated his confession would garner. Adrienne marveled at how such arrogance and self-loathing could coexist, in equal measure, in one man at one instant. He could spend hours talking about what a wretch he was, but if ever he was faced with the prospect that somebody did not find him remarkable, he would respond with stark bewilderment.

"Maybe it would be better if we spent a little less time together," she said, and she stood up.

Howie looked from side to side. Slowly he rose and moved toward her. He had left his coat hanging over the edge of the love seat, and when she realized he was trying to figure out some way to hug her, she pulled back and stepped around him. She picked up his coat and turned slightly to face him. Now he was standing with his back to the door. She held his coat out. He stood fixed in place with his arms almost imperceptibly spread, looking distraught and still bewildered.

"I have a lot of things to figure out about our wedding," she said, which was misleading, since she and Maynard hadn't so much as discussed what year they would be married and his giving of the ring had really just been a gesture of vague promise. "You need to accept the decisions I've made. When you've done that, then you can call me. I don't want to see you until then."

And, knowing that Howie was likely to stay in the same place whimpering for the next several minutes if she let him, Adrienne turned and walked upstairs to her bedroom, closing the door behind her. He might still stick around to see how serious she was, but she doubted that he would be ballsy enough to follow her up here and knock on the door.

That meant that for the time being she would have to wait. She sat down beside her bed and cupped her chin in one hand, picking at the threads of the carpet with the other, cursing Howie and wishing him gone from her life. And following on the heels of that wish like a dog begging for food came the doubt, doubt about her engagement, and the realization that she was close to wishing Maynard was gone too and that there were no decisions to make. She looked up at the clock on her wall and counted down the minutes until she would have to get ready for work. Her life would so much simpler, she thought, if she didn't have to deal with things like love, the giving or the receiving.

20. Hits!

Wayne, on that same Tuesday night, was for the first time in weeks not alone. He was one unit in a collective and he moved with the others. They walked in snow and snow fell around them. The falling snow was made up of huge, soft flakes that pulsed and shifted, sometimes moving towards Wayne on their way down, sometimes moving upwards, sometimes landing on his face, where they tingled, and the tingling coursed through his entire body: it began where the snowflake touched, then spread, as the cracks of a windshield will spread when cold air makes the glass contract, until he felt it in his toes and the tips of his fingers. When he closed his eyes to blink, Wayne could still see the snowflakes glowing a soft yellow on the backs of his eyelids, and when he opened his eyes again the snowflakes would still be yellow for a moment, still glowing.

He could feel the tickle of moisture on his forehead and his cheeks, and when he wiped his hands over his face nothing happened, he could still feel the tickle. Inside his mouth crawled a kind of film, over his teeth, around his gums, and down the center of his tongue. When cars passed, the noises they made—the whoosh of displaced air and the hiss of tires on wet pavement—stretched along, lingered briefly with Wayne, then snapped back into silence.

"It's so cold," said the guy walking next to Wayne. Stewart, Stewart Something. His voice came to Wayne as if through a pillow, but when the words unscrambled in his head, they echoed.

Wayne scratched the scruff of beard on his chin and it sounded like thunder. "Yes," he said. "It is." And he shivered, but beneath his heavy coat and beneath his black sweater and his tee-shirt he was sweating. He could feel the sweat coming from each pore. He shivered. "Where the fuck are we?"

"Yeah," Stewart said. Then he looked at Wayne. "Where are we?" he repeated, and Wayne nodded. "We're on Eighth. We're going to Cheesman Park."

They were on a strip of sidewalk that kept repeating itself. They had walked past this fenced-in playground over and over again, and that red minivan had already passed them and pulled into that Conoco. The same street corners kept coming up on them, and further ahead there was a set of stop lights that refused to get any closer, the lights themselves all wrong, shades of blue and violet and bright white. Wayne looked at his watch once and it was 9:20, and when he looked at it again later it was 9:07.

Others had been with them, but the others had left, gone back to the house. Now it was just Wayne and Burke and four whose names were lost to Wayne. These were strangers. Why was he with them? The snowflakes looked like they were shooting out from their bodies rather than landing on them.

Wayne understood that none of this was happening, that the sensation of movement was why they called this a "trip." Their bodies were back at Stewart and Fisk's house, and it was their minds responsible for taking them off to these strange places. All these sounds and visions were products of Wayne's imagination, and if it was too cold, and if the blister on the heel of his right foot bothered him, it was only because his imagination was negative. To escape discomfort, he had only to conceive of pleasant things. Fisk and Teri had done it just a few minutes ago, and those other three guys had done it much earlier, when they turned back two blocks away from the house, which wasn't really a house, but a construct in their collective consciousness of comfort and safety. Wayne wasn't on a *walk*, because walks were merely things his mind had created to distinguish one state from another, like snowboarding, which they had just been doing before they stopped in this copse of trees to rest, and to point at the stars. Wayne saw the stars, then looked out from the trees at the dark. Toby and Jessica were out there still, snowboarding somewhere, and Wayne and the others he was with were just letting time pass.

Wayne sat down and took the boots off his feet, the boots that the girl Teri had told him she had picked up from a dumpster a few weeks ago. They were big, heavy Doc Martens, and somebody had abandoned them. Before they had left the house, Wayne had decided to try them on, because he hadn't wanted to wear his shoes in the snow.

"The boots!" one of the girls shouted when she saw him pull them off. Wayne put his hands in to them and they changed shape to fit over his hands. "These damn boots!" She took them away from Wayne and clapped their soles together, then set them in the snow next to the sidewalk. "These boots give everybody blisters. We're going to leave them here, where some bum can find them. You're better off just wearing socks."

She was right. His feet felt free, and they could breathe. It was better. This is what Wayne had to do: he had to get rid of all things produced by the negative energy in his mind. Now that the *boots* were gone, he had to get rid of the cold and the hunger. All he needed was discipline. Once his mind was free of the bad, he would be back at the house. The trip would be done. Wayne tried to think of good things. What was good? He imagined Burke, and Burke was lifting him up, and they were walking again. Burke was talking, but Wayne didn't know what he was saying. The snow was soaking through his sea-green cotton socks. Burke and the girl were beside him, and Stewart was up in front them with another, and Stewart kept pointing across the street at things and saying their names. Burke's girlfriend was up there, too, looking back over her shoulder at Burke and Wayne, smiling.

Then they were back at the house, and all the lights were on. But something was wrong. Burke wasn't here. Neither were Wayne's parents. The house was a mess. Furniture was broken, and there were thick dark puddles on the floor. Wayne walked in loops, in the front door, through the kitchen, into Fisk and Teri's room, and out the back door. In the back yard, the swimming pool was barren, and the table beside it impossibly purple. Wayne turned and walked down the alley beside the house, stumbling over garbage bags, and back up the front porch, and inside again. Three people were leaning against the kitchen counter laughing. Wayne kept walking. A bunch of the collective were lying on their backs in Fisk and Teri's room, chattering, but Wayne could only discern random words from their conversations. His feet were cold. He went outside the back and watched the snow fall, and then he turned around and did the loop backwards. This was starting to make sense. He picked up a pair of sunglasses from the kitchen counter and twisted them in his hands until they snapped.

The laughing stopped. Stewart came toward him and said, "Dude, what are you doing?"

Wayne pushed Stewart away and went back outside. He saw his car, the front end crumpled, crashed onto the sidewalk. Stewart came out behind him and clapped him on the back. "There's no problem between us, right, Wayne? Did I do something to upset you?"

Wayne shook his head. The sadness that he had been trying to bury welled up in his chest. "No," he said. "I'm sorry."

This was not the way people were supposed to act. He was disappointing everybody. His father would be ashamed if he could see him. His thesis committee at Berkeley would be ashamed. From inside the house, he heard laughter again.

"You going to be okay?" Stewart asked. Wayne told him yes, even though he was beginning to understand how artificial the question was. In his mind he could see the face of his aunt in Colorado Springs, shaking her head as his aunt in Colorado Springs, shaking her head as an admonishment. He thought back to the weeks leading up to this moment, to getting drunk in the hotel room and passing out in the bath tub, the shower drumming his vomit-caked chest, and now here beside his wrecked car on the street outside a stranger's house. The police would be here soon, that was what happened when you did drugs. With a tremor and a tiny sigh, Wayne faced the truth.

The laughter kept coming through the open door, where Stewart had gone back inside, to report, obviously. The truth was that the trip had never happened, that the acid was not real. Acid did not even exist. Life as Wayne had up to that point understood it was a joke at his expense. Now that he had gotten it, none of the others were pretending to be tripping anymore. They were all enjoying themselves and congratulating one another. Each had had a part to play, and they had played it well, eliciting from Wayne all the appropriate thoughts and emotions to bring him to this point, and to break him.

He reeled and stumbled back inside, not bothering to shut the front door. Around him, the words of the others corroborated his revelation. In Fisk and Teri's room, he heard somebody shouting about George W. Bush. They were laughing, they all thought that was a good one. Wayne himself could almost force a laugh, thinking about how worried everyone had once been that Bush would order the invasion of Iraq, never knowing that *Bush* and *Iraq* and *invasion* were all arbitrary names and ideas. He thought about the apartment he rented in a basement, and about watching three minutes of *It's a Wonderful Life* on Christmas day. He thought about his aunt and uncle, not missing him because they didn't even exist. All the people Wayne had met in his few months in Denver, all were delusions, as was his entire past. And this friendship with Burke—it had come so easily to him, and every other relationship had been so trying. He should have known then. It was too forced, unnatural.

Wayne sat down on the floor and blinked. Around him, people he had imagined were his friends—or acquaintances at least—were getting ready for whatever they would do next, smiling patronizing smiles at him, all so proud of their joke. "This is sick," Wayne said to God. And in realizing that life was an illusion, he realized too that death must be. Death had been what motivated him this far, the possibility of giving himself to death and abandoning his aloneness. Without death, he had nothing. This loneliness and this pain would be with him forever.

His socks were wet, and now his feet were throbbing, not just the blister that had formed by the boot, but the whole things, all of the feet. They were cold and the cold stung. He peeled the sock off his right foot and held it with his hands but it did no good; his hands were cold too.

"How's it going, Wayne?" said one of the girls. She sat with somebody else down on the couch above Wayne. He wondered if they had jobs or something, and would they carry on existing in some metaphysical plane? Were they just actors? Or had they played a role in the orchestration of his demise?

He answered, "Okay," in a mumble to the girl's question. He let go of his foot to pull the left sock away.

"Oh my God, look at his feet."

He held his left foot in his cold hands.

"Dudes! Somebody come in here and check out this guy's feet!"

There was still some of this that Wayne had to work out. It seemed that he was stuck here now, in this house with these people, because the world beyond this now didn't exist, and could never exist again, because the truth had been revealed. If he had been better, or wiser, perhaps he could have come to the truth at another, happier time in his life, and spent eternity in that moment. With his father, perhaps.

"Holy shit. Was he walking out there without any shoes?"

"He was wearing those fucking Doc Martens when he left. He didn't want to wear the shoes he had brought."

"Oh, shit. *I* took those from him. At Cheesman."

"You *took* them?"

"Fucking A, dude, look at his feet!"

"He took them off when we stopped, and he showed me the blister. I wanted him to stop hurting."

People stood around Wayne talking. He knew they were talking. They had to figure out what to do with him. His feet hurt.

"He's fucking wasted. How many hits did he do?"

"Those damn boots!"

"I gave him four. He'd never tripped before."

"Four?"

"Fuck, man, *you* gave him four? I gave him six."

"Six?"

"This is his first time?"

"Somebody get some hot water."

"Cold water."

Wayne let go of his left foot and he crossed his legs so he was sitting Indian style. That's what they called it when he was little. His mind must have created that, too. Indians. Cowboys. He was sitting so his right foot was beneath his left calf and he had his left foot tucked into the crook behind his right knee, keeping it warm, even though it hurt to put pressure on it, and he held his right foot with his hands again.

"Just regular water. In a big basin."

"A fucking basin."

"There's a tub underneath the sink. Use that."

"Stewart, you said you gave him six hits?"

"Wayne, can you hear me? I need you to let go of your foot."

Abby was what he had called the girl who was pulling on his foot now. What he wasn't sure of was whether that name was chosen for her, or had he assigned it to her? He didn't know how much he had done himself and how much had been done in advance for the set-up.

"He asked me how many he should take. I didn't know Burke had already given him some."

"Yeah, but *six*?"

"Here, lift him up to the couch."

"I'm tripping so hard right now."

"Look at his *feet*!"

A person was holding each arm. Burke was on his left. It was really Burke. Then he was sitting.

"Jesus, they feel like fucking ice cubes."

His feet were being held by somebody else now, Abby was holding his feet. And then they were in water. The water felt like fire.

"Maybe we should call 911."

"Look at those socks, man. Those socks are...Jesus, look at them."

"I'm looking."

"We can't call 911."

"I figured, this was his first time, he'd want to trip balls. You don't want to have some weak-ass trip your first time out."

"My first time, I had a whole ten-strip."

"That's what I'm talking about."

Wayne could move his toes again.

"He has shoes, though, right?"

"We don't have to call 911. His feet just got cold. They're fine now."

They were fine. Wayne leaned his head back and smiled. His feet still hurt, but there was no danger. He was being taken care of. People cared.

"Look at the water!"

"I am so fucked up."

"Wayne, how are you feeling? Are you feeling okay?"

Wayne smiled and looked at the ceiling. Burke's girlfriend was nice. She was so nice. Burke was important to have around. "I am okay," Wayne said.

"Get a towel. Pull his feet out. Dry them off."

"I am okay."

21. Howie's relocation

At the empty club where Howie was slouched against the sticky wall hugging a bottle of Cutty Sark to his chest, his precarious hold on consciousness was hardly helped by the sound of knocking at the front door. He did nothing, sure that whoever was out there would eventually come to the conclusion that the place was empty and that he would then be left alone.

Alone. What had always been a curse in the big picture of his life was at this tiny, particular spot a wonderful blessing. Nobody could comfort him, true, but at least nobody could look down on his shivering, huddled form and shake her head and despise him for the wreck he had become.

The knocking had only subsided for a moment when it was followed by the sound of the door opening. Howie pushed himself up from the sleeping bag and set the bottle down beside him. There was no heat in this place. To ward off the cold he was wearing his two pairs of pants, a sweater, wool mittens, and a fleece ear-warmer that wrapped around his head. He didn't own a hat.

"Howie?"

Howie gasped and he kept the air in his lungs. He didn't recognize the voice, and the architecture of the club kept him from putting a face to it. The building was shaped like a short, fat L, with the top of the L pointing west, and the doors around the corner on the far north wall. Howie had arranged his living quarters, on the insistence of Fisk's cousin Danelle, in the westernmost corner, in case anybody chanced to peer into the little windows on the doors and caught a glimpse of him.

"Howie?" the voice repeated, and Howie heard footsteps coming near the corner. "It's Adam."

Oh. Howie let out his breath. Of course. Fisk's cousin and Adam had bought this place together. They were going to turn it into another club. After all Howie had gone through, he had pushed from his mind many of the facts that didn't relate directly to him and Adrienne. It was only then, as Adam rounded the corner, that Howie recognized how preposterous his own misery was. Suddenly he was facing, across a dusty concrete floor, the pale light from the window behind him casting the man's features in striking black and white, someone whose life had gone through such drastic upheaval that the throbbing of Howie's own heart seemed callow. "Hello, Adam," he said.

He figured this was it. He had been staying here for three weeks. It made sense that Fisk's cousin would send her disassociated business partner to demand that Howie find someplace else to stay. Adam, already tall, seemed even taller from where Howie sat, his long, narrow face the epitome of authority. "Howie," he said. "We should go."

Howie looked at his meager pile of belongings in the far corner: four good-size boxes, a crate, and a duffel bag. With the sleeping bag and the pillow behind him, it was all he had left. "I'm sorry I'm still here," he told Adam. "I've just had a really hard time—"

Adam made a slashing gesture with his hand. Howie stopped talking. "We've got to get you out of here."

Howie nodded and stared at the floor.

"I don't think Danelle had any idea how long you were—"

"I know, I know," Howie said.

Adam scooped up Howie's pillow and his sleeping bag. "I'm sorry, Howie. Danelle would have invited you to stay at her place if she had room. And I was so busy...it never occurred to me."

"I know," Howie said. A sob wracked his body. "I'm so sorry." He felt Adam's bony hand squeezing his shoulder.

"Sorry?" Adam repeated. "Howie, you've got nothing to be sorry about. We've been complete shitheads about this. Come on, grab some of your stuff."

The hand fell away, and Howie looked up in time to see Adam pick up his duffel bag and turn the corner. His tears faltered and his curiosity impelled him forward, to follow Adam in slow, shuffling steps. By the time he turned the corner, Adam was already on his way back in. He stopped to clap Howie on the shoulder, then passed him and picked up the crate.

Howie turned around and went back to grab one of the boxes. He carried it outside. Adam, on his way back in, gestured toward a little black car that was parked in the alley alongside the building. Howie set the box inside. He leaned against the trunk and wiped his hand over his forehead. When Adam came back out with the second box, Howie smiled weakly at him. Adam nodded and they went back in for the last two boxes together. The bottle of Cutty Sark still stood in the corner near where Howie had been slouching. Howie looked at it meaningfully. Adam followed his glance.

"You've been drinking, Howie?"

"I have."

"Well, you won't want to leave that bottle," Adam said. He picked up a box. "Put it on top of here."

Howie fetched the bottle, checked to make sure the cap was on tight, and set it on top of the box Adam was holding.

"On its side," Adam said.

Howie turned the bottle on its side. It rolled down toward Adam and Adam lifted his chin to let the bottle fall into the crook between his neck and the edge of the box. Howie watched him anxiously. Then, as Adam left, Howie picked up the last box and followed him.

"I've got an extra room at my place," Adam said. "You'll have to sleep on a futon, but I guess you can manage."

They loaded the boxes into the trunk, and Adam wedged the bottle in against the wheel well. This whole thing seemed like it was happening to somebody else and Howie was just watching. Adam went around to the driver's seat and Howie sat down in the passenger's seat beside him. "How have you been?" Howie asked, when he trusted himself to speak. It was still hard to accept the notion that Adam really was driving him away from the dark and cold empty to someplace with a bed.

"I've been okay," Adam said. "These past couple of weeks have been hell, but I've been getting better. You know. We live."

"Yes," Howie said. The way Adam said it, *We live* was neither a celebration or a lament, but a simple statement of fact. Things came at you, and sometimes you tried to dodge them, and sometimes you held on to them for dear life. It didn't matter if you were weak or strong, sentimental or oblivious. When it all came down to it, choice wasn't even in issue. "We live," Adam was saying, and it was as simple as that.

"I'm sorry," Howie added after a moment. He wondered if he should add "for everything you've been through," so Adam wouldn't think he was just begging his forgiveness for having wronged him, as he wronged everybody, as every decision he made complicated somebody's life somewhere and made the whole "We live" idea harder to swallow. But he didn't have to earmark the apology. As soon as the words were out, Adam said, "I've found ways to cope." Howie felt better about all the crap life had flung at him. Adam was a paragon of human resolve. He had lost everything in the span of days, and he had found ways to cope. That his difficulties outweighed Howie's no longer seemed significant; all that mattered was that he had learned that he could move past his anguish. Surely if he could do it, then Howie could.

Howie blinked and in blinking realized how heavy his eyelids had gotten. With his next blink he kept his eyes shut. His head toppled forward. The next thing he knew

Adam was saying his name and shaking him by the arm. The car was parked in the driveway of a house. Howie rubbed his eyes.

"We'd better bring your stuff in now," Adam said. "This neighborhood used to be safe, but nothing is safe now."

Howie stepped out of the car and looked up and down the street. Dusk was coming, but even in the long sinister shadows the area looked pleasant. He felt as safe here as anywhere. It all seemed safe.

They carried Howie's things in and deposited them in a room with conspicuously bare shelves. "I was robbed," Adam said curtly when he noticed Howie looking. "They violated my home."

Howie nodded. "I'm sorry."

"Sorry isn't enough, Howie," Adam said. He left the room and Howie, after hesitating for a moment beside his pile of things, crowned by the bottle of Cutty Sark, followed him out and found him leaning against his kitchen counter, his arms folded over his chest.

Howie was going to ask him if he wanted any whisky, but he wasn't quite sure if he should yet. "What'd they steal?" he asked. There was an entertainment center in the living room, with a big TV and a DVD player and a really nice looking CD player, one of those 100-disc deals. "Books? Did they steal anything besides books?"

"They were comic books," Adam said. "Hundreds of thousands of dollars worth of comic books."

"Hundreds of thousands!" Howie whistled and shook his head.

"Thousands, anyway." Adam chewed on his lip. "I'm not sure. I haven't priced them in a while."

Howie nodded and sat down at Adam's table. He wondered if he should offer Adam a glass of whisky now. "And they didn't take the CD player?" he said, instead. "Or anything else?"

Adam sat down across from him. "I know. It's odd. The enemy is unpredictable. My father first, then my mother, and now this. It boggles the mind."

"Yeah," Howie said. "That's something." Adam looked like a wreck now. Before, he seemed pretty okay, but now that he was thinking about his parents again, his face was just wretched. He looked like he could really use a drink. "That's why I brought you here tonight, Howie." Adam looked up now, into his eyes. Howie scooted his chair back a centimeter or two. "This enemy is more pernicious than anybody ever knew before. It's certainly worse than I ever expected. And something must be done. To stand by idly in the face of all this evil is as bad as the evil itself. Or worse, maybe, because the evil knows it is evil and does what is its nature."

"Yeah," Howie said. He stood up. "I'm going to go get my whisky. Do you want a drink?"

"Howie!"

Howie froze.

"I'm talking about making a difference!" Adam said. "Doesn't that mean anything to you?"

Howie sat down. He nodded.

"It killed my parents," Adam said.

"Yeah, I know," Howie said. He wasn't sure what they were talking about now. "Wait, what killed your parents?"

"The cancer," Adam said.

Howie couldn't say for certain, but he thought Fisk had said one of Adam's parents had had a heart attack. Whatever. It was rotten timing: one a heart attack, and one cancer. "One was a heart attack, wasn't it?" he asked Adam.

"That's just it," Adam said. "It's a mark of how pervasive the cancer is, and how insidious. Yes, my mother had a heart attack, but it was because of the strain on her heart from watching the man she loved wither away."

His voice was trembling. Jesus, he needed a drink. Howie reached across the table to pat his hand, which, both of them, were pressed flat against the table, fingers splayed. "I'll go get the bottle," Howie said. "I'll be right back." He stood up again.

"But you see, right? There's no reason to distinguish between the two. Cancer, heart attack. I used to specify, but then I realized—"

"Keep talking," Howie said. "I'm just going to..." He headed toward the room, walking backwards so Adam could still see him and see that he was paying attention. "Don't worry, I'm listening."

"I realized that what killed my mother is no different than what killed my father," Adam yelled after him.

Howie plucked the bottle from the top of the boxes and brought it back to the table.

"Cancer is more than a disease," Adam told him. He stood up so he could look Howie in the eyes. Howie held the bottle by its neck. "Cancer is everywhere in the world. Cancer is the part of every man that drives him to evil acts." Howie looked into the kitchen and counted the cupboards. "Cancer steals and kills and rapes, and everywhere else in the world people just watch it happen."

"Do you have some glasses?" Howie asked in a soft voice, not wishing to throw off Adam's rhythm. "Just point."

"For a long time, I just watched it, too." Adam grabbed Howie's arms, effectively holding him in place. "But the other night I had a revelation. Something clicked, Howie. I realized, we can just keep zapping away at cancer cells with radiation 'til the end of the world. We can pay taxes to pay the payrolls of the police to catch criminals and lock them up. But none of it's going to make a real difference, is it?"

Howie shook his head. "No." He was about to suggest that Adam should keep going, and he'd find the glasses himself, but Adam didn't give him the chance.

"We have to change the very fabric of society is what we have to do, Howie. We have to rid the world of all the things that allow cancer to thrive. We have to fight."

"Fight," Howie repeated.

"I have some Talisker," Adam said. "Do you want that instead?"

"Huh?"

Adam let go of Howie's arms and he walked into the kitchen. He opened the cupboard above the stove and pulled out a bottle. Howie squinted at the bottle, then looked down at the white label in his hand, and he put his bottle on the table and padded over to Adam. "Talisker?"

Adam set the bottle down and when he turned away to open another cupboard Howie picked it up and uncorked it. "Danelle gave it to me for Christmas," Adam said. Howie smelled it. "It's great. One of my favorites. But I'm not drinking now." He set a glass down, and Howie filled it. "Easy, Howie."

"You say you're not drinking now?" Howie asked, looking up from his glass. Adam shook his head. Howie shrugged and put the cap back on the bottle. He picked up his glass and carried it with the bottle over to the table. Adam hesitated near the cupboard, but then followed Howie, empty-handed.

"Ooh, that's good," Howie said. He smacked his lips. "That's really good. It tastes like a little piece of God."

"Yes," Adam said. He nodded. "I'm not drinking now, though."

Howie's mouth felt warm. "Why aren't you drinking?"

"The fight," Adam said.

Oh, yeah. The fight. Howie took another sip. "You mean the fight against cancer."

"Whatever you call it," Adam said. He seemed a little bit more composed now. "It's going to be hard, Howie. I already went out there once, and I failed." He hung his head.

"Out where?" Howie asked. He took another little sip and let the whisky rest on his tongue. After he finally swallowed, he said, "Listen, this Talisker is really great. By the way."

"It's an Island malt," Adam said, lifting his head. "It's pretty smoky. Some people really hate that taste, I know. But it's one of my favorites."

"You mentioned that."

Adam nodded.

Howie took another sip, and he realized suddenly that he hadn't thought of Adrienne for the past half hour, since Adam had picked him up. When was the last time he had gone this long without thinking of her? And what did it say of his love for her, that it could be distracted so easily by the disruption of routine and the introduction of single malt scotch? He put the glass down and frowned.

"I might just have a taste, though," Adam said, reaching out gingerly. Howie slid his glass forward. Adam took a sip, then set the glass down and pushed it back toward Howie. "Yeah, that's good."

He was right. It was good.

"Anyway," Adam said. "I realized after the other night that I can't do this by myself. I need somebody to watch my back, and to be there for me if anything goes wrong again."

Adrienne had to know what had happened to Adam, hadn't she? Actually, now that Howie thought about it, he was pretty sure Maynard was friends with Adam. Damn. Yeah, he was.

"That's when I remembered you," Adam said. "I had heard about your...about what happened with you. Losing your job, and I guess you sort of had a breakdown, didn't you?"

Howie half-nodded.

"And I thought, maybe it's all part of the same thing. Maybe what's got a hold of you is the same force that destroyed my father and that stopped my mother's heart."

Wait, but...Adam was friends with Adrienne first, wasn't he? Now that he thought about it, Howie was pretty sure he and Maynard had met Adam at about the same time, at one of Adrienne's brother's parties. Adam had gone to school with Adrienne's brother or something, and he and Howie had talked a long time at the party about the music scene in Denver. Maybe Maynard had hung out with him a few times after that, but that didn't mean he had exclusive rights on the guy. Howie took another drink.

"I wanted to ask for your help, Howie. And in helping me, you would be helping yourself. You would be helping the world."

Adam was a good friend.

"Will you fight with me, Howie?"

22. WAYNE FINDS HIS WAY BACK

A few blocks away, Wayne lay on his back on the carpet. He hadn't noticed precisely when it happened, but the world had stopped twisting. It no longer heaved, swayed, or trembled. With each breath he could feel his back push against the floor. He turned his head slowly to the right and he could see feet. He saw a couch, and underneath the couch were things, in the dark, things he couldn't make out. In front of the couch were feet, and when Wayne focused on the feet he could hear voices coming from above the feet. They didn't seem to be talking about him, which he found curious. He wondered what they would do now, the owners of the voices. Where they would go.

Turning his head to the left, making with his line of sight a parabola over his prostrate body, he saw the heads that were producing the voices. Above them he saw the wall turn into the ceiling, and then the ceiling turned back in the wall, but in a reasonable and steady fashion, not streaking, leaving no trails behind. At the base of the wall on the left he could see part of the table that the television sat on. Next to the table were his shoes.

They seemed impossibly far away. But when he reached out his arm, his fingers brushed over them effortlessly. He didn't even have to stretch.

"Hey, my friend," one of the voices that belonged to the feet said. "Where are you going?"

Wayne could see the whole person now. He sat up and pulled his shoes to him. He wondered if he could speak;

earlier in the evening, speaking had taken an inordinate effort. Slowly, he said, "I think I want to go home."

The person with the voice leaned forward and put a hand on Wayne's shoulder. "I don't know if that's such a good idea right now. Why don't you stay for a while, hang out?"

Wayne looked around for his socks. He couldn't remember what he had done with his socks. His feet throbbed. He did not want to put his shoes on if he couldn't find his socks. "I would like to go home," he said, more to assure himself that he could, indeed, speak, than anything.

"Yeah, we'll all go home eventually. But right now I think we should all just hang out here, you know?"

This was not what Wayne had missed. This was not why he had left society. Where was Burke? "I'm tired," he said.

"Sure. Yeah. That's cool. Do you want to sleep? You can sleep here, and when you wake up in the morning, we can all go home."

Wayne looked around for his socks.

"I'll get you some blankets," the person said. The owners of both pairs of feet stood up together, and the one who hadn't been speaking to Wayne said, "You can sleep on the couch, Wayne."

He tipped his head back to see them and their faces. They were faces he knew. They had names.

"Here." One held his hand out to Wayne. Wayne took it, and he was pulled nearly to his feet. His feet screamed. Without standing all the way, with most of his weight on the hand being held by the other, Wayne pivoted on his heels and moved past the two who had been sitting and fell into the couch. Hands moved him to lay his body down. The couch was long enough. How few couches were long enough to lie on! Wayne, with his face pressed into the cushions of the couch, could almost find it in him to smile. Instead he exhaled and his breath came back to him. He pushed himself up and turned to face outward. A girl was helping, moving a pillow underneath his head. The other person had gone. It occurred to Wayne to wonder at their generosity. Then he wondered if he had been right. He realized gradually, his mind working through the problem like his studless tires through thick snow in his first winter here, that these people were not just players. The drug was real, and now its effects were subsiding. Wayne could see that now. He could even say he knew it.

"Thank you," he said. The other was coming back now with blankets. He was with somebody. *Fisk* came to Wayne, a name for the face of the somebody who was coming with the other. Fisk lived here. Lived, really. He did not just fake this for Wayne.

"Is he going to be okay?" Fisk asked the one who was handing the blankets to the girl who spread them out over him. *Yes*, Wayne wanted to say, but instead he closed his eyes. It was enough to know that the question was phrased with real concern. There would be no reason to carry the charade this far, once Wayne had seen through it. Therefore, it wasn't a charade. The fabric of reality could be stitched back together.

The next time Wayne opened his eyes the house was dark and quiet. He was too hot. The heat was what had woken him. He pushed the blankets off of him and sat up. His feet were still cold but the rest of him was hot. He was sweating. *The drug*, he remembered. He shook his head. There was no reason to be here. The experiment was over. Death was still an option.

His shoes, he knew in spite of the dark, lay on the floor nearby. He bent at his waist and leaned forward to grab them. Then, holding them with the index and middle finger of his right hand, Wayne stood. His feet were numb. It felt like he was standing on Styrofoam. No, that's not what it felt like. Wayne shook his head. To put the shoes on now would be an act of self-hatred; his feet could not take them, they would protest. What he had to do was get back to the hotel, back to what he knew and where he was fit to make decisions. There he could wash his feet and perhaps soak them in warm water, then wrap them in a towel and have a drink, sit and figure out what he would do next.

Still holding his shoes, he hobbled toward the diamond of light that suggested a window of a door. His left arm, extended, found the knob. He twisted it and pulled. Nothing. He pushed, and with a creak the door opened. A rush of cold air came in, and a sliver of moonlight that revealed to Wayne the crumpled mass of his coat beside a chair on which sat a girl, sleeping, who murmured and turned her back to the cold and hugged herself. Wayne let go of the door knob to scoop up his jacket. Then he stepped outside onto the stoop and shoved the door shut with his shoulder. For the moment, he let his shoes drop to the ground and he pulled his jacket on. There was a familiar, comforting weight to it. Wayne patted his pockets. His phone was in one, his wallet in the other with the key to his room at the hotel. These were tangible things. His mind would survive.

He picked his shoes up, tucked them under his arm, and stepped out onto the sidewalk. The sidewalk was cold, but not so cold that it bothered his feet, at least not as much as it would bother him, he was sure, to put his shoes on without the socks. He turned to the left and headed the direction he was pretty sure he had come from. It seemed like it had happened in a different life, so the memories had to be dredged up from an abyss and reexamined, searched for a useful, distinguishing feature. If he could just get to Colfax, he was sure he would be okay. He could find the hotel from Colfax, and he didn't have to worry about what direction to turn onto Colfax, because even from here he could see the big blue Qwest sign on the skyline, like a beacon for downtown. All Wayne had to do was get on Colfax.

He had to hobble, too. His feet weren't quite as numb as he had thought they were; he could feel the cold of the sidewalk. The roughness wasn't a concern. It was smooth enough that the soles of his feet would not be getting chewed up, but it was cold. He curled his toes to make fists of his feet. Colfax was coming up. He turned to his left and crossed the street.

The question of what to do next was not going away, even as it was being pushed aside by more immediate concerns. He knew he had to get back to the hotel, but beyond that, and beyond the solace of momentary seclusion, he was at a loss. He didn't know how tonight's experience fit in to the grand scheme or what light it shed on the matters that had been troubling him in the weeks leading up to it. When he had put that list together, the prospect of losing his mind had held a certain allure, but now that he had gotten so close to seeing the losing of his mind as a concrete possibility, he decided that he was grateful. Whatever decisions he made from here, he would make them with a sound mind. That had to count for something.

Ahead of him the street was veering to the right. Wayne let out a sigh. The veering meant that Colfax was turning into Fifteenth Street. Before long he would be seeing landmarks that communicated some measurable fact and he would know exactly how far he was from the place that had become his home. Then he would be there, at home, resting and deciding.

He had wanted to see what the world was like without him in it. Tonight—no, last night; it had to be nearing dawn, although Wayne had deliberately chosen to leave his watch behind at the hotel, so he had no way of knowing for sure, but he had done so much since then that it had to be a new day—so last night, he had met Burke and his friends at a coffee shop up on Fifteenth Street, somewhere further north from where he stumbled forward right now. Burke's friend talked with another guy who showed up and they made plans to leave. Nobody mentioned Wayne's disappearance. It was like he had never left. The experience was a bit confusing, like a scene from a movie about a character similar enough to Wayne that he could relate to him, but not Wayne. He felt nothing for these people. Something was missing.

They went to a house Wayne had never been to before. He recognized the people who lived there from the band that had been playing at the first party he went to and understood that the girl he had slept with that night was the drummer's girlfriend, but none of these people had been part of the group he had latched onto when he had been getting to know Burke. It was a bit bewildering.

Watching Burke interact with all these people, Wayne got the impression for the first time of how huge Burke's society was, and he understood then that the people he, Wayne, had been spending so much time with since that first party were only a tiny sub-section of that society. That might have been the first moment he understood how fortunate he was to have established such an intimate connection with Burke. Even before now it had flattered Wayne to know how highly Burke seemed to esteem him, but only because of his own fondness for Burke. Witnessing last night what a small part he was of Burke's social make-up had made Burke's estimation of him even more remarkable. For a few short hours Wayne could stop worrying how he was considered by all those others, faces and names that had seemed so meaningful a few weeks earlier, but which were fading now in his memory.

Wayne blinked. He had gotten to Larimer Street. The Oxford was just a few blocks away. He had made it. The reason for his blinking, though, was not the street sign, but the blueness of the sky above him. It was still a dark blue, but it was blue. There was color in it. The sun was coming up behind him. A new day really was coming. He looked down at his feet. They were pink, nearly white. They didn't *appear* painful. Just a few more blocks. He turned to the left.

Did it mean anything that this new group of people had seemed willing to embrace him in their fold? It might have, he thought, except that it was the drugs that had united them, and any group might have embraced Wayne if they were bonding over some hedonistic ritual. The matter of the value of his own life and the effect he had on others was still as mysterious as it had been when he wrote his letter to Burke, and still he had no way of knowing if he was missed. He had not addressed the crucial judgment, just postponed it.

"God morning, sir. Welcome back."

The doorman was smiling at Wayne, holding the door open for him. He had recognized Wayne before Wayne had even recognized the hotel. That meant something, didn't it? No. It only meant that he was spending money here. Of course that made people happy. Ah, well. It was good, at least, to be indoors and walking on carpet. He waddled to the front desk, where he was greeted with a wide smile from a greasy guy with a five o' clock shadow. "Morning, Mr. Talbot."

"I was wondering," he asked the clerk, "do you have any aspirin, by any chance. Or ibuprofen?"

"Rough night, huh?" The clerk chuckled. For a moment, it seemed as though that might be the only response Wayne would get. The clerk leaned forward and looked to his right. Wayne followed his gaze to the dark windows of the gift shop. "Gift shop won't be opening up for another hour."

Why hadn't he worn his shoes? His feet were starting to throb again now that they were warming up. Where the hell had he put his socks?

"Tell you what." The clerk rapped his knuckles on the counter, calling Wayne's attention back. "Let me check our first aid kit, all right? I'll be back in a sec."

The clerk disappeared into a back room. Wayne rocked slightly on his feet. He needed to get back up to his room and get them in some warm water. God, they burned! Why hadn't he worn his fucking shoes?

"Aha!" came the clerk's voice. He walked back out, looking at a little packet in his hand. "You're in luck, Mr. Talbot. This was the only thing in there. Take a look." He set down a little packet of Bayer. Two tablets. Wayne wanted so much more. But,

"Thank you," he muttered. He slid it off the counter with his left hand and made his way to the elevator.

Now that Wayne was indoors and the prospect of relief so imminent, his feet were positively howling for action. Inside the elevator he put all his weight on the handrails to lift his feet from the ground. When the elevator stopped, he let his feet down slowly and hobbled as fast as was comfortable to his room. The shoes fell from underneath his arm as he rooted around in his jacket pocket for his key. He pulled the key out of the wallet, fit it into the lock, and stumbled inside, letting the door swing shut on his shoes. In the bathroom he sat down on the toilet. Taking the pressure off his feet alleviated the pain slightly, but momentarily. He turned on the hot water in the bathtub and stopped up the drain. He lifted his legs into the tub and the water around them turned murky with the dirt of Denver's sidewalks. The warmth was soothing and stinging at once, but it would get better. It had to.

He pulled his jacket off and tossed it out into the hallway. Now that his feet were completely immersed, he shut off the water. The packet of aspirin was still curled up in his left fist. He unfolded his fingers and tore the packet open with his teeth. He swallowed the pills as they were, without water.

In the tub, his submerged toes wiggled and flexed. As soon as they started to feel normal again, he would pull his feet out, wipe them dry with one of the Oxford's nice plush towels, then get in bed and sleep for however long it took. No. First, he would turn the heat up to 80. Then he would crawl into bed, pull the covers over his head, and when he woke up the last remnants of the drug would be gone from his system. The new day would begin in earnest. But for now he would just rest and let his wretched feet soak up the warm water.

23. Howie's next assignment

Late in the morning on the day after Adam had left Danelle's place, Danelle stopped by and rang the door bell. She waited a couple minutes and when nothing happened she pushed the button again, holding it down for a good eight seconds. Adam's door bell sounded like an old-fashioned telephone, like a real bell. When you held that button, the ring just kept going. It was impossible to ignore. Danelle was determined to ring for as long as it took until Adam answered the door. She didn't expect the door to be answered by somebody else.

"Morning," Danelle said, a little flustered.

Her cousin's bassist stood holding the door open, wearing only his boxer shorts. His body was white and tiny, with a cavity in his chest, and a disproportionate belly. He was squinting and looking at the ground a few feet past Danelle. He didn't say anything when he opened the door and didn't say anything to Danelle's good morning.

"Adam here?" Danelle asked.

Fisk's bassist smacked his lips. Still not looking into Danelle's eyes, he said, "I'm not sure. I just woke up. I need some water." He turned away from the doorway and fumbled toward the kitchen.

Danelle stayed for a second on the stoop trying to figure out what Fisk's bassist was doing wandering around Adam's house in his underwear. After a moment she stepped inside, closed the door behind her, and called out to the kitchen, "Are you staying here now?"

Fisk's bassist didn't answer. A couple of weeks ago Fisk had asked Danelle if it would be okay for his bassist to crash at the club on Josephine for a few days. Danelle had said yeah, sure, just don't make it too obvious, and after Fisk had stopped by to pick up the keys, she had sort of forgotten about it.

Howard, that was his name. He stood in Adam's kitchen holding an empty glass of water. His eyes had opened all the way, but they looked a little glazed. His hair stuck straight up from the top of his head and was matted down on the sides. His little belly was heaving, and a thin stream of water dribbled down from the corner of his mouth. "Hey," he said, "you're Fisk's cousin, aren't you?"

Danelle nodded. Howard turned toward the sink and refilled his glass, then drank it all in one go and let his hand fall. More water dribbled down from his mouth through his stubble. His little belly moved up and down, up and down.

"Are you staying here now?" Danelle asked.

Howie shrugged. "I stayed here last night," he said. "Adam came and picked me up from the club. Where is Adam, anyway?"

Danelle didn't know, either. "That's what I asked you when I got here," she said.

He shook his head. "You asked me if he was here."

"Obviously, then, I don't know where he is." Danelle walked away from the kitchen and called Adam's name, but there was no answer. When she turned around, Fisk's bassist was sitting at the dining room table. His glass was full again, cupped in his left hand. "His car's here," Danelle said.

Half of Howie's mouth smiled at her.

"When did he pick you up?" Danelle asked.

"Last night."

"And what happened then?"

"We moved my stuff over here. Then we drank."

"You drank?" *We*, Fisk's bassist had said. Both of them, then. Adam had been drinking. That was a relief. Adam's

154

blood alcohol had been tested at the hospital and the data had pointed to cold sobriety. His sitting at home drinking suggested that perhaps he was allowing his mind to be distracted from notions of revenge, or whatever it was he had been trying to exercise out in Five Points. Fisk's bassist had been through his own sort of misery. Maybe Adam had brought him here so they could wallow in it together.

"How are you doing, by the way?" Danelle asked. Then, to make the question feel more personal, she quickly added, "Howard?" She was horrible with names. As soon as she said it out loud, it sounded wrong. Fisk's bassist didn't immediately respond. She wondered if she should apologize.

"Oh, I'm okay," he said. Yes, Howard. That had to be right. He didn't look insulted. "I guess I...well, being around Adam sort of puts things into perspective, doesn't it? I mean, I've got a broken heart, sure, but a broken heart is all I have."

Danelle smiled. She let herself stop worrying about where Adam was for a moment. There was a Safeway only a few blocks away; maybe he had decided to walk. "You want some coffee, Howard?" Danelle asked.

Howie took a small sip of water and said, "I could drink coffee."

Danelle went into Adam's kitchen and put the kettle on to boil. While she pulled out the French press and the coffee, she called out to Howie, "How did he seem last night?"

Howie wasn't looking into the kitchen. His gaze was fixed in the distance. He sat with a slight slouch, his hand on the table holding the glass. His frowned and furrowed his brow. "He seemed...angry," he said. Satisfied with that, he nodded. The expression melted from his face and he took another sip of water.

Danelle put a couple of spoofuls of coffee into the pitcher of the press, then went and sat down at the table opposite Howie. "You didn't hear about Friday, did you?" she asked.

Howie started. He finally looked into Danelle's eyes. "What do you mean I didn't hear about Friday?"

"About Adam?" Danelle said. "About the whole Batman thing?"

Danelle could almost hear the click in the back of Howie's mind. A brightness came to his eyes. "Batman?" he asked.

"He was found over in Five Points dressed up like Batman," Danelle said. "Somebody had beat the crap out of him. We're still not sure what happened to him."

Howie took a long drink of water. His glass was empty again. He slid it toward Danelle, shaking his head.

"He won't talk about it," Danelle said, "but we think he was trying to *be* Batman, to actually fight crime."

"He talked to me about it," Howie said in a soft voice.

The tea kettle made a few anticipatory sputters announcing its intention to whistle. Danelle ignored them. "He did? Last night, you mean? He talked about dressing up like Batman?"

Howie nodded. "I sort of forgot it until just now when you mentioned it," he said. "Sorry. Look, I was pretty drunk last night, and the whole thing sort of confused me. I think I thought he was just messing around, so I went along with it."

The tea kettle whistled.

"Went along with what, Howard?" Danelle asked.

"He wants me to be Robin."

It was a loud whistle. Danelle whistled herself and shook her head. She walked to the kitchen and took the kettle off the burner.

"I don't know what I said last night," Howie said, "but I'm not going to wear those little green short pants. No way."

Danelle poured the hot water over the coffee grounds. She put the lid on, grabbed a couple of mugs, and carried everything out to the table.

"I'm glad Adam asked you to live here, Howie," Danelle said. "For your sake, as much as his. It was Fisk's idea to put you up at the club, and with everything that was going on here, well, I sort of forgot about it. But that's no way to live, without heat or furniture or anything. And Adam's got the space, so you might as well use it."

Howie smiled wanly.

"And, anyway," she said, "we're all still pretty worried about Adam. So if you're sticking around here, it kind of relieves the burden on the rest of us. We were worried he might take it as an invasion of his privacy if we were always over here checking up on him. Now, you can just let us know if there's anything we should be concerned about."

Howie picked up his empty glass, held it to his face, then set it down. "Okay," he said. "But what do I do if he asks me to be Robin again?"

"You tell him no," Danelle said, maybe a little too forcefully. "Obviously. If you can, engage him on it a little bit. Try to figure out *why* he's doing it, and then try to convince him it's the wrong way to go about it."

Danelle filled one of the mugs and slid it toward Howie.

"I could do that, I guess." Howie took a tiny sip of coffee and grimaced. "Does Adam have any sugar?"

Behind them, the door opened and Adam came in wearing a running suit, surrounded by an aura of steam. He swung the door shut and pulled off his shoes.

"Adam!" Danelle called. She stood up and walked over to the door. "You're running now?"

"New year's resolution," Adam said. He took his jacket off and tossed it onto the back of a chair. "I saw your car outside. How are you doing?"

"I'm good," Danelle said. "I'm good. How are you doing?"

Adam shrugged. He walked past her and past Howie, who was now turned away from the table holding his head in his hands with his elbows propped on his knees. In the kitchen, he filled a glass with water. Danelle walked back to the table. "Want some coffee?"

Adam shook his head. He took a long drink.

"It was a bit of a surprise to see Howie here," Danelle said. "I think it's great that you're taking him in."

Howie sat up straight in his chair. "I think I have to vomit," he said. He stood up and rushed toward the bathroom. Adam watched him go with a deep frown. He looked sad.

"Hey," Danelle said. "Jarvis and Kathryn were going to have a little get-together on Friday. Sushi party. You interested?"

"I can't," Adam said. "I have plans that night."

Plans?

"Maybe I can come by in the evening," he added. "What time will it start?"

"I don't know. Six, seven."

"I'll be there at six. I can't stay too late."

Danelle wanted to ask Adam what his plans were, but her fear of seeming intrusive held her back. "All right. Give me a call on Friday. And tell Howie about it, too."

Adam nodded.

"Okay, well," Danelle couldn't think of an excuse to stay. "I'm heading out then. I just figured I'd stop by since I was over this way. I'll see you Friday."

"Yes," Adam said. "Looking forward to it."

24. Wayne gets preoccupied

When he woke, Wayne called down to the front desk to ask if he could have a little jar of Tylenol delivered to his room. When he said the words, he was suddenly struck by the fear that they would not know what he meant by "jar," but he could not think of what the appropriate term was. *A jar*, the sadistic pedant in him insisted, *is a very specific receptacle. A jar is what you would store strawberry jam or pickles in. A jar is made of glass, or maybe in some instances of plastic, but a jar is always transparent, so that, aside from however the jar is labeled, you can see its contents. Tylenol is never kept in a jar.* But what, then, he wondered, do you call those little plastic containers of Tylenol?

"Mr. Talbot," said the woman on the phone, "I'm sorry, but all we have in our gift shop are the travel-sized packets of Tylenols. Would you like us to send you up some of those?"

Was it bottles? No, bottles were tapered at one end. Bottles made even less sense than jars. "No," he said to the woman, and afraid that if he tried to be too specific he would only confuse the woman and damn his chances of relief, he added simply, "I need more than just a travel-sized. I'm really feeling awful. Could you send somebody out to a drugstore or something? To pick me up a bigger...thing? Of Tylenol?"

There was a pause. Then, "Sure, Mr. Talbot," the woman said. She had some kind of accent. He was not used to hearing accents in Colorado. "There's a Walgreen's nearby, and I could send a bellman out to pick up some something for you."

"Yes," Wayne said. "Do that."

"Would you like me to send him up to get some money from you now?"

"No. Sorry. No. If possible, I'd like for you to send him out right away. If you could give him petty cash or something. I'll pay when he gets back. But I don't want to have to wait."

The two aspirins he had taken earlier in the morning had allowed him maybe two hours of sleep, and that only because his exhaustion had discounted the pain. Now his feet were in agony. Even the Tylenol he was sure would hardly help, but it would help more than nothing. He lay in bed with the covers kicked off onto the floor, his body sticky.

"Sure, Mr. Talbot," the woman said. She had taken another pause. "We'll send the bellman out now. He'll bring the Tylenol to your room with the receipt."

"Yes," Wayne said. He rolled onto his side and dropped the phone onto the cradle. His feet were angry at the rest of him. They hadn't gotten anything transcendental out of the drugs, but they hurt now because of the carelessness those drugs had encouraged. Wayne, lying again on his back, tilted his neck and flexed the muscles of his belly to look down at his feet. The toes looked darker, but he wasn't sure if it was a trick of the lighting, or they really were darker. Without even trying he knew he could not walk on them. He let his neck fall and lifted his legs, still putting a strain on his abdominal muscles. There had been a time in his life that he did sit-ups regularly, but that time had passed, and the strain reminded him of that. When this was over, maybe he ought to pick up the habit again.

He swung his legs over off the edge of the bed and rolled over onto his belly. When he bent his knees, the soles of his feet were parallel with the ceiling, and he could lower himself off the bed, onto his knees, without his feet ever touching anything. On his hands and knees, with his calves held up slightly, it was a natural inclination to curl his toes, but curling them caused almost as much agony as touching anything to them might have. He forced himself to keep them as relaxed as he could and he crawled toward the doorway to get his wallet from the jacket on the floor. It was empty. As soon as he saw it he remembered pulling the bills out the night before. He had worried that he might spend the money or do something stupid with it if he had access to it while he was on drugs, so he had taken all the bills out before leaving the hotel and put them in the drawer of the desk. He sighed.

Leaving the wallet behind, he turned again and crawled back into the room proper, past the bed, and to the desk. He pulled himself up by the chair and opened the desk drawer. There was a thin stack of bills inside, fifties and hundreds. That was all he had for cash, no smaller bills. He took a fifty, folded it twice, and put it into his breast pocket. The chair he was holding, he noticed with a certain childish thrill, had wheels. There was no need to crawl. He lifted himself into the chair, spun it away from the desk, and let his legs sprawl out before him with only a tiny portion of his heels touching the floor. He allowed himself a smile. In an instant, he had made the tremendous evolutionary leap from an australopithecine quadruped to a master of such wheels as would inspire awe in a Neolithic. The vodka was within reach, too, now that he was sitting in the wheeled chair. He wondered what the vodka would do for the pain in his feet, even as a disinterested voice in his head asked whether he hadn't read somewhere that the acetaminophen he was planning to ingest could, when taken with too much alcohol, lead to liver damage or stomach bleeding, or something like that. But the screaming of his feet was louder than the disinterested voice. He pulled the corked cap from the bottle and took a drink.

As far as Wayne knew, LSD use wouldn't result in anything like a hangover, but he felt like a wreck now, and he wondered where he had gotten that impression, whether it had any basis in fact. He should have asked for a salve for his feet, too, although now that the thought occurred to him, he wasn't sure what kind of salve would be appropriate. His first thought was Ben Gay, because it was the closest thing to a balm that he knew of, but then he imagined the warming sensation that the menthol provided. Just imagining it made his feet burn. Aloe, though, would be perfect. It was used on sunburn, and if his feet felt like they were burning, aloe could cool them as well as anything. He looked at his toes again. They were definitely getting darker.

When the bellboy came back with the Tylenol, Wayne would give him the fifty dollar bill and ask him to go back out and pick up some aloe. With enough Tylenol to deaden the pain and enough aloe to soothe the burning, he could postpone making a decision about whether to get help from a hospital for another couple of days at least. He took another drink and set the bottle down on the desk beside a book with a fat spine, an immense novel he had been reading intermittently for the past several months. Its heft was the primary reason it was here now, or possibly the only reason: When Wayne had been packing things from his apartment before coming to the hotel, he had planned to bring only essentials. At the last minute he had decided he would want something to read, since he expected to have a lot of time to fill. He hadn't wanted to bring several books, though, because of how difficult books were to move. When he noticed the thick blue and white spine of *The Idiot's Tale*, which because of its weight had been leaning against one row of books and acting as a bookend, he had pulled it down and stuffed it into his backpack, then left.

For all his love of reading, he had never been one for fiction. There was too much important stuff to learn about the world as it really existed, and novels struck him as a useless indulgence, but he had read about two-hundred pages anyway, after picking the book up at Capitol Hill Books last summer. The purchase was an impulsive move, made mostly because Wayne had been a few feet from the cash register when he saw the "Buy 2 Get 1 Free" poster, and *The Idiot's Tale* had been lying on a little shelving cart right next to the sign. Since Wayne had already found the two books he had really been hoping to find, *The Idiot's Tale* just seemed like the best deal, being physically so much more substantial than anything else that occurred to him at that moment. Over the past few days that he had been staked out at the Oxford, he had read one-hundred and thirty pages more. That left over seven-hundred. Now, waiting for the bellboy to show up to ease his pain, Wayne decided that the book would be a passable distraction from that pain. He opened it on his lap to the page he had marked with an index card on which was a list of vocabulary words he still hadn't gotten around to looking up, and he began to read.

If asked, Wayne would have only been able to give the most primitive of synopses for the book up to that point. There were many names, and many convoluted scenarios, and many months had gone by since he began reading. At the moment that he picked it up again, anyway, he wasn't concerned with understanding the plot. He was looking for something to distract his mind, and in the book he found it. When the room phone rang minutes later, the pain in his feet had grown almost as remote as the idea of happiness. He picked up the receiver and said hello like hello was a question.

"Mr. Talbot," said the voice of a woman, "the bellman is waiting at the door. He didn't want to knock because you still have your 'do not disturb' sign up."

"Ah," Wayne said. "Yes. Okay." He closed the book. "I'll go answer the door." Then he hung up and turned in the chair to push himself away from the desk, within reach of the bed. He pulled himself along the bed, then to the short hallway, and pulling himself by the walls he reached the door. He opened it to a tall pear-shaped man in a vest and a tie, who stood holding out a plastic bag. "The total was fifteen dollars," he said. "The receipt is in there, too."

"Okay," Wayne said. He reached into his breast pocket and took out the fifty-dollar bill. "I forgot…or, I didn't think about it before, but I want some Aloe, too. Like for sunburns? If I give you this," he wiggled the fingers that held the fifty, "can you put it toward the Tylenol, then use the change to go out and pick me up some Aloe? You can keep whatever's left after that."

The pear-shaped man nodded. Wayne wasn't sure, but he thought the guy looked a little dejected. Maybe he should've offered a bigger tip. "Yeah, sure," he said. He handed Wayne the plastic bag and took the money. "You want your shoes?"

Wayne blinked. He stared at the bellman. The bellman gestured toward the floor and Wayne looked down and saw his shoes where he had dropped them in the hallway. They had been polished and laid out next to one another. "Um, yes," he said. He bent and picked the shoes up. "Thanks."

"I'll be right back," the bellman said.

Wayne let the door swing shut and tossed his shoes onto the floor. His feet were dancing and singing and he had to remind them that they would not be getting relief immediately. The maximum daily dosage according to the box that he pulled out of the bag was six, and he planned to take that now, but the gratification could not be instant. He knew that. His feet would have to accept that. But the vodka was already helping, and the book had helped, too. After he swallowed the six pills, Wayne would go back to the desk, take the book, and crawl again into bed. Then he would read or sleep or do whatever he had to do to stop thinking about the pain.

25. More bridges burned

It didn't matter to Howie, huddled beside the dumpsters in back of Johnny Rockets and wiping a spot of vomit from his mouth with the corner of his hat, that Adam's scotch was responsible for his condition. Lately it was easier to count the days in the month that he had woken up without a hangover, easier than trying to count the hangovers, and he was sure that signified some kind of tipping point: from here he could either stop, and take a few cautious steps backward into sobriety, or he could keep going as he had been and lose himself completely in the abyss of alcoholism. Things being what they were with Adrienne, or rather being what they were not, and with his career and with his music, he could think of no reason to step back. If he continued to produce hangovers that crippled him like this, then the pain of failure became peripheral; because when not even water would stay down and he was left retching up ropes of bile, the vomiting was all that mattered.

But with Adam's proposal he had an out, and that was why he did not resent the hangover today, and did not resent Adam for delivering it. As absurd as Adam's quest might have been, it offered the potential, however remote, for some sort of future success. Once Howie's brain had tentatively acknowledged the possibility of considering to weigh the pros and cons of the proposition, he had taken a step toward legitimizing it. From that point, a cycle formed, and the more thought he dedicated to the idea of becoming a crimefighters, the more rational the idea became. At worst, he would get beaten like Adam had been on his first night out, or he would be arrested. Arrest was something he could deal with, he knew that now, and being beaten... well, surely there was no drubbing that could be more degrading than what he had been putting himself through over the past few weeks.

Also appealing was the idea of making a decision not based on his misguided love for Adrienne. So much of his life had centered on convincing her of his worth, and he hadn't even realized it. Now, he was leading his life without even thinking of her, and he felt liberated. He was his own man. And if, in acting in his own selfish interest, he also impressed Adrienne with his apparent selflessness, would such an act be regrettable? If she heard through their network of shared friends that he was doing something noble, making a real difference in a shitty shitty world, then she'd think back to how awful she had been, and wonder what in the name of hell had convinced her to close off her heart to him and treat him like some kind of dog. Howie wasn't even sure that he would forgive her when the time came.

"Howie? Man, you have been out here for a while." Alejandro was peering around the corner of the dumpster. "Are you okay, man?"

Howie balled up his hat and hurled it to the ground. The social experiment was over. There was no reason to keep humiliating himself here. He stood up and stepped on his hat. He unbuttoned the matching shirt—he still had a white tee-shirt on underneath that, so it wasn't too big a sacrifice—and he threw it down on top of the hat. "You know what, Alejandro?" he said. "Fuck Johnny Rockets. I'm out of here."

"Sure," Alejandro said. "Fuck Johnny Rockets, man."

Howie reached out and shook his hand. "Have a good life," he said. "I'll see you in the next one." He shivered. This goddamn weather. He picked up his shirt again and put it on, but it didn't make too much of a difference. Halfway out of the parking lot, he remembered that his coat was still inside, and his coat had his wallet and the key to

Adam's house, so he turned around. The kitchen guy was still standing there, watching Howie with a little smile.

"Hello, Howie," Alejandro said. "Again."

"I forgot some stuff," Howie muttered. He walked back inside. The supervisor, Sonny, asked him where the hell he'd been, not really sounding angry, just curious in a friendly way. He was standing in the way of the locker room, so Howie couldn't get to his coat without answering. "I'm not feeling so good," he said.

"Yeah, you look pretty wrecked, bro," the kid said. "You going to make it through your shift?"

Alejandro came in behind Howie, pulling the trash can, and he stopped, because Howie and Sonny were blocking the hallway. He handed Howie his hat, which he had pressed flat again, but which still bore the muddy trace of Howie's footprint.

"Um, thanks, Alejandro," Howie said in a small voice. He tried to brush the mud away from the hat. He couldn't look into Sonny's eyes. "I think, uh, yeah. I'm pretty tired." Leaving Neuartig had been easier than this. Howie remembered with a tremor all his awful shouting matches with Steve Biggs and the horrible stuff Steve Biggs had said about him, but remembering it now didn't make him angry, not outraged like he had been then, or even irritated like he had been outside just a few minutes ago. He just felt sad and defeated. He could not tell Sonny to fuck Johnny Rockets. "I'd like to go home, if that's okay."

"I don't give a shit," Sonny said. "But, really bro, I can't give you the okay. Just tell Josephine you've got the flu. She'll send you home. We're slow."

Howie made himself as small as he could and squeezed past Sonny into the locker room to grab his coat. "I'm going to go home," he said. "I guess if Josephine wants to fire me over it, that's okay. But I'm going to go."

"Escuse me, Sonny," Alejandro said, and he dragged the trash can past the doorway.

Howie put his coat on.

"Sure, bro," Sonny said to Howie. "Cool. Whatever. I'll tell her you got the flu and you had to go quick."

"Yeah," Howie said, "do that. Thanks," and he left.

Adam's place was only a ten-minute walk from the restaurant, more convenient than when he had been living in the vacant club. He had almost made it there before he had to stop and vomit into a stranger's barren flower bed. He had thought at work that he could keep down at least a child's size cup of Sprite, but even that had proved too provocative for his roiling stomach. Here now again he was dehydrated and aching, his head hanging and his hands on his knees, but he was almost home, and, home, he could sleep. With a deep breath, he straightened his back and kept walking.

When he opened the door, he saw first that the furniture had all been pushed toward the wall, and then that Adam stood in the middle dressed in black latex, delivering a series of kicks to the air. He could get his leg up pretty high. Howie was sure he couldn't do half as well in the best of circumstances, and at the moment even balancing on one foot would have been a harsh demand.

"Howie," Adam said. He stopped kicking the air and turned to face Howie. The costume he wore was a bit too big and it sagged in places. Also, the bat on the front was just a big black thing the same color as the rest of it, so you could hardly tell who he was supposed to be without the little hat thing and the cape, neither of which he was wearing right now.

"Isn't there supposed to be like a yellow circle behind the bat?" Howie asked, stepping inside and closing the door behind him.

Adam looked down at his chest, then back up at Howie. "Actually, in the original comics, there wasn't a yellow disk. That didn't come along until the sixties. Anyway, the first suit I had had the yellow, but that's gone now." He sort of grimaced. Howie guessed that he probably didn't know what had happened to the first suit, only that he hadn't seen it since he had come back from the hospital. "That one cost too much anyway, and it was stiff. It was made of, like, rubber, and it was nearly impossible to move in. I just got this today, and—" Adam turned away and walked toward Howie's room, adding, "Check this out."

Howie padded after him, wondering when he'd be able to crawl back into bed and sleep. Adam reached into a box that lay at the foot of Howie's bed and pulled out a latex top a lot like his own. He let it unfold and held it up in front of him by the shoulders. "All the Robin costumes I could find looked pretty much like pajamas, so I figured you could be Nightwing. It'll be easier for you to hide in the shadows that way." He tossed the shirt to Howie, who made not even the feeblest attempt to grab it. It fell in a crumple at his feet.

"Um, yeah, Adam?" he said. "Listen, I don't think I'm going to wear a costume, if that's okay. It's just, I don't think I...well..."

"Howie!" Adam barked. Howie knelt quickly, picked up the shirt, and hugged it to his chest. "We had an agreement."

"Yeah, yeah," Howie said. "No. I mean, I know. Yeah. No, it's just, yeah, I still want to help you. I think what you're doing is important. But I don't think I should wear a costume."

"A suit," Adam said.

"Sure. It's just, listen, I really do want to help. I just thought I'd be more like a sideline figure, like, you know. Like the butler. Alfred." Howie wiped the back of his hand over his forehead. He felt awful. Adam wasn't planning to go out tonight, was he? Howie set the shirt down on one of the wooden shelves near his elbow, then moved past Adam and Adam's stony glare and sat down on the edge of the futon. He really needed to sleep. He needed water, too, but he was pretty sure his stomach would reject it.

"I'll still go out with you," he added, because Adam was just staring at him. "Of course. But, really, Adam, I'm not much of a fighter. I'd probably do more harm than good if I entered the fray with you. But I'll be there, you know, looking out for you, so if anything goes wrong—" Howie snapped his fingers—"I'm there."

Adam folded his arms over his chest. He looked down at the box and then at the shelf where Howie had left the Nightwing shirt. After a few moments of deliberation he nodded slowly. "You're right. It makes more sense this way. I don't need to put anybody else in harm's way. This is my fight."

Howie nodded more emphatically and he smiled. "Great. Listen, I'm going to try to get some sleep, okay? I don't know about you, but I'm feeling like I just got hit by a bus. After last night I mean. That's why I left work early. So, I'm going to lay down for awhile, and when I wake up, we'll talk some more about this, okay?"

Adam nodded. "Sure, Howie," he said. "We need our rest. Tonight's going to be a big night."

He made it sound like he was planning to start this thing already. But it was a Wednesday night. Going out tonight, that would be bananas. Surely they would wait for the weekend. Howie pulled his shoes off with his feet and curled into a fetal position on the bed. The pillow was still a foot or two from his head, but he didn't want to bother reaching for it. He just pushed his face into the cushion of the futon and hoped to forget his hangover long enough to fall asleep.

26. A man engaged

For Wayne's part, sleep was never too elusive. The problem was that he had a hard time distinguishing waking from sleeping. When he was awake he was drinking and rubbing aloe on his feet, swallowing Tylenol and reading *The Idiot's Tale*. When he was asleep he was dreaming about his feet, about drinking, and about the book. If he had been asked, in life or in a dream, what the plot of the book was, he wasn't sure he could provide an answer. There were so many names, and he never knew when he was reading who exactly those names corresponded to, but he kept reading, and when he wasn't reading, he tried to keep straight the difference between people he had met here in Denver and the characters populating the novel. They were all souls wandering a city, interacting with each other, in the book as here, and the souls in the book didn't know who he was, so what he did made no difference in how they carried out their lives, the lives that were being determined for them by the author whose book Wayne was holding.

When he had begun reading, Wayne had been irritated by the apparent lack of story. He could see no relationship between the events in the life of one character, and the events following, in the lives of others. There must be some point to it, a purpose, to hold his interest, and early on it didn't seem like there was one. So he had closed the book on his fingers and turned it in his hands to read the blurbs on the back again. Knowing that readers before him had found it worthy was enough to keep his attention in the beginning. Now, all that kept him going was the distraction that keeping going provided.

"I'm not going anywhere with this," Wayne read from the page. "I know you must be wondering how all these stories are going to be woven together, but that's not really the point." Wayne straightened up slightly. He had been lying nearly flat, with the heavy book resting on his chest and angled toward his face. Now he pushed himself into something more like a sitting position, but still lounging.

> The point is this, what I'm doing now. It is nothing. All the rest was sound and fury. This whole thing so far has been nothing more than a joke, and you were taken in by it. Of course, you're not the first. Just look at the back of the book. Read those accolades. All those people read this and apparently they loved it. Even this part. Why is that, do you think?

Wayne freed one hand to rub his eyes. He went back to the beginning of the paragraph to read it a second time.

> Don't you suppose all those readers felt cheated when they found out this was a farce? You feel cheated, don't you? You've got to be pretty indignant, mad at me and mad at those bastards whose high praise sold you on the book. It must be becoming obvious that there's no chance they enjoyed this as literature, but they still wrote all those flattering things. You're left to wonder *To what end?* Why write such good reviews of a work that clearly has nothing to offer, that—worse than being merely bad—deliberately deceives. It promises greatness, only to reveal itself as a meaningless joke.

Wayne didn't bother looking at the reviews again, but he stopped reading long enough to summon them to mind. Maybe the reviews had been made up like the rest of it. Or maybe people actually had read it, and they had been annoyed and confused just like Wayne was now, but they hadn't wanted to confess their gullibility.

> There's that whole episode with the Duke and the King in *Huckleberry Finn* where the townspeople who wasted

money on the first show didn't immediately break out the tar and feathers because they wanted to make sure their neighbors suffered the same humiliation. That commiseration was more important to them than retribution.

Is that what's going on here? Does human nature compel the victims of fraud to act complicitly with the perpetrators of fraud to take in others? Try to imagine that. All the people who have read this before you are too proud to admit that they fell for my scam, so they're making sure they're not the last, maybe even taking comfort in their own deceit, trying to nullify the sting of their being duped by duping another. Nobody, at least nobody you're aware of, has come out and told the truth.

Wayne frowned. He pressed his thumb against the edges of the pages on the right-hand side of the book and fanned through them to the end. There were still something like three-hundred left.

There are three-hundred and twenty-four pages left. Now you're wondering where I'll go from here. To all appearances, I've devoted six-hundred-some pages of tiny typeface to introducing characters and establishing setting, all just to say, *Ha ha! Got you, fucker!* That in itself seems stupid and childish. What can I possibly have planned for the rest? Am I going to keep on in this weird conversational tone? Somehow, I convinced every reader before you not to spoil the secret, and you must be wondering how I managed that. Sure, you might not put up with this for 324 pages, even though you're kind of enjoying it, or intrigued by it at least, not like with the fiction that preceded it, but you're curious. You don't have much else to do, and your feet are killing you, so you might as well keep sitting there, to see where I'm going with this.

Wayne stopped reading and lay the book on his belly. The heft of the book demanded putting it down to accomplish anything else, not like a mass-market paperback that you could keep folded open with one hand while you used the other to scratch an itch or lift food to your mouth. Wayne wasn't sure he wanted to continue devoting his attention to it right now. And what was that bit about the feet? What was that supposed to mean? He looked down the bed at his own feet and wiggled the dark red toes. They still throbbed. For a moment, Wayne was arrested by the irrational fear that the line he had just read was addressed directly to him. He pulled the book up and read it again: "You don't have much else to do, and your feet are killing you."

He supposed it was a common enough complaint. Most people his age, the age of the book's target audience, worked jobs that demanded a large share of standing or running around. Obviously the author was counting on their being tired, making the reasonable assumption that their feet would hurt. Wayne supposed he had just been struck by the synchronicity.

There were fourteen pages until the four-fifths point. He would take some more medicine. If he fell asleep while reading, then so much for the better, because it would spare him the pain of his own morose imaginings. He set the book down next to his pillow and slid to the end of the bed, carefully moving his feet out of his way, and he leaned across the gap to reach the bottle on the desk. Getting a glass would be too much effort, so he sat back against the headboard and took a pull from the bottle. He could almost feel the sting leaving his feet. Even as he acknowledged that the sensation was likely psychosomatic, he took another drink, to celebrate. He would need this, all of it, if he was to sleep through the night.

27. ADAM AND HOWIE SALLY FORTH

Adam had alternately rested and prepared his body through the day and at midnight he roused Howie and went outside to wait in the car. After five minutes, he went inside and roused Howie again, this time staying in the room to make sure he stayed awake.

His first outing had convinced Adam that he could not do this on his own, and Howie was the only person he could think of whom he knew well enough to trust, but who hadn't treated his idea as an act of madness. To demand that his sidekick also be as committed as he was would mean more waiting, more searching, and more delays. He decided, watching Howie clumsily dress himself, that this display of commitment was enough; anything greater would have to come later, once Howie came to see the importance of what they were doing.

Adam drove them a few blocks farther east from the lot he had parked in on that first night. He had Howie wait outside the car to keep a look-out while he donned his cape and cowl. He checked himself in the rearview mirror, then took a deep breath and stepped out of the car. Howie shivered. "Come on," Adam told him. He led the way to a dark alley that seemed as good as any a place to begin their night. Adam stepped into the shadows.

Howie yawned. He clapped his hands and rubbed them together. "So what do we do?" he asked. "We just sit here and wait?"

Adam nodded.

Howie pulled his jacket closer to him. "I suppose going inside is out of the question?"

Adam didn't respond.

"Hn," Howie said. He went over to the wall opposite Adam and slid down it to sit cross-legged on the concrete.

"Why are you sitting down?" Adam asked.

Howie scrambled up to his feet. "Sorry," he said.

"You need to be ready."

Howie looked to the end of the alley. No one was out there. They hadn't seen anybody on the streets yet. "We just, what, we stand here all night?"

"We stand here as long as we need to."

Howie blew on his hands and rubbed his arms. "What if nothing happens? I mean, this is just one little corner of the whole city. What are the chances of something happening right here?"

Adam grunted.

"In the comics, they usually just show the crime, huh?" Howie said. "Batman just shows up in the middle of it, out of nowhere."

Adam said nothing.

"Huh?"

"It's not always like that," he said. There was a lot of planning involved in it. Maybe he needed to plan better. Batman was as much a detective as he was a warrior, after all.

"Yeah, I know," Howie said. "But if he's not fighting like the Joker or something, and he's out on the streets, then they don't show where he was beforehand. He's just, BAM! There he is, isn't he?"

Adam pulled his cape around him and looked to either end of the alley. Then he looked up.

Howie followed his glance. "Yeah, huh? Whenever he stops a crime, he usually comes flying down from somewhere high. I bet he just hangs out on roof tops."

Adam dropped his gaze and looked again out toward the entrance of the alley.

"That's what we should do," Howie said. "We should go up to the roof—"

"You can't just jump off the roof and tackle somebody, Howie," Adam said. "I've already thought about it." It was a mistake to use Howie's name. Now, since nobody was around, he could forgive the lapse, but it was a thing he would need to work on.

"Well, maybe not *jump off*," said Howie. "But at least if we went up to the roof we could see farther, more than just one little alleyway. We could see for blocks."

Adam nodded. Howie sat down again. "I suppose we could wander around for a little while," Adam said, "and see if there're any roof tops we could access." He tried to picture parts of the city he knew.

"There's a fire escape in Lodo," Howie said. "Where the Tattered Cover is."

"We can't go to Lodo. Lodo is safe. We would be useless in Lodo."

"Yeah," Howie said. He looked out toward the street again, and he asked, "Are we being useful now?"

Adam walked away. At the mouth of the alley he paused and scanned the area for pedestrians. Howie had gotten to his feet and hurried after him. "We'll go this way," Adam gestured toward Lower Downtown, "but not *into* Lodo," he turned to Howie to make sure Howie understood. Howie nodded emphatically. "There are a few decent-sized buildings over there. Maybe we can find a way on to the roof of one."

They left the alley and hurried down the street. Adam kept to the shadows, but Howie just trotted along beside him, oblivious to the light. "Hey, Adam," Howie said. "You're doing this because your parents died, right?"

The short answer to that question was yes, but how honest was that? Would it convey the full significance of their mission, or would it cheapen it?

"Adam?"

"I'm doing this because there is injustice in the world," he said. He stopped walking. For Howie's benefit he pointed across the street then ran to the spot he had pointed to, in the shadows of the opposite side and into the nearest alley. When Howie caught up he slowed down, but he kept moving. "My parents' death was one example of that injustice, and maybe it was only with their death that I could be made to understand that I had to do something about it. About injustice." They walked out of the alley and across the street into another. "So, yes," Adam said. "I guess you could say that's why I'm doing this."

"But your parents died of natural causes, Adam."

Adam sighed and shook his head. For Howie to keep calling him *Adam* out here was potentially worse than his calling Howie *Howie*.

"Whoops, sorry," Howie added. "Batman, I mean."

"My father died of cancer," Adam said. "There is nothing natural about that."

That silenced Howie for a moment. They kept walking. In each new alley, Adam would look at the side of the buildings and then up, but there was never a way up.

"I guess so," Howie said, "but I mean, it wasn't like you could have stopped it from happening, is what I mean. Not like with what you're doing now. Out here, you're wanting to beat up muggers and rapists and stuff. It's kind of different."

Dammit. Howie was beginning to sound like all the rest. Nobody understood how important this was. They lived in a world where suffering was meted out arbitrarily, and so what point was there in living your life in any way that denied the inevitability of that suffering? Why did they behave as though they could avoid it? Why not rush out and meet it head-on? Some would say that the very inevitability of suffering rendered worthless any attempts to combat it. Was it worthless to live, since death, too, was inevitable? Sure. But they ate and they slept, they earned pay checks and bought shiny toys, despite the fact that they were dying anyway, and with their actions they were only postponing death, not avoiding it. Adam had simply made the decision to stop pretending that suffering didn't exist.

"Hey, look," Howie said. "Will that work?"

He had found a fire escape. Its lowest rungs stopped just a few inches from Adam's head. With a little cooperation, they would be able to climb it at least as far as the top floor of the building. Adam, craning his neck to see where it stopped, decided they would probably be able to help one another onto the roof from there. "Yes," he told Howie. "It'll work."

28. "IT'S WORSE TO BE ALONE."

Several minutes later, Howie stood looking down at the dark streets. From up here, the city didn't look quite so dead. They could see cars moving, and some people. Adam stood watching with his arms folded over his chest. Howie thought he looked pretty imposing. He wondered what he would do if his own parents died. Probably things wouldn't be much different, even if they died really close together like Adam's had. They were far away, in Minnesota, and he didn't see enough of them to be traumatized by their absence from his life. That wasn't to suggest he didn't care for them—he did, and deeply—but their death would have no great effect on the way he lived.

Now, Adrienne, on the other hand, was very much a part of his day-to-day life. If anything happened to her, his life would be wrecked. He would grieve for years, never dream of taking another lover. Well, taking a lover. His soul would be a husk of a soul, and he would have to leave Denver, for good this time. He would have to go away to find a new place to become a new man, some place where nobody knew him and he wasn't limited by their preconceptions. Iceland, maybe. Reykjavik was supposed to be a good city.

"You know, Batman," Howie said, "sometimes I think about what would happen if the people I love died. I do this. I think about how much it would hurt, but then, when it all comes down to it, I'm a resilient person. I think, if they were gone, I would cope. I imagine whole courses of my life, and all the things that I would do, and then I get so satisfied with the way I see my life unfold that I start to feel guilty, like maybe some part of me *wants* them to die, because of how drastically their deaths would change everything. It makes me feel horrible." Picturing Adrienne dead, he found his eyes tearing. He sniffled. "Do you ever feel that way?"

"My parents' dying was the worst thing that ever happened to me," Adam said. His voice came out all raspy, it was great. Howie figured that's just how Batman would talk. "I've gone through it in my head, and nothing else in my life comes close. There's something sobering in that idea, but it's also liberating, in its way. It puts things into perspective. It's so hard to imagine anything hurting more than that, you're willing to try anything, to take any risks. Let life do to you whatever it will."

Howie wondered what the worst thing that had ever happened to him was. All in all, he figured he had led a pretty charmed life. Things hadn't started to get bleak until recently. After that he supposed it was all relative. Losing his job had been kind of shitty, but he had wanted to be out of that place. Getting arrested wasn't nearly as bad as he would have imagined. And anyway, it all came down from Adrienne. She was the root cause. Maybe meeting her was the worst thing that had ever happened to him.

Howie shivered. "Hey," he said. "I'm getting kind of drowsy. You want to get some coffee somewhere?"

Adam glanced at him, then away, to the streets. Howie figured that was enough of an answer.

"Yeah, I guess you're right," he said. He nodded. He rubbed his hands together. He shifted from one foot to the other and bounced up and down on the balls of his feet. "How about I go down..." He was pretty sure he had seen a 7-Eleven sign on their way here. "I go down and get some coffee and bring it back?" He started toward the fire escape, but Adam grabbed the sleeve of his jacket and pulled him back gently.

"We don't need coffee," he said. "We need to keep watch."

"*I* need coffee," Howie said. As soon as Adam let go to cross his arms again, Howie moved away. "I need something. Don't worry. Listen, I'll be right back. And if something happens while I'm gone..." He got to the edge of the roof and he hesitated. "Well, I don't think anything'll happen while I'm gone."

"Howie," Adam said in a stern voice.

"Don't worry," Howie called back. "I'll be right back." He hurried down the fire escape and jumped to the ground, then walked quickly to the end of the alley. He looked to his left, then his right. He couldn't figure out which direction the 7-Eleven was. After a moment he decided that it didn't much matter and he started walking. There were 7-Elevens every few blocks in this city. Where they were missing the void was filled by little shops with names like *Scott's* and *Zeke's*, or even, as the sign above the one he saw up ahead across the street, simply *Store*. More important, there was a liquor store just a few doors further on. Howie decided to stop in there first for a half pint of Cutty Sark, and with that tucked in his pocket he headed back out to the store. As he did, he noticed a gaunt old man stumbling toward him with his hands extended. He towered over Howie. His hair and beard were long and thin and white, and he wore a diarrheal stench like coveralls over his tattered clothes. His eyes flashed with what almost seemed like rage, but his voice was gentle and supplicant: "You got thirty-seven cents on you?"

Howie patted his pockets because that was what he did when confronted with the homeless. He patted both hands against his thighs, then against his torso, and in the past it had always been a reflexive gesture, since he never carried cash, but tonight he had a wad of ones in the side pocket of his pea coat. He felt that with his left hand and felt the Cutty Sark with his right. Then he felt a twinge of doubt.

"Oh, I don't carry cash," he told the old man, offering a feeble shrug. The man let his hand drop. "But, listen, tell you what," Howie added, "if you wait here for a couple minutes, I'll bring you something from the store."

"Yeah, sure, I'll wait here for you. I'll wait because all I've got is time, and I can just stand here, right in this spot, and just stand and wait, and wait for you to bring me food."

"Okay," Howie said, moving away from the old man. "I'll be right back."

"You'll be right back, Jack. You'll leave and come back, and I'll stand here, right here, stand here." He did as he said and kept saying it the whole time, standing in the very spot where he had stopped to ask Howie for money, unmoving except for his mouth, like a talking, stinking extension of the sidewalk.

Howie went into the convenience store and let loose an involuntary shudder. He immediately felt guilty for it.

"How's it going, dude?" the guy at the counter asked.

"Cool," said Howie. "Do you have any coffee?"

"No, dude. I can make some."

"Don't worry about it," Howie said. He went to the back of the store to the coolers and took out two cans of Rockstar. He wasn't sure what Adam would think of it, but he figured Batman would be more likely to drink Rockstar than coffee, anyway.

"What're you up to tonight, dude?" the guy at the counter called.

Howie was making his way over to the doughnuts, but when he heard the question he stopped suddenly and looked up. "Nothing," he said. "Why?"

"Yeah, dude, it's boring as fuck in here tonight. Man. I can't wait til I get off."

"Oh," Howie said. He picked up a package of miniature powdered sugar doughnuts and brought them to the counter.

"Is this shit any good?" the guy asked when he scanned the bar codes for the Rockstars.

"It's okay."

"Five thirty-two," the guy said. "Does it get you fucked up?"

Howie looked at the green digital readout and then at the guy's outstretched hand. "Uh, no," he said. "No. It's just caffeine, really." He pulled a handful of bills from his pocket and counted off five ones.

"Yeah, I hate these fucking bums, dude." The guy took the money and punched a button to open the cash drawer. He put the bills in, then stared thickly at the change slot.

"What bums?" Howie asked, less because he was interested than because he felt compelled to fill the dense silence.

"These bums," the guy said. He shook his head, took out three quarters, and dropped them in Howie's hand. "Fucking homeless guys everywhere. They always come in and don't buy anything and they fucking stink, man."

"Oh," Howie said. "Yeah. Yeah, I guess so." He raised his purchase in a little salute and said, "Thanks."

"Cool," the guy said. "Take her easy, dude."

Standing in the same spot just a few feet from the doorway was the old man, muttering to himself. "I got you some doughnuts," Howie said, holding the doughnuts out. The old man took them without a word and without looking at Howie tore them open with his teeth.

"Have a good night," Howie said. He tucked the Rockstars underneath his arm and began walking back towards where he had left Adam. Behind him, he heard the sound of spitting, and when he looked over the shoulder he saw the old man following in his footsteps. He was picking pieces of plastic from his mouth. Howie turned his gaze forward again and quickened his pace.

"I like the cinnamon ones," the old man said. "These ones are okay, but the cinnamon ones, oh, God! God!" he shouted.

Howie kept walking.

"It's a cold night to be out, isn't it?" the old man asked around a mouthful of doughnut.

Howie didn't respond.

"Isn't it?"

"Yes," Howie said. "It sure is."

"If I were you, I'd be inside somewhere where it was warm and there was a fire crackling and you had a blanket and maybe a girl to curl up with, or even, maybe, not even a fire crackling, but a vent blowing out hot air from somewhere that you don't even think about because all you have to do is throw a switch and the hot air comes out, and you never think about what's burning. Sometimes that's even better than a fire. You can stand on the grate in your naked feet and just wrap a blanket around your shoulders and the hot air will go up your whole body, but it starts with your feet."

Howie resisted the impulse to cast another glance at the old man. At the next intersection he turned abruptly to the right without responding.

"I changed my mind," the old man crowed. He was still right at Howie's elbow. "These are better than the cinnamon! The powder sugar ones are better than the cinnamon! No wonder they're more popular!"

Howie looked up to the top of the buildings on the opposite side of the street, trying to pick out Adam's comic silhouette, but he was suddenly disoriented and gripped by a manner of panic. He hadn't paid close enough attention on the way to the store, and he couldn't pick out the building now.

"Sometimes," the old man bellowed, "though, it's better to be outside. Even if you have a blanket and a fire crackling or warm air coming from somewhere through a vent in the floor, even if you have those things and you know you'll be warm inside no matter what, sometimes you don't want to be inside because, inside, you're alone, and it's worse to be alone, and really, when it comes down to it, you'll never be warm when you're alone. Never. No matter what." There was a slight pause, and Howie shivered. Then, his mouth full again with doughnuts, the old man garbled, "Go left on Champa."

Yes, that looked right. Howie crossed the street and started walking down Champa.

"There are worse things than being alone," the old man said when he'd swallowed his doughnuts. His voice was soft now. Although Howie's father was nowhere near his mind, the word *fatherly* occurred to him when the old man went on: "There are lots of things that are worse, but when you're alone that doesn't matter. You don't think about those things. You only think about the cold, and the alone." They were nearing the building where Howie had left Adam. He recognized it now. He looked back at the old man, not sure he had heard everything right.

"You can go ahead and drink your whisky now," said the old man. "I'm not going to ask for any. And anyway you should probably drink it before you go up there." He pointed not up, but at a pile of boxes Howie and Adam had assembled to climb up to reach the fire escape. Howie followed his finger trying to decide if he had put the bottle of Cutty Sark in his pocket before he had seen the old man, while he was still in the liquor store, or afterwards, outside. Maybe he was just assuming. He must have seen Howie leave the liquor store at least. Howie pulled out the bottle and took a long drink.

"Thanks for the doughnuts!" the old man said. "You take care of yourself, and I'll see you next time. I'll have the cinnamon next time, if they've got them. Even though I liked these ones fine." The old man walked away, muttering and waving his hand over his head. Howie had another drink, then climbed up the boxes.

29. Wayne with a sinking soul

Wayne woke once in the night—and waking on this night was not the clearly demarcated shifting of consciousness that it had always been before, but a sluggish, viscous transition between two states differentiated primarily by the increased awareness, awake, of his feet, and of the thudding of the heart in his chest—and it occurred to him that there might have been some permanent change rendered on his psyche by those ten tiny tabs of paper. He wondered in that moment that he was awake if this brain would ever again be able to recognize the patterns in his environment that everyone else around him was recognizing. It seemed entirely possible that the drug had caused his neurotransmitters to misfire, that from here on he would be imagining patterns where no patterns existed, and that he would be tormented for the rest of his life by the doubt of what was real.

Somehow, despite that fear, or because it seemed so inevitable that it was beyond concern, Wayne oozed back into the state that had always been sleep. For a few hours longer he didn't worry.

30. ADAM AND HOWIE ON DEATH AND VIOLENCE

After Adam and Howie had been out here for a few hours, Howie looked like he was losing focus, and in his waning focus a new doubt was born in Adam. He needed a partner who was reliable and committed. Howie could hardly keep his mind on the task: he kept bringing up the death of Adam's parents and talking about the damage the death of loved ones could wreak on a person's psyche. What troubled him about Howie's ramblings was the implication in them that, had his parents lived, Adam would be inside now and disinterested in this quest. He was calling Adam's entire moral fiber into question.

"I know this one guy," Howie said. "I don't know him, I mean. There's just, ah, there's a song I know about him." His words were coming out a little thick, bleeding together, like his body was working so hard to keep warm that his mind was suffering for it. "Ever heard of Hayden? He's the guy who wrote the song. It's great. I'll make you a CD. Remind me when we get back."

Adam was tired of telling Howie to be vigilant, so he was doing all the watching now. The little life that had been in the streets below them when they first climbed up to the roof had drifted away now, and for several minutes now, maybe even hours, Adam had seen nothing worth his consideration.

"Anyway," Howie said. "Hayden's got this song called 'Skates,' about a kid who's working at a department store, and one day an old man comes in and asks him for a pair of skates. This old man just looks awful the way he describes him. His eyes are heavy and glazed over and he's got deep lines all over his face, with this sad, tired mouth just sort of hanging open. The kid goes over to him to find out what he needs and that's when the old man says he wants ice skates. It's the middle of summer, so they don't have much in stock, but the old man tells the kid he wants the best pair they've got and he doesn't care about the price. The kid goes into the back and finds his size, and as he's helping the man try them on, he asks the man if he's a pro. The old man frowns and says, 'No.' He says, 'These skates are my last hope.' Then he tells the kid that earlier that summer his wife had drowned in the river behind their house. He didn't know how to swim and he couldn't do anything to save her. The river took her, and the old man needs to find her. So he's going to wait until it freezes over, then he'll skate as far as it takes, to find her and bring her back home."

Adam took a long, deep breath. He didn't turn around, but behind him he heard Howie shuffle. After a moment, he said in a voice loud enough for Howie to hear, "There was nothing I could do when my parents were alive. You cannot understand how horrible a feeling that is. So now, yes, I will do whatever it takes."

Howie smacked his lips. In a smaller voice he said, "But you can't bring them back."

"I can do my best to make sure they are not lost forever."

For a while, Howie was silent. Adam, in the silence, considered leaving the roof. Whatever good they could do would not be done here. Howie smacked his lips again. When Adam turned around he had his hand inside his jacket. He looked a little startled.

"You have to believe we can make a difference, Howie. Otherwise there's no reason for you to be here."

"I do," Howie said. He pulled his hand out and nodded animatedly. "I do."

Adam flexed his fingers. The leather of his gloves made a faint, pleasant creaking sound. "Good," he said, and he walked past Howie toward the edge of the roof on the other side, where the fire escape was.

"It's just," Howie said, padding along beside him, "I was thinking about the whole quest for justice thing, and about violence as punishment. For the sake of retribution." They got to the edge and looked down at the fire escape. Adam paused. He eyed Howie. Howie peered over the edge of the building, wiped his hand over his forehead, and went on. "If it's going to work, then the punisher's got to be more powerful than the punished, right? And that means that right-ness can only be established when it coincides with, ah...with mightiness." There was enough light for Adam to see Howie's face contort slightly. "Anyway," he said, "by this model, justice depends on the good being stronger, *physically*, than the bad."

"But the good aren't always strong, Howie," Adam said. "Which is why what we do is so important. We need to be strong for them."

"Yeah, but, see, that's what I'm getting at. If the powerful are doing the enforcing, then it's inevitable that they'll assume goodness, and the weak, regardless of their moral stature, will remain victims. If we grant your method validity, then there's no incentive to be a moral being. There's only incentive to be strong."

Adam adjusted his cowl. The mask was irritating his face. "What are you trying to say?"

"Only I guess that we have to love our enemies. We can't bash them into submission."

"There is real evil in the world, Howie. Somebody must rise up to face it."

"Sure, sure. I'm just saying, if we're going to say that force is justifiable in certain circumstances, then there will be people who will justify it for any circumstances. Like, in a few days, Bush is probably going to declare war on Iraq. If you asked him, he'd say he's rising up to face evil in the world, but what would you do if we were walking through the streets tonight, and you saw some big guy all the sudden start beating the crap out of another guy? You'd save the other guy, wouldn't you? You'd try to stop the beating. Maybe, though, the big guy thought the little guy had a knife, and maybe he thought the little guy was going to stab him if he got the chance. In his mind, he was a moral agent, acting not only in his own interest, but ensuring the safety of others who might've fallen victim to the knife. And if he was more powerful, his morality would be cemented by the act. But if you show up in the middle of it, and you're more powerful, then you can establish your own moral code, even if it's completely opposite his. You're just going to protect the little guy, and for you, that's noble."

No, Howie was not the right man for this. "There are some absolutes, Howie," Adam said gruffly. "Some evils are evil in every circumstance, not just dependent on our perceptions. These are the evils we face."

"Yeah, but—"

"Love our enemies, you say, but can you find it in your heart to love a cancer? Will loving a cancer render the damage it wreaks on those you love any less hideous?"

Howie sniffled. "I guess I didn't think about it that way," he said.

"We have to fight, Howie. Not fighting makes us as bad as what kills us."

31. A TALE TOLD BY AN IDIOT

The next time Wayne really woke up light was shining again through the curtains and his feet were on fire. They weren't really on fire, he checked. But the pain felt like fire, was as constant and consuming as fire. He was wet, and his sheets were wet, and when he put his palm to his forehead, it came back sticky and wet. How hot was it in this room? Had he set the thermostat this high? He must have, when he came back in from the cold. He had been so miserable and shivering, he must have turned the heat up really high. Now he was uncomfortable with the heat but he couldn't do anything. He couldn't move, because to move would be to rely on his feet. What did the book have to say about this?

The Idiot's Tale lay on its spine beside him, and it was open to a point where most of its pages were on the left. He might have read that far, but how far he had read was increasingly a matter of little apparent importance. Now, looking at the words, he struggled to make sense of his misery.

The abandonment of what even heretofore could only in the most generous sense of the word be considered a plot raises some questions. Forget even about the plot: the abandonment of the *narrative* raises some questions. Can a novel, in its middle, stop suddenly being a coherent narrative, and turn into a book of ideas? Of ruminations on the human experience? Can it do that without losing the good will of its readers?

Wayne thought it could.

Probably the answer depends on the nature of the readers, and how receptive they are to the ideas being presented. Anybody who has devoted as much time and energy to reading this as you have is probably a little more likely than most to command a great measure of patience and discipline. Does it even matter that you got a little attached to some of the characters? The story would have ended eventually anyway, so what real difference is there to ending it now, hundreds of pages before the end of the book itself, or ending it with the last word written? One way or another, you would have had to leave this world.

He had already resigned himself to the leaving. He wasn't interested in that. The book seemed overly concerned with defending its decision to abandon the story, and it appeared willing to devote several pages to that defense. Wayne turned to a spot deeper in. He was lying on his back and the covers had been kicked to the floor, so it was just him on the bed, and the book. He was half-heartedly propped on his right shoulder, leaning to his right and twisting his head so he could see the book without picking it up. He flipped the pages with his left hand and he read.

If you'd rather not read the last few pages, that's fine. We just thought it was better to build up to this slowly. If you think you're ready, then by all means, dive right in. It probably helps that you're suffering from septic fever right now, so everything feels a bit confused already. And you're still not convinced that all that acid you ate hasn't had some serious, long-term residual effects, so you won't panic too much when we tell you that up until now you have only glimpsed a tiny, insignificant portion of existence. For all your inquisitiveness and search for knowledge, you have gained virtually nothing. What knowledge you have gained is useful only within its own boundaries. Beyond the system you and your forebears have established, beyond the walls of language and scientific formulas, everything you hold true falls apart.

Of course, we have no wish to discount all the work that has been done. It really is a remarkable system, and much good has come of it. Now, though, it is time for you to put away your childish things, as it were. Two nights ago you ingested a drug, and under the influence of that drug you came to the conclusion that your life was an elaborate joke, and that each person you interacted with was a partial architect of the joke. Say, instead, that life is an elaborate stage play, and nobody knows he is playing in it. They are all laboring under the same ignorance. What we're doing is giving you the script. How you use it is up to you, but you cannot change the core truth. Do not imagine you have more power than you do. Right now, for instance, you have to go to the bathroom, and you're wondering how you're going to manage that, because the skin from your feet is flayed and you know that walking is not an option. Still, you cannot take away the pressure on your bladder without discharging your body's waste. The need troubles you. In spite of your pain—which is tremendous, far greater than any pain you have experienced before in your life—you are still aware of the discomfort caused by the need to urinate. That discomfort, rather than distracting you from the agony of your feet, seems to be exacerbating it. The chair is still close to the bed, and you could try to roll on that as you had earlier, but the fever has made you weak, and the notion of pulling yourself from the bed is too daunting to be seriously contemplated.

Wayne lay back on the bed and let his arms fall by his side. He lacked the strength to hold himself up any longer to read the book.

That doesn't matter. Reading was a formality.

He let his muscles relax. A rush of warm liquid washed over his thighs. Somehow he would have to figure out a way to change his pants without worrying his feet. For now, he thought he would try to sleep some more. He wondered what Burke was doing.

Ever since he had gotten that letter, Burke was acting all shitty. He'd never crack any jokes, never wanted to hang out. If you could talk him into hanging out, he would give up after only a couple of drinks. It was like all the fun had been bled from him. They'd have four or five drinks, Stewart would just be getting into everything, and then Burke would freeze up. He'd start talking about Wayne, wondering if Wayne had killed himself yet, and if he had, whether it was Burke's fault. As petty as the thought was, Stewart sometimes found himself wishing Wayne *would* kill himself, or at least stop contemplating it. *Shit or get off the pot*, was the way Stewart looked at it.

Since the night they had all tripped, Burke's moods were even more erratic. He was like turning into another Carissa. Stewart didn't want two girlfriends; he wanted Burke back, the way he used to be, all laid back and funny. Shit, the man used to be funny. But after Wayne had slipped out of the Unnaturalists house the other morning, Burke started really freaking out. Nobody knew what had happened to him. It had been two days now, and he was just gone.

"He was already gone," Stewart would try to remind Burke. "We never knew where he was staying before. There's no reason to worry about it now."

But Burke couldn't be calmed. He was on about it again this morning, when Stewart stopped by his apartment before work. "Maybe somebody should call the cops," he suggested, which Stewart figured was about as miserable an idea anyone could come up with.

"Awesome," he said, sitting down at Burke's little kitchen table and clearing off a spot in front of him. "Should we tell them we fed him copious amounts of acid before he wandered off?" He lifted the strap of his shoulder bag over his head and set the bag on the table. Burke was pacing in the kitchen, pulling at the little tuft of hair below his lip.

"We don't have to tell them about the acid," he said.

Stewart sighed. They had gone over all this last night, too, he was pretty sure. No matter how many times he offered the McCormick's bottle to Burke, it kept coming back to Wayne, even after they had killed the bottle.

"Man, I am fucking wrecked," Stewart said. "How are you feeling?"

Burke glanced at him and shook his head slightly. "I didn't drink too much last night."

Stewart opened his shoulder bag and pulled out the Toad. "I feel like hammered shit," he said. "I feel like a piece of shit that's been hammered by another piece of shit." There were five or six CD cases stacked near his elbow. He took one of them from the pile and wiped it against his shirt, then set it down next to the Toad. He put his bag on the floor.

"Shit," Burke said. He stopped pacing when he saw the Toad. "That's a good idea."

Stewart's sister had brought the Toad back with her from her trip to South America a couple years ago. It was a little stone thing about the size of your fist, and if you pulled the head off, there was space inside to keep your stuff, like you were keeping it inside the belly of the toad. What Stewart liked about it was how the inside was all smooth, like glass. There weren't any little cracks or rough spots where you would lose tiny grains of cocaine. Stewart pulled his wallet out and used his King Soopers card to scoop up a little pile of the white powder and dump it onto the cover of the CD. Burke came over and sat down across from him. Burke put the head of the Toad back in its place and Stewart began to chop the powder with his card into four haphazard lines. His hands were shaky from the hangover. Burke took a Bic pen from the Avalanche mug next to his phone and disassembled it. He laid the end pieces and the ink tube down next to the mug, then took his scissors and cut the barrel of the pen in half. He cut one of the halves in half and handed a piece to Stewart. Stewart snorted a line from the CD case, rubbed his nostril, then stood up and walked to the sink for a glass of water.

Burke snorted the next line and set his straw down. "We could just tell the cops we haven't seen him in a while," he said, "and we're worried."

Stewart drank his water.

"And, I mean, we could say he was really drunk when he wandered off. That would be reasonable."

"But it's not like he just vanished," Stewart said. "He went in to hiding. We know that. It's nothing mysterious."

"I know, but he was so fucked up that night." Burke snorted another line. Stewart sat down again and snorted the last. Burke picked up the King Soopers card and scraped the remnants together.

"Yeah he was. He broke my fucking Smiths, man."

"I just want this to be over," Burke said. He snorted the last little bit of coke, then ran his finger over the case and rubbed his finger against his gums. "Think about it, if I hadn't called him that time Abby and I were fighting, this never would have happened."

"If you and Abby weren't fighting, then you never would have called him."

"Yeah."

"Fucking women," Stewart said. He took the Toad's head off and lifted out another measure of coke. "Honestly, though, man? That's pretty much your M.O., calling random people to hang out. You're always so desperate to expand your social circle. So of course it was just a matter of time before it came back and bit you in the ass."

Stewart made the lines a little neater this time. He took the first one, then slid the CD towards Burke. Burke hesitated with the hand that held the pen barrel hovering over the table. "I've got to be at work soon," he said. "Do you have any more of this? We could do some tonight when I get off."

Stewart nodded. He took a drink of water. "Fucking A, man. It's Friday."

"I think it's Thursday," Burke said.

"Yeah, whatever. You going to do that line?"

Burke nodded. He did the last line. This is what happens when you're not around.

32. Deciding how to save a life

I never did read *The Idiot's Tale* all the way through. Like most people who have attempted it, I began to lose interest after a few hundred pages, sometime around the part where the one character, whose name I forget, was wrestling with God in the Nevada desert, a sequence that went on for dozens of pages without any resolution in sight. Actually, *losing interest* might not be the best way to describe what happened; I was still enjoying it, I think, but I got preoccupied with other things. I became immersed in other books. In the back of my mind I intended to finish it, but I kept forgetting it was there, until so much time had passed that I didn't think I could rightly pick up where I had left off. I figured I should start over, with a fresh perspective, but then that prospect was sort of daunting, too, and the starting over kept being postponed. Then, when I was leaving Denver, I was trying to unload a bunch of my things, and a friend of mine really wanted to read *The Idiot's Tale*. Since it was such a beast to tote around, I gave it up, always planning vaguely to pick it up again some day if I ever saw a used copy somewhere.

Nobody I know personally has finished the book. Most tell me stories similar to mine. The friend I gave my last copy to lost it while he was moving. "It's in my parents' garage, I'm pretty sure," he tells me. "I left a bunch of boxes of books there. I do want to finish it, though. Some day." In my more imaginative moments, I wonder if there isn't some property of the book that repels readers who aren't ready for what it reveals. Either way, it seems like no great leap to believe that the text of the book isn't as important as the personal interpretations of whoever's reading that text. I prefer to devote my energy to less esoteric literary pursuits.

I mentioned already the *Westword* article about Adam Lister. When the guy who wrote it was doing his research, word traveled pretty quickly among Adam's circle of friends. A few talked to the journalist, but most resented the idea. As Danelle put it to Maynard and Jarvis, "The article's going to make him look like a wack job. It'll ruin his reputation."

Jarvis wasn't so sure that Adam's reputation could be salvaged by that point, and he suggested as much to Danelle. Then he looked out toward the bar for the waitress.

"The only people who really know about the whole thing are pretty close to him," Danelle insisted. "They know what he's been through. The newspaper won't take that it into account. If they print this story, a whole lot more people are going to recognize his name, and they're only going to know him as that crazy dude who thought he was Batman."

"I don't think there's much we can do to stop the article," Maynard said. "What we need to think about is damage control, make sure Adam doesn't make it any worse for himself."

"I thought my cousin's bassist would keep an eye on him," Danelle said. Jarvis forgot about the waitress for a moment. He looked up and said, "Howie?", stifling a smirk. He shifted his eyes to Maynard for a second, then back to Danelle. "He's not playing with Fisk anymore. You do know that, right?"

Danelle shrugged. "I haven't seen Fisk in a while. Anyway, I talked to Howie about looking after Adam, but last night I tried calling Adam's, and nobody was there. I went over to the house, and nothing. I'm afraid he might have even gone out again."

"Aw, they were probably just out getting loaded," Jarvis said. He looked back out over the bar. "Man, where the hell is our waitress?"

Maynard cleared his throat and said, "Okay, here's a thing. Either of you know Calvin Dougherty?" Jarvis knew him, but he was pretty sure Danelle wouldn't. Maynard kept going: "Well, he knows Howie from way back. And, also, he's doing a play with my little sister right now. They had a rehearsal this morning, and I guess he told Abby he had seen Howie earlier—like really early, three or four in the morning—and Howie was with some guy in a Batman costume."

"Awesome," Jarvis said. The waitress was finally coming over. "You guys want another round?" she asked. Jarvis told her she could bet her ass they did.

"Wait, where did he say he saw them?" Danelle asked Maynard.

"North of Lodo, apparently," Maynard said. "Out on the streets. They were talking to homeless people. She said Calvin was a bit hazy on the details."

"What was *he* doing out there at three or four in the morning?"

"I asked Abby the same thing. Apparently the guy's a complete lush, and he likes to wander around Denver at all hours. He had probably been out all night when he saw Howie and Adam.."

"I don't know," Danelle said. "After that *Rocky Mountain News* article, a lot of people were claiming they saw Adam out there. Way more than could have possibly seen him in one night."

"I don't think Calvin had read the article. He didn't seem to know anything about it. Abby said she didn't mention Adam's name, and Calvin just had a laugh over it, like it was a weird freak thing."

The waitress brought their beers out. Jarvis took a long drink, then said, "Yeah, I know Calvin. Calvin's a fucking mess, man. He does that, too. He wanders around Denver and talks to random people, says he's doing it to improve his craft, like learning the voice of the people. But, god-damn, he's a mess."

"Still," Danelle said, "why would Adam and Howie be talking to homeless people? Doesn't make sense."

"Maybe they're looking for informants," Jarvis said.

"And why would Howie be with Adam?"

"Howie's a lost soul," Jarvis said. "He's in a bad place right now. Impressionable." Jarvis kept checking Maynard's face when they talked about Howie, just to see how the whole thing sat with him. His face didn't seem to change much.

"I think we've got to assume Adam's still at it, Danelle," Maynard said. "And we need to figure out a way to stop him before he gets hurt again."

Danelle stared at her beer. One glass still had a few sips left, and she hadn't touched the one the waitress had just brought. "I don't know how, though. He won't even talk to you about Batman if you try. He just looks at you like you're nuts. And if you talk about anything else, he's fine. Seems completely sane."

"He won't talk to *us* about Batman," Jarvis said. "He'll talk to some people."

"Like who?"

"Like Howie, obviously. He convinced Howie to go out on patrol with him, looks like. Howie's who we should be talking to right now."

"What if Howie won't talk to us?"

"Get him down here and feed him a few glasses of Scotch." Jarvis nodded toward the bar, the wall behind it lined with a huge array of single malt whiskies. "He'll talk then."

"Sounds good to me," Maynard said, maybe a bit too quickly. He'd probably want to talk to Howie about Adrienne, too. If that was his goal, Jarvis was pretty certain he'd be disappointed.

Danelle nodded to Jarvis and Jarvis pulled out his cell phone. He hesitated. "Howie disconnected his cell service.

I think he threw his phone at the wall when he totaled his apartment."

"Call Adam's house."

Jarvis nodded. He dialed, and after a moment Adam picked up. "Hey, Adam. Jarvis. I'm actually looking for Howie right now. He there?"

"Yes," Adam said. "He's...I think he's sleeping. Just a second."

The phone was set down. Jarvis tried to imagine what was going through Adam's head. Did he think nobody knew about him? Like, did he think he had a secret identity? Whatever it was, the whole thing seemed pretty awesome to Jarvis. Who's to say it was crazy? It wasn't any more crazy than the rest of the world, assholes sleepwalking through their lives working jobs they hated until they died.

"Hello?" came Howie's quivering voice over the cell waves.

"What's up, big man?" Jarvis said. "We're all out at Pints right now. You should come down. I buy you some whisky."

"Who's we?"

"Ah, me and Danelle."

"You said 'we're *all* out at Pints,' " Howie said.

Jarvis rolled his eyes. "Yeah, well, it's just me and her now, but more people might be coming down."

"Who?"

"It'll probably just be you, me, and Danelle, really. Anyway, I think Maynard's out of town ..."

"Fine," Howie said. "I'm on my way. Give me twenty minutes."

Jarvis closed his phone and put it in his pocket. He grinned at Maynard. Maynard didn't look pissed or anything, just frustrated. That was reasonable enough. There was no way Adrienne would ever leave him for Howie, so it wasn't like Howie was a threat. But it must be galling to have to put up with a guy so unapologetically infatuated with your old lady.

"So, what?" Maynard said. "Am I supposed to leave?"

"Nah," Jarvis said. "I just told him that to get him out of the house. It's not like he's going to turn around and walk out the door when he sees you."

"Yeah, but, you told him I was out of town?"

"I said I *thought* you were. I was wrong. You showed up right after I called."

"Maynard," said Danelle, "it'll be fine. Don't get worked up about it. This is about Adam, remember? Not you and Howie?"

"Yeah," Maynard said. "I know."

33. Jarvis and Maynard form a plan

But Howie wouldn't even make eye contact with him when he got there. Maynard didn't have any problem with the man, but he couldn't say really that he *liked* him, either. Howie would never give him a chance to get to know him well enough to like him. Maynard used to try to get Adrienne to invite Howie along when a small group of them went out, but Howie always had other plans, so Maynard hardly ever saw him. Only recently had he begun to suspect that Howie was deliberately avoiding him. That phone call of Jarvis's had pretty much clinched the suspicion.

For a little while when Howie got there, he and Jarvis made small talk and the other two sat back and listened. When Jarvis ordered Howie his third drink and it seemed like his vocal folds might be sufficiently lubricated, Danelle leaned in and asked, "So what'd you do last night, Howard?"

Howie looked startled. His eyes darted from Danelle to Jarvis. He kept spinning his glass on the table. "I, uh, just hung out," he said. "Adam and I hung out. At his place."

"You didn't go out anywhere?"

"Huh? Oh, yeah. Uh, we went out." Howie nodded. "Yeah, we went out."

"We heard," Jarvis said. Howie looked at him and almost winced. He seemed pretty miserable. "You saw Calvin Dougherty, right?"

"Calvin," Howie said. For a moment he looked serene. "Yes. We saw Calvin."

"You and Adam?"

"Yes." Howie took a deep breath. "Listen, Adam saw some guys standing around a trash can fire and he wanted to talk to them. Calvin was one of the guys."

"And Adam was in costume?"

Howie nodded. His face was making all sorts of little spasms, it was horrible. Maynard almost felt bad for him, but more than that he was fascinated. For all his discomfort, Howie might have been facing interrogation in a Mexican jail cell, rather than sitting in a comfortable English pub getting soused.

"What the hell, man?" Danelle said. "I thought you said you were going to keep an eye on him?"

"I was," Howie said, a touch indignantly. "I did. Look, Adam wanted me to dress up, too. He wanted me to be his sidekick, but I told him I couldn't do that. And it's just, I figured I couldn't stop him physically, so I thought it would probably be best for everybody if I went out with him. That way I could watch out for him, and...and make sure he didn't get hurt again."

"Howie," Maynard said. "This isn't healthy."

Howie looked at a spot of the table in front of Maynard, then back at Danelle. "I know," he said. "I know. But I didn't know what else to do."

"Talk him out of it," Danelle said. "Tell him it's fucking nuts."

"I tried," Howie insisted. "He just, when he starts talking about fighting crime, he gets in this zone. It's amazing. He won't talk about anything else."

Through all of this Jarvis was sitting back in his chair with a look halfway between disinterest and amusement. Maynard didn't know how much he was really paying attention or if he was just blissfully drunk. After Howie started talking about fighting crime, Jarvis pushed his chair back and walked away from the table toward the bar.

"Does he say why he's doing it?" Danelle asked Howie.

Howie squirmed. He looked at his empty glass and frowned. "Listen, you know what I think? Didn't his parents run some kind of volunteering program?"

Maynard and Danelle nodded. When they were in high school, Adam used to spend his Christmas breaks putting together gift boxes for low-income families, which was just the aspect of their non-profit work that Maynard was most familiar with. But they had always had stuff like that going on. Their philanthropy had granted them a certain sort of celebrity in the city. You could see it at the funerals last autumn. They were packed. You could have sold tickets to the damn things.

"Well, I was thinking," Howie said, "if community service was always such a huge part of his life, maybe Batman just sees this a another way to serve the community—"

"Adam," Maynard said.

Howie flinched. "What?"

"You called him Batman."

"Oh." His cheeks went red. He still wouldn't look Maynard in the eyes. "He always wants me to call him that. At least when we're out."

Jarvis came back with another glass of whisky and set it down in front of Howie. Howie looked up furtively at Maynard, winced, and took a sip. Maynard wondered if any kind of friendship could ever exist between them. Adrienne hadn't talked about Howie as much recently, even in spite of how spectacularly his life seemed to be falling apart, and Maynard took that to mean that perhaps they were spending less time together. He hoped that if they spent less time together, Howie would start to abandon his dreams of wooing her away, and that as he abandoned those dreams he would become more comfortable with Maynard, at least to the point that they could drink together without both secretly longing to be somewhere else.

"Do you think," Danelle asked, "there's any way we could convince Adam that there's a better way to help the community?"

Howie shook his head even more fiercely. "Listen, I've tried that. Believe me. He'll just say, like, 'we have to do *something*,' and even if we can't stop the evil completely, at least by fighting we're showing it that it has no hold over us. Or something like that. That's how he talks when he has the suit on."

Danelle stared at her drink. For a few seconds everyone was quiet.

"What we got to do," Jarvis said, "is just tell Adam there's somebody else out there doing the job. I mean, what'd you do last night, Howie? Anything?"

"We just hung around, yeah. He didn't beat anybody up or anything."

"There you go. After a while, he's going to get tired of this. All you have to do is say you saw somebody else out there smacking bad guys around, and obviously he doesn't need any help."

"Yeah," Howie said. "Yeah, that might work, actually. Yeah. Cause, he wouldn't want to just stop, cause he doesn't want evil to keep, you know, messing things up. But if you could tell him, 'Hey, evil's out there, yeah, but don't worry about it. So-and-so has it under control.' "

"Superman, maybe."

"No," Howie said. "That's stupid."

"Doesn't matter who you say it is," Maynard interrupted. "It'll work. Also, it'll mean more if it comes from a few different sources. We can all mention that we've seen somebody around, another superhero, and say this new guy seems to be taking care of the city just fine."

"What the hell is wrong with you people?" Danelle blurted out. It caught Maynard way the hell off guard. "Superheroes? Jesus fucking Christ. It's bad enough that Adam thinks he should be doing this at all. We need to tell him the police can take care of this without him."

"Superman's more romantic," Jarvis said.

"No, no," Maynard said. It had nothing to do with romanticism. "Adam knows the police are out there, and he decided to do this thing anyway. That means he doesn't think the police can handle it. This way, there's a new development, and Adam can bow out gracefully, knowing everything's going to be okay."

"Hell," Jarvis said. "I'll even dress up like Superman myself, if that's what it takes. I could take Adam in a fight."

"Not Superman," Howie said. "It's got to be something more real."

"Nobody's dressing up!" Danelle insisted.

"Danelle's right," Maynard said. "There doesn't actually have to be another superhero out there. Adam just has to think there is." This would work. The way Maynard saw it, they were reaching out to Adam on his level, so nobody was calling him insane. They were just saying, *Yeah, you fought the good fight, but there was only so much you could do.* After a while maybe Adam would just go back to being the way he used to be and this whole quest could just fade away. Maybe a few years from now it would be something they could all laugh about. Adam would have worked through his grief and Howie might've even found a girlfriend for himself. They could all sit around in this same spot and share some drinks. There'd be no hard feelings. Everybody would be happy.

34. On the possibilities of romance and heart-break

Before Howie had left Adam's house to meet Jarvis, Adam had told him to make sure he was back by midnight. Howie said he'd try but he didn't really mean it. After Jarvis bought him all those drinks, though, they encouraged him to go. Fisk's cousin told him to try to convince Adam not to go out, but if it seemed like Adam absolutely wouldn't budge, then Howie should go along and keep talking about rumors of another superhero. Keep wearing him down. Howie agreed because he couldn't find the words inside him to argue, but when he left he was feeling really low.

Adam had been busy that day, too. Their route for the night was all plotted out on a map he had bought, and he gave a copy of the map to Howie. He had also bought a pair of little walkie-talkies with earpieces, and he told Howie that what they were going to do was split up, just go out in a small circle, never more than five blocks apart. If Howie saw anything suspicious, he was supposed to call Adam right away. Howie told him sure, that was no problem. When they separated it was already like one in the morning. He was still a little drunk and he was relieved that he didn't have to hang out with Adam the whole time.

What had Jarvis been thinking, inviting him out for drinks with Maynard there? Jarvis said he didn't know Maynard was going to be there, but he should have thought of it. It was like they were punishing Howie, trying to humiliate him. Heck, Jarvis probably even liked Maynard more, too. Everybody probably liked Maynard more.

Maynard had his shit together. Maynard had a job, Maynard had a car. He could buy you drinks and laugh loud and make everyone feel comfortable. Howie just made people miserable. His own miserableness was like an airborne pathogen. If he stepped into anyone else's circle the misery flew out and infected them all. Of course no one wanted to spend time with him, least of all Adrienne. She had probably known Howie was going to be there at Pints earlier. That's why she hadn't come. She couldn't even bear to see him anymore.

"Nightwing, come in," said Adam's voice in Howie's ear. Howie had been shuffling along aimlessly, and the voice startled him. His hand went quickly to the radio in his breast pocket and he pushed the button in and said, "Uh, yeah, go ahead Batman." There was a long pause. It didn't seem like Adam was going to respond, so he said again, "Batman?" Then he realized he was still holding on to the button. He let go.

"—utton. Dammit, Howie."

"What?"

"Nightwing?"

"Yes?"

"You need to let go of the button after you call. I thought you said you knew how to use these things."

"I do," Howie said. "Sorry." Adam's voice was piercing. Howie found the volume knob and turned it way down.

"How are things looking on your end?" Adam asked, his voice getting smaller and smaller with each word, until when he finished it was a gentle whisper.

"Nothing to, uh, report, Batman," Howie said.

"Ten-four. Keep your eyes peeled."

Howie nodded. He started to shuffle forward again, and then a loud, booming voice came over his shoulder, asking, "Who you talking to?" Howie's whole body jerked. He checked the volume on the radio reflexively, but of course it wasn't the radio. He turned around and saw an old man standing there, right behind him, his shoulders at the same level as Howie's eyes. It took Howie a moment, but he realized it was the same old man from the other night.

"Oh," Howie said. "I'm just talking."

"If you just talk out loud and nobody else is around, people think you're crazy," the old man said. His big white beard was spotted with something dark, and in the pale glow of the streetlights it almost looked like blood.

"Okay," Howie said.

"Where're you headed?" the old man asked. "You mind if I join you?"

"No. I guess not."

They started walking down the sidewalk together. The old man asked him if he could remember the last time in his life he had been really happy. Howie told him he couldn't.

"You're in love is why, am I right?" the old man asked.

Howie nodded.

"You're in love and the one you love doesn't love you or she loves another more, am I right?"

"Yes," Howie said. He pictured Maynard's stupid smiling face.

"Everybody thinks love makes you happy," the old man said. "But you know it doesn't always, don't you?"

Howie sighed. There was a bus stop up ahead of them, a bench inside a Plexiglas shelter. Howie told the old man, "I'm going to have a seat here, okay?"

"I'll join you," said the old man. Everything he said was loud, not like he was deaf and couldn't hear his own voice, but like his exuberance couldn't be checked by decorum or common sense or even by nature.

"I'm sorry," Howie said as he sat, "but I don't have any cash on me."

"That's not an issue," the old man said. "I think no less of you for that." He didn't sit down. He stood in front of the bench facing Howie and he moved in close, so Howie could smell again his stink. With the booze already roiling in his belly and with his nerves being what the were, the stink was almost enough to make Howie vomit. He breathed through his mouth.

"And if a love doesn't make you happy," the old man said, "why hold onto it, huh? Why not let it go?"

Howie frowned. Everyone always pretended it was so easy. "Listen, you can't just *let it go*," he said. "That's not how love works."

"I didn't say it was easy. No. But you can let it go. It doesn't always go away easy, but if you keep trying so hard to hold onto it, it won't go away at all."

How hard had he been holding on? Hope kept rearing its head, but it was becoming an increasingly unreasonable hope. How obtuse was he to continue to foster that hope? "I just," he said to the old man, "I need some kind of closure. That's what I need. That's why I keep holding on. It's the uncertainty."

"Ah, but it's not really that uncertain, is it? Is it? You're just pretending it's uncertain because when you stop pretending that's it, it's over. You give up. So the uncertainty is a product of your hope."

Howie studied the cracked cement at his feet. "No," he said. "The hope is the product of the uncertainty. I wait and wonder because I'm unsure of how she feels."

"It comforts you to think so," said the old man, "but you are not an idiot. Only an idiot could be unsure of how she feels. You know, but you are afraid to acknowledge." He stroked his beard and stared down at Howie, his dark eyes intense, unsettling.

"What I wonder about," Howie said after a long silence, "is how things might have been different if she had been single when we met. To leave her boyfriend for me would be a mark of a fickle heart. Honestly, I'm not even sure I'd want to be with a woman who was so quick to abandon the man she loves. What I'm afraid of is, maybe she's holding on longer than she would have otherwise because of some sense of obligation. Like, maybe she doesn't want to be in this, but she's afraid to break up with him for the wrong reasons, so she holds on, without ever even knowing what she really wants."

"And you think you know what she wants better than she does?"

"I only want her to be happy."

"You want her to be happy with you," the old man said. "It would be no easier for you to accept her unwillingness to be with you if she was single when you met her."

Howie shivered. Such a rejection would be a much more personal one, but it would be easier to accept than a rejection rooted in circumstance.

"Is that what it would take?" the old man asked. "You will only acknowledge her lack of attraction if she expresses it in a vacuum, where you are the only thing she possibly could be attracted to, and her repulsion holds?"

It was a nasty way of putting it, but Howie supposed the old man was right. All extenuating circumstances had to be eliminated. It was the only way to know for certain.

"And without knowing for certain, you will still clutch on to hope?"

"I will," Howie said.

The air tonight was still. In relation to the nights preceding it, this could almost be considered balmy, but he imagined the cold that would come with Adrienne's unequivocal rejection and let out a long shivering breath. He would survive, anyway.

"What about this," said the old man. "What if she came to you today and said, 'This is it. It's over. We cannot be.'? Knowing that, would you still love her as you do?"

"It wouldn't stop immediately," Howie answered. "It couldn't."

"The love, you mean?"

"Yes," Howie said. "The love would linger."

"But for how long? How long would you let it, knowing there was no chance of its realization?"

"I suppose," Howie said, "that I could let it rest with time. If I knew there was no chance."

"You would pursue nothing, if your love was doomed?"

Howie felt a tremor pass through his entire body, as though recognizing the possibility that his hope of a future with Adrienne might be doomed was the same as recognizing the doom itself. Remarkably he felt no temptation to cry. The entire experience was almost clinical. "I would pursue nothing," he said. The old man didn't move. Howie looked up into his eyes. The eyes looked like they were smiling, but his mouth was concealed completely by his mustache. After a moment, he let out a loud laugh. "Ha!" he said at the end, to emphasize the laughter. "If you had a chance to sleep with her, you'd take it. You wouldn't pass that up."

Howie squirmed. He tried to push the image of sleeping with Adrienne out of his mind. "Listen, if she wanted— that's different. I said I wouldn't pursue anything if I knew she didn't have any feelings for me. Obviously, if she wanted to do *that*, well, I don't know. It's different."

"Hey, maybe she wants to get her rocks off one last time before she goes off and settles down," said the old man. "Ever think of that? Maybe she'd want somebody she knows she wouldn't be emotionally attached to, eh?"

"Adrienne's not like—" Howie shook his head. He couldn't look at the old man anymore. "*Women* aren't like that," he insisted. "For women, sex is a means, not an end. It's the start of something more, the foundation. When you're talking about men, yeah. Men are the ones who're always looking for that one last conquest, because for men, sex is the final thing. It's what everything else leads to."

"Not in your case, though." The old man sat down beside him and dug an elbow into his ribs. "Right?"

Howie put his hand over his nose and mouth. "I just meant most men are like that," he said.

"But some of them aren't."

"I'm not."

"So maybe some women aren't just like you imagine, too. Huh? Maybe some of them look at sex as the final act, and nothing's worthwhile after that."

"Sure," Howie said. This was nuts. He just wanted to be left alone. "Maybe you're right."

"And if the object of your affection was like that?"

"No," Howie said. "No. If Adrienne... No. I wouldn't go for that. That's not what I want."

"Ha ha!" the old man said. "You think you can be reasonable in the face of your body's greatest desire. Ha!"

The old man was wrong. Knowing he was wrong was almost liberating. Just saying no to a hypothetical situation involving Adrienne was more than he could have managed a few months ago. He was getting better.

"I've got to get the hell out of here," the old man said. He slapped his knees and stood up. "It's not cold now, but it's going to be. I have no doubt of that. It's going to be cold, and it's going to be wet, and if I don't go find some place to put my head where it will be dry, if I don't do that now, then I don't stand a chance. I'll be buried. I'll freeze. I'll suffocate."

Howie imagined being without the hope of a future with Adrienne and for the first time he did not imagine being smothered by that future. She would go her way, and he his, and never would their paths cross again. Neither of them would be irretrievably unhappy because of it. There would be subsequent highs and lows, but none insurmountable. Howie heard his name in his ear, like a whisper carried along the wind: *Howie? Howie, come in. Are you there? Howie?* The old man shuffled away from Howie on the bench at the bus stop, away from the pool of light that surround them, into the dark. "*Howie!*" came the voice. Howie's eyes fell closed.

35. Respite for Wayne

Wayne saw himself sitting on the couch in Burke's apartment. The preceding weeks were only a foggy memory, and for Burke they were less than that. Wayne at least remembered disappearing, remembered envisioning his suicide and reaching out to Burke. For Burke, nothing had changed. Wayne had not left. He had sent no letter. He had let life go on as it would. Now he was here, in Burke's apartment in a stilted silence, Wayne sitting on the couch holding a cushion on his lap, Burke pacing in the kitchen, pulling at the little tuft of hair below his lip. A shrill buzz jolted Wayne's attention away from the pattern on the drywall he had been studying. Burke walked quickly over to his door and pushed a button on the panel next to it. The buzzing stopped and Burke undid his deadbolt.

"Stewart," he told Wayne. He went back into the kitchen and sat down at his table. Wayne took the cushion from his lap and set it next to him on the couch. He tried to understand his inability to understand what was happening and chalked it up to a hangover.

The front door opened and Stewart came in. He saw Wayne first. He hesitated a moment, then came in and pushed the door shut behind him. He went into the kitchen and grabbed the chair across from Burke, but the chair was loaded down with Wayne's things, his bag and his heavy jacket. Wayne must have stayed here last night. "This your stuff?" Stewart asked. Wayne nodded. Stewart nodded back. He sat down instead on the couch beside

Wayne and llifted the strap of his shoulder bag over his head.

"Man, I am fucking wrecked," he said. "How are you guys?"

Burke shook his head wearily. Wayne couldn't come up with an answer.

Stewart opened his shoulder bag and pulled out a fist-sized sculpture of stone, which he set it on the coffee table. Wayne leaned forward to look at it.

"I feel like hammered shit," Stewart said. "I feel like a piece of shit that's been hammered by another piece of shit." He looked around the room, and when he looked at the kitchen table where Burke was standing he stood up. There was a pile of CDs on the table near the phone. Stewart took one and wiped it against his shirt.

"Shit," Burke said, looking over at the coffee table. "That's a good idea."

The thing Stewart had taken from his bag was shaped like a squat toad, sculpted, Wayne thought, from limestone. He picked it up and turned it in his hands. Limestone felt right. It wasn't too heavy. There were just enough details to suggest amphibianhood, with bulbous eyes and a slightly ridged back, and big, flat feet. Wayne flipped it over to look at its belly, and there was a muffled thud of something hitting the carpet at his feet. He looked down and saw the toad's head, and a cloud of fine white dust.

"Oh," Stewart said. "Fuck you. No."

The toad's head hadn't been attached to the body. It had just come right off.

"No," Stewart said. "No fucking way. No," but Wayne wasn't watching him. The dust settled into a little pile on the floor. It looked like powdered sugar or something. Stewart pulled the toad roughly out of Wayne's hands and got down on his hands and knees in front of the spill. He took out his wallet and used a credit card to scoop the powder back into the body of the toad. His hands were shaking. Burke came over from the kitchen and crouched down beside him. "Shit, man" he said.

Stewart was whimpering. He got as much of the powder into the belly of the toad as he could, mixed with whatever dirt was already on Burke's unvacuumed floor, and he set the toad back on the coffee table.

"Sorry," Wayne said.

Stewart pushed his face into the carpet and sucked in through his nose. He whimpered. He angled his face so just the right side was in the carpet and he pressed his left nostril shut with his index finger. He sucked in everything he could. He moved up and down the carpet, in circles, sniffing and sniffing, and when he finally pulled his face up there were red marks all over it.

"Sorry," Wayne said.

Stewart sneezed four times in quick succession, then looked dejectedly back down at the carpet. He repeated the performance with the left side of his face, then stood up and walked into the kitchen to the sink, sneezing as he filled a glass with water.

Burke ran his fingers over the carpet.

"Sorry," Wayne said.

"That sucked," Burke said. "Shit, man."

"You make people feel uncomfortable," Wayne read from the pages of the book. He was still reading. "Even if none of this had ever happened, if you had never disappeared and sent that letter, your presence would be a burden."

Nobody missed him. He was in his hotel bed, the bed sheets soiled now, wearing a sheen of sweat like a second skin, with more sweat coming through the pores of that skin, perpetually. *The Idiot's Tale* was still here, open beside him, and it was doing for him what Burke had been unable to do.

That was your primary mistake. You were relying on Burke to be your liaison to the world you left. His concern for you was supposed to be a constant by which you could measure the variables. The hypothesis that you so desperately hoped to disprove, that your existence did nothing to enrich the lives of others, depended on an agent whose loyalty you could take for granted.

Burke Russo is a man with many friends, and he wears a different mask for each of them. That these masks are all drastically dissimilar stems not from dishonesty or insecurity, but from the sincere pleasure he derives from bringing pleasure to others. What you felt was an intense personal connection was for Burke just another fleeting diversion. As you spent more time together, if you spent more time together, he would keep trying new masks, and each one would feel wrong. Soon, he would sense your desperation, and it would drain whatever measure of enjoyment he had been gleaning from your encounters. Spending time with you would become a chore that he didn't feel compelled to perform. He would drift away.

His feet had gotten worse. The toes had blackened and withered, and they looked like they might soon vanish completely. He wondered if they could do that, just disappear. Where would they go?

The skin is turning into brittle flakes and falling away. A hoard of bacteria has made its home in your blood stream. The toxins they're secreting will destroy even more tissue. They'll generate a gas which, in expanding, will open and separate internal tissues that haven't been touched yet. This is what's causing your fever. And, really, it's disgusting. Let's go back to talking about how little everyone you know cares about you.

It was really not too surprising. It was what he had expected, even. The people whose paths had crossed his were almost faceless now. He had a hard time linking names with identities.

You probably care less about sex than you ought to. You could have had a lot of fun here.

He wished he could have been satisfied with such exploits. Others he knew would have been. But he wanted a deeper and more meaningful connection, one whose existence did not have at its root the base evolutionary instinct that would reduce him to the state of a stud horse. There was something backwards about approaching a girl with a pretty smile or shapely legs, maybe vaguely hoping that they would develop a more profound appreciation for one another with time, without having any substantial reason to suspect that they would. It was better to separate the two needs, to lump sexual attraction in with hunger and sleepiness as inescapable biological urges and to consider his drive for companionship a trait elevated above such urges, and by its elevation elevating him, too, above them if not quite out of their reach. After all, had those sexual encounters availed him anything? Was his absence from the scene any more noticeable to those women than it had been to the others?

> You have a point there. It's too bad. The answer is no. Nobody missed you, not even the women you bedded, or back-seated. True enough, when you pulled your stunt, they were horrified, and they wept over the idea that you might decide to end your life because nobody cared for you, but their care at that point was abstract, having less to do with you than with your situation. Had Burke kept his mouth shut, as you implored him to and expected him to, they would have stopped thinking about you and gradually forgotten you altogether.

> Nobody missed him.

> It doesn't bode well for your future, does it?

> No. It didn't.

> You were going to base your decision to continue living on how much your life affected the people around you. Knowing that it didn't affect them at all, you cannot with any modicum of pride decide not to kill yourself.

Wayne had no pride, not by this point, but the thought of death still frightened him and the fear was powerful. It was fear that had kept him alive this far. Even now he didn't know if he could summon the courage to roll onto his side, reach across the bed, and open the drawer where his gun lay hidden behind the Gideon's bible.

When you planned this, Wayne, you planned for an *act* of suicide, and that is daunting. To put that gun in your mouth would demand courage enough, and to pull the trigger then would demand the mightiest will. But what's beautiful is, you don't have to act now. The suicide has already been set in motion by your circumstances. You have no idea how horrifically you wrecked your body when you walked home the other night. Since your fear of exposure kept you from seeking help beyond that request for Tylenol, you have rendered the damage nearly irretrievable. Your frostbitten feet have already succumbed to gangrene. Without any prevention, you will soon find yourself in septic shock. Your body will be unable to cope with the infection and your heart will stop pumping blood. When the blood stops reaching your brain, you will drift into that final *nox durmienda*, the night of sleep and perpetual dreams.

Now, any action on your part will be toward salvation. That is what will take courage. If you do nothing, you realize your plans. You get what you wanted. All you have to do is sit there.

36. Mr. Midnight and the Dark Knight

At Pints, Jarvis and Maynard had stuck around after Howie and Danelle had left. They kept drinking until the waitress told them the bar was closing. Jarvis suggested they stop by the liquor store to pick up one last pint of whiskey before two. Maynard was game, and he even offered to pay, since Jarvis had spent so much on Howie that night. They got a bottle of cheap bourbon and started weaving toward Jarvis's loft. Maynard wondered out loud how Howie and Adam were doing. "Do you think Adam's really going to accept that there's another superhero out here?" he asked Jarvis.

"Sure," Jarvis said. He couldn't really fathom the mindset, but he figured if Adam was willing to dress up like Batman himself under the assumption that he could change the world, then his ability to suspend belief had to be a notch or two above average. He passed Maynard the bottle. Maynard took a long drink. "Thing I think we should do is go out there." He gave the bottle back to Jarvis. "We find out where they are and we go out and see how they're doing. If it looks like Howie's not convincing him, then we help out."

"Yeah," Jarvis said. "Fucking A. I'll be Superman, man, and you can be Wonderwoman, and we'll be like, 'Batman, lay the fuck off!' " He giggled. Something about Maynard in a brass bikini tickled the hell out of him.

"All we have to do," Maynard said, "is give you a mask, drape a towel over your shoulders, and then you tell him you've got everything under control. Tell him he can go home, and the city will be taken care of."

It sounded reasonable enough. "But what if he still doesn't want to go?"

"He's *got* to want to go," Maynard said. "You heard Howie. Last night, they didn't do anything, just wandered around in the cold. Adam's going to get sick of it really quick. You're just helping things along, making it easier for him. This way, he can go home without giving up."

"He will be giving up, though."

"Not to the bad guys," Maynard said. "That's what counts. You just have to make him believe that you can do the job better than he can."

Maybe it would work. Jarvis liked the idea of making a costume. He had a drama mask at home that he could wear, just a plain smiling face thing. It would look pretty cool if he could cover the rest of his head and then make a cape out of something. Not a towel, though. That would be stupid. "One thing," he said to Maynard. "What if Adam wants to fight? Isn't that what always happens in the comic books?"

"Fuck him," Maynard said. "You can take Adam."

"Yeah," Jarvis said. He used to punish Adam ruthlessly in junior high, shove him around and pin his arm back behind him and shit like that. "I could."

They had gotten about halfway through the pint when they reached Jarvis's apartment. Jarvis took the drama mask down from the top of his book shelf and tossed it to Maynard. "Figure out a way I can put that around my head," he said. Then he went into his bedroom and opened his dresser. Buried at the bottom of the bottom drawer were his leather pants, which he hadn't worn in years. In the mid-nineties, when he was first getting into the promotion business, he used to call himself Mr. Midnight. He'd make himself part of the shows, introducing the bands in those pants and a leather blazer, with a black silk shirt and satin tie, his hair all spiked up, wearing eye-liner even. He'd tell jokes and flirt with the girls in the audience from the stage. Everyone lapped it up.

In more recent years, any reminders of that era made him cringe, but tonight when he picked up those pants he felt only the swell in his heart of nostalgia and a longing for the exuberance and ego of his youth. It was as Mr. Midnight that he and Adam first met Danelle. When Adam and Danelle started to make plans to open the bar, Mr. Midnight was going to be part of it. He was going to bring in the bands from all over the country and the Manor was going to be the venue of choice. They were going to change the face of the Denver music scene.

Things didn't turn out quite as Jarvis had dreamed. They all got wrapped up in the numbers side of the business and it became another job. They did reasonably well for themselves, and he certainly didn't have any illusions of a better life with a forty-hour work week and a 401k, but the romance of it had long since faded. After all this shit with Adam got sorted out and he was finished mourning his parents, they'd have to plan something huge, to remind Denver there was still shit out there worth getting excited about.

"I put some holes in the side with a pair of scissors," Maynard said. He was standing in the doorway looking down at the mask in his hands. "And I tied a rubber band to them. I think it'll work." He looked up as Jarvis stood and he noticed the pants. He grinned. "That what you're wearing?"

"Yeah," Jarvis said. "I think so." He turned toward his closet and pushed past his shirts to find the blazer, which was all the way back. "I was thinking maybe I'd just be Mr. Midnight, but as a superhero, you know?"

Maynard didn't respond immediately. Jarvis grabbed the blazer and tossed it onto his bed with the pants. He had long since lost or gotten rid of that silk shirt, so he'd have to find a black enough replacement.

"I dunno," Maynard said into the silence. "*Mr. Midnight* sounds more like a supervillain, doesn't it? We don't want Adam to get the wrong idea. And besides, he'll probably recognize you. He'll recognize the name and the suit, anyway, even if you're wearing the mask."

Jarvis stopped searching. Damn Maynard. He was right, but damn him. Where had they put that whisky bottle?

"Still," Maynard offered, "you should wear the pants. Those'll be awesome." He was trying to make Jarvis feel better. "And do you have a black turtleneck or anything? That would look really good." Maynard found a black hoodie that would cover up the rest of his head and hide the shoddy rubber strap of the mask. When he pulled the drawstrings to tighten the hood, enough slack was left over to be tied to the old black sheet that they draped over his shoulders, clasping it below his chin. All they needed then were gloves.

"I should wear the blazer over the hoodie," Jarvis said. "It'll look more mysterious that way."

Maynard had his misgivings, you could tell by the look on his face, but Jarvis pulled the blazer on before he could voice them. "Just don't call yourself Mr. Midnight," he said, after stepping back and looking Jarvis over. "I think you'll be fine."

They went into the living room, Maynard grabbed what was left of the whisky, and they headed back outside to the night.

"I could just call myself the Dark Knight," Jarvis suggested, but Maynard shook his head. He was right about that, too, but Jarvis couldn't think of anything else. Maynard had pierced the holes a little too low in the mask, so that with the rubber band over his ears, the eyes of the mask were just about level with Jarvis's eyebrows. He'd pull it down, and it would be okay for a moment before sliding back up. He could still see out it then, but not quite as well. He hoped they could get this over with quickly.

"So where are we going?" Maynard asked. They were leaving Lodo in the direction of Five Points. Jarvis realized suddenly that he didn't have any idea where they would find Adam and Howie. They had tried to figure out from Howie earlier where they might be hanging out, but

Howie had said over and over again that it wasn't up to him. Jarvis remembered then too that he never had gotten around to finding the gloves to complete his costume. He stuffed his hands into the shallow pockets of his leather pants. "I don't know," he told Maynard.

They walked down Arapahoe, chasing the white clouds of their breath as they sent it forth. Maynard passed Jarvis the bottle, and Jarvis lifted the mask to fit the bottle underneath it. As he drank, a tall, grizzled figure appeared from around the corner like a ghost. The closer he got, Jarvis realized that the old man wasn't gliding, but that had been the first impression. In spite of his long legs, the man shuffled toward them at the most modest of paces. Jarvis handed the bottle back to Maynard and looked at the ground. He felt foolish for the first time.

Nobody said anything as they passed each other. After Maynard and Jarvis turned the corner that the old man had just come from, Maynard suggested stopping for a moment. "There's a bus shelter up there," he said. "Let's have a seat and finish this bottle. Then we can figure out what to do next."

Jarvis nodded. It seemed like a good enough idea. They sat down and Jarvis took the bottle from Maynard's extended hand. He looked up and down the street, then across. Another bus stop faced them, where sat another homeless man. Jarvis pushed his mask up to the top of his head, the act of which necessitated the loosening of his hoodie's draw strings, which in turn loosened the knot of the sheet cape at his throat. He took a long drink. The bottle was nearly empty. He passed it to Maynard and squinted at the huddled figure across the street. The guy seemed pretty well dressed for a bum, but he couldn't well be anything else. He certainly couldn't expect a bus to pick him up at this hour.

"Shit," Maynard said, sputtering over his last shot. "Is that Howard?"

"Howie!" Jarvis yelled, only half-certain but excited anyway. The figure at the other bus stop didn't move. Jarvis stood up. "Howie!" Maynard stood up next to him and they jogged across the street. Jarvis kept calling Howie's name. Finally, when they were just a few feet away, Howie's body jerked and he lifted his head. Jarvis and Maynard stopped in front of him. Howie jumped up to his feet.

"Howie," Jarvis said, grinning.

Howie stared at him blearily, then his eyes went out of focus, and he cocked his head. He put his hand to his chest. "Sorry, Batman," he said, and Jarvis noticed that Howie was holding a little mic that had a cord leading from it to a dark thing in Howie's ear. "Yeah, everything's fine, there was just some, ah, interference." He looked up at Jarvis. Jarvis clapped him on the shoulder and raised his eyebrows. He pulled the mask down over his face and asked, "How do I look?"

"No, really," Howie said. "Everything's fine here. Over. What are you guys doing?"

"Is that Adam?" Maynard whispered loudly. "Is Adam on the radio with you?"

"Where is he?" Jarvis asked. His own breath came back at him, like whisky, and his voice was muffled. "We're going to fight him!"

Howie looked at Jarvis, then at Maynard, then quickly back at Jarvis. "Um, really, I'm not sure," he said. "Listen, how'd you find me?"

Jarvis rolled his shoulders.

"Luck," said Maynard.

"Tell him to come meet you," Jarvis said. "You told him about me, right? I mean, about the other superhero?"

Howie shook his head thickly.

"Tell him you saw something," Maynard said. "Over by the elementary school. Say you're not sure what it was, but he should come check it out."

Howie didn't look at Maynard. He was still staring at Jarvis, his mouth hanging open slightly. Jarvis nodded adamantly. Howie hesitated a moment longer, then lifted his hand to the mouthpiece of his radio and said, "Batman? Ah, I think I saw something." He looked up the street.

"There's a school or something a block away, and I think somebody's in there. I'm going to go check it out." Howie winced and held his hand up to his ear. "Look," he said to Jarvis, "he wants me to stay here. He says he's coming." He looked down to the nearest intersection, then held the mouthpiece up again and said, "I'm at twenty-fourth and Arapahoe."

"Awesome," Jarvis said. He gave Howie a thumbs up and made as if to head down the street, then hesitated. Jarvis looked down at the bulge in Howie's pockets and asked, "Hey, can I borrow your gloves?"

37. Maynard's remorse

Jarvis and Adam fought on a Saturday morning, at an hour that the very hip would still call Friday night. Adrienne found out about the fight much later in the day. It was an hour that everyone in that time zone would agree belonged to Saturday, but one at which Maynard was even then feeling a little toxic, enough that he couldn't offer much in the way of details. He could tell her that they had had to take Adam to the hospital again, but he couldn't remember what exactly led up to that moment. Jarvis was, by all reasonable expectations, going to be passed out well into the evening, so the only person that Adrienne could turn to for a complete story was Howie, who was remarkably the most sober one that night, or at least the most sober one not now in a medical coma. Adrienne called Adam's house first. When she couldn't reach Howie there, she tried Johnny Rockets. Over the span of Howie's entire lunch break, she had him go over the story twice all the way through, asking for as much detail as possible.

When she heard a voice calling his name in the background, she thanked him, turned down his offer to talk more about the whole thing later in the evening over dinner maybe, and she hung up. Maynard had come out from the bedroom while they spoke. He was lying on the couch with a pillow over his face. After Adrienne said goodbye to Howie, she and Maynard sat in silence for a few minutes. Then he asked, "What'd Howie have to say about it?"

"How much do you remember?"

"I don't remember Howie," he confessed. "I don't remember anything after leaving Jarvis's. We shouldn't have gotten that pint. Shit."

"Jarvis told Howie to tell Adam to meet him at the playground," Adrienne told Maynard. "When Adam got there, Jarvis was standing at the top of the slide with his hands on his hips, and he told Adam to go home. He said he was the protector of the city and Adam wasn't doing any good."

"Okay. Yeah," Maynard said. He pulled the pillow away from his face and set it on his chest. "I sort of remember that. I was hiding behind the merry-go-round."

"Adam refused to leave," she continued. "Finally, Jarvis jumped down from the top of slide to tackle Adam. He missed and he landed on his face in the gravel. Adam jumped on top of him and put him in a headlock. Howie didn't know what to do. Howie's a pacifist—you know that, right?"

Maynard groaned. He covered his face again with the pillow.

"So you came running out from your hiding place," she said, and Maynard started punching his face through the pillow, "and clubbed Adam upside the head with an empty bottle."

"I didn't want to hurt him," said Maynard's muffled voice. "I was afraid he was going to kill Jarvis."

They couldn't be sure now whether Maynard had hurt him, or how badly. The blow to the head wasn't what had hospitalized him. "Howie told you and Jarvis to get out of there," Adrienne said. "Do you remember that?"

Maynard didn't respond.

"You ran out of the playground. Howie tried to keep Adam cool, but you know Howie, he's not one to fight. How's he going to hold Adam back? Adam took off after you and Howie after him. You got as far as Park Avenue. You and Jarvis got to the other side, and Adam went right after you, not even looking. Howie said the car that hit him was flying." She told Maynard this much because part of her wanted to obviate the guilt that would inevitably come.

"There was no traffic at all, and out of nowhere came this SUV. Howie didn't even see what kind it was, much less the license plate. It hit Adam almost dead on and just kept going."

Maynard sat up suddenly, letting the pillow fall to the floor. He looked like hell and Adrienne didn't know if that ratcheted up her sympathy for him, or made his behavior more deplorable. She had certainly had her share of nights in oblivion, but those days were supposed to be over. Maynard was the one she imagined would lead her into adulthood and away from the destructiveness of her youth.

"Wait," Maynard said. "Is he okay?"

"Hm?" she said.

"Adam. Is he okay?"

She shook her head. "He's unconscious now. They were working on him all morning, I guess. He landed on his face, and there might be some damage to his spine. Danelle's been over at St. Joe's all day, and Adam's uncle's on his way down from Montana. Driving, I think. He should be here tomorrow."

"We should be there," Maynard said.

"You should sleep," she said, with perhaps more venom in her voice than she had intended. "You and Jarvis can visit him tomorrow." It almost felt liberating to be angry with Maynard now, to have some tangible flaw to point to as the cause for her blossoming reticence.

"I know this sounds weak," Maynard told her, "but we really did want to help him." He stood up, leaned forward, and got down on his knees in front of her. She let him take her hand. "Things got out of hand. We definitely shouldn't have drank as much as we did. But this wasn't just a prank. This was supposed to—"

"Maynard," she cut him off. "You still smell like whiskey. And you look like shit. I mean it, you should go back to bed and sleep this off. Adam's still alive. That's what matters."

38. The purposelessness of suffering

Death was waiting at the bedside, a stupid, unpredicted death, not ominous, but like a fat dog on its haunches licking its chops and salivating. Wayne had never felt worse, wasn't sure now whether he could move and, if he could not, whether he would ever move again. The shivering was constant. Sometimes it would come in great spasms, wracking his entire body, but beyond that he did not move. He was aware of a fetid air hanging over him but he did not have the energy to be offended by it. He was ready to die.

Ready?

Maybe not ready, but reconciled.

You're willing to accept it.

He was resigned to the prospect that he must accept it.

Wasn't this what you wanted?

Wayne wasn't sure what he wanted. His life had not been going as he had expected for years now, but lately, since he had really made a concrete plan, it had been consistently off. The worst scenario he had imagined involved Burke telling him the truth, that nobody had asked about him. In that scenario Wayne would be confident in his decision to end his life. He realized now that, married to the assumption that Burke would be honest was the unconscious conviction that there would be at least one person around to talk him out of the decision. Perhaps a small quarter of his imagination harbored the vision of Burke arguing passionately, and of him turning resolutely away, his mind made up.

You wouldn't have admitted as much to yourself, but you were actually counting on being welcomed back with tears and hugs into the fold of the community as you had imagined it to exist.

He wouldn't have admitted to that hope when he wrote his letter to Burke. Such a fantasy was almost laughable in the face of the truth. Even his worst expectations had fallen short.

Would you have found it any easier to accept this if you had predicted it? If there was any logic to your behavior before, it can only be more logical now. You were prepared to end your life if you learned that everyone you knew except Burke would not mourn its end. Now that you have learned that everyone you knew *and* Burke would not mourn its end, shouldn't your resolve be strengthened?

It should be. It was. He was ready.

Reconciled.

But he felt empty.

Here is a truth: You would have had the courage to pull the trigger of that gun with the barrel in your mouth if you believed Burke cared about you. It could have been anyone, but you needed to think that somebody would be hurt by your choice. Believing that your absence would detract from somebody's life meant believing the converse, that with your presence you enriched a life. Now you feel you have nothing to offer.

Was it too late, he wondered, to offer something to the world?

There was a time in your life that you accepted freely the notion that your body is a complicated machine and your mind was a piece of that machine. Consciousness was, then, just a construct engineered by that machine to ensure that you made the most of all you were endowed with so your DNA would be passed on to future generations. Such a notion precluded the utility of words like *decision* and *desire*, and when you did use such words, you were aware that you were using them with a different meaning than the meaning people around you ascribed to them. "I want to go to the movies," you would say, and in your mind you said, "The synapses that set my body in motion toward the movie theater have already fired, and once my consciousness was made aware of the motion, a new set of synapses fired to form the words *I want to go to the movies.*"

In the last year, you have thought about such things less. You had other concerns on your mind, and the fixation with free will seemed like a luxury. You started believing that you could choose whether or not to die.

He was going to die.

Of course you're going to die. The easy way to die is to keep doing nothing. That is the quickest. The alternative would be to muster every bit of your strength to roll onto your side. Then you will be close enough to the edge that you can reach the phone, and once you pick it up, it will ring downstairs. Just tell them to dial 911. What follows will be nearly as painful as your immediate death would have been, but after that your death will be further away, harder to fathom.

Wayne's head lolled to the left and he could see the phone. It was not so far away. The decision had been made, though, hadn't it? There was nothing he could do to change his death.

The decision will be made when you roll over, or not. You will merely accept it.

What would it mean, though, to die this way? What does it mean to be unloved by these people you have met? Are you in a position to blame them? You have not loved, either. You have not made real, emotional connections.

For you, these people were objects, chosen as you choose a book or a CD, for how it makes you feel. You accessorized your life with the lives of others, and now you are suffering with the realization that your accessories have no interest in being a part of you. Had you made any genuine attempt to improve the world you live in, you would have found yourself in the company of individuals—of persons, not mere things. And then you could welcome death.

He had not lived well, had not been living well, but his life had living left in it. Or it could. The suffering of these last few weeks did not have to be purposeless, not if he called for help now, but it certainly would be purposeless if he did nothing. He had done no great good in his life so far, maybe, but he could still change the world, or even just change the world of one other. He could do anything. All he had to do was close the book and pick up the phone.

39. Hearts following the lead of a city in winter

The next Monday, Howie went after work to see Adam. He didn't change out of his work clothes because he didn't expect to stay for very long. Adam was still out of it, so all Howie could do was stop in and look at him. Then he'd head home and drink until he slept. With the jacket on and buttoned up, you couldn't really tell he was wearing work clothes anyway, except for the white pants. And his shoes looked like hell. There was grease in the air of that kitchen and everything just sort of settled on your shoes. He should get a separate pair of shoes for work. Everyone else there wore sneakers.

Tonight it was snowing. One of his customers had said it would be snowing all week. They said this was going to be a blizzard. Howie didn't think much of that prospect.

This late, there'd only be one or two nurses on the floor, and Howie didn't have much interest in looking good for them. If he had known he'd see Adrienne in the lobby, he certainly would have taken the time to change. But if he had gone home to change, he would have missed her. He paused in the doorway, not sure whether to bless his luck or curse it. Adrienne hadn't seen him yet. She was looking at the floor. Howie stepped inside. The guy at the reception desk ignored him.

"Hi," Howie said, just as Adrienne was looking up. Her eyes were all red, and her nose.

She seemed at first startled to see him, but slowly she smiled, a not entirely happy smile. "Wow," she said, her eyes drifting up to the top of his head. "It's really coming down out there, isn't it?"

"Hn?" Howie said. His head was wet. He shook it and brushed his shoulders. The snow came off in great chunks. "Yeah," he said.

She looked into his eyes. Without meaning to, he sucked in his breath. "Do you want to go out?" she asked.

"Um," Howie said. He glanced past her to the elevator.

"Shit," she said. "Sorry. You're here to see Adam, obviously. I wasn't—"

"That's okay," Howie said. He reached forward, to touch her forearm, to reassure her he wasn't offended, but before he could he yanked his arm back and stuffed it in his pocket. "Were you up there?"

She nodded.

"How is he?"

"He's still asleep."

There was no reason to see him if he was still asleep. "That's all I wanted to know," Howie said. "I wanted to be there if he had gotten better, but I don't want to see him like that again. It's fine."

"What's that?" she asked. She seemed distracted.

"We could go out for a drink," Howie said. "I mean, if you still want to. I'm off tomorrow. I was going to hang out here most of the day, so I don't really have to be here right now. I could use a drink," he added, almost out of desperation. He was afraid she had lost interest already.

She exhaled and smiled again, but more warmly. "Okay," she said, "let's get a drink."

Something inside of Howie tightened, something roiled. She didn't hate him! Everything would be okay. They were going to go out together, just the two of them, and he wouldn't say anything stupid. He'd just sit across from her and talk about the things they used to talk about. What did they used to talk about? They would talk about music, yes, that was something. Music and books and films, those were always great. Before he got so wrapped up in being in love with her, those were the things they used to talk about, just like any other pair of friends. Art, and then maybe more substantial stuff like religion and politics. Then, as the night wore on, their inhibitions might drift away, and they could talk about what was close to their hearts.

"Did you work tonight?" she asked. They couldn't really look at one another. The snow was blowing right into their faces, so they had to walk with their heads down. That meant she could see his pants. Dammit.

"Yes," he said. "I worked tonight. It's nice being there. So much less stressful than Neuartig." Maybe in general that wasn't true, but tonight it had been dead. He didn't miss the office culture.

"Did you hear the news?"

He didn't know what news she meant, but his heart suddenly sped up and he had a flash in his mind of Adrienne and Maynard fighting. Maybe she was mad at him about what had happened to Adam! Maybe she had told him she needed some time to re-think things!

"Bush addressed Congress tonight," she said. "We're going to war."

"Oh." Jesus, was that all he could think to say? "Asshole," he muttered.

"I know," she said. "It's supposed to be part of the war on terror. He keeps insinuating that Saddam was responsible for nine-eleven, without ever saying it right out."

With everything that had gone on in these last few days, Howie had sort of forgotten that the prospect of war had been looming over them. "Yeah, you're right," he said.

"And, really, even if he was responsible," she said, "Bush is still missing the point."

"Lion's Lair?" Howie interjected softly. They had come up to Colfax, just down the street and across from the bar where, he suddenly remembered, he had last played with the Unnaturalists. That had been nearly two months ago. "Or," he added quickly, "we could go down to Squires. I think I'd rather go to Squires."

Adrienne looked up. "Sure," she said. "Let's go to Squires."

They shuffled through the snow toward Squires. Howie encouraged her to keep going. "You said Bush was missing the point," he offered.

"Yeah. He thinks you can defeat terrorism by bombing the shit out of people. It's completely fucking ridiculous."

Howie opened the door for her. She walked in, shook the snow off, and went up to the bar. She ordered a double vodka cranberry and paid for a glass of whiskey and bitters for him, and they took their drinks to a table in the back. The bar was nearly empty. They were the fourth and fifth ones in. The bartender had the TV on to Fox News.

"Listen," Howie said to Adrienne, "I've been thinking about this stuff a lot. Not just with Bush, but with... Well, I talked a lot about it to Adam. Not the war. I mean, a little with the war, but the whole idea of changing the world with violence. It can't work."

Adrienne nodded. She took a hefty drink and said, "It can work. It'll change the world, just not for the better."

"Exactly." Howie took a sip of his drink. It was vile whiskey, but he had known Adrienne would insist on paying for the first round, so he had ordered from the well. "And, look, people are going to hear about Adam, and everybody's going to say he's crazy. It'll be one thing everybody can agree on. But with Bush, people support it. They think it's okay for him to act like this, to just go off pummeling his enemies, or anybody he thinks might be his enemy."

Adrienne nodded. Howie had gotten used to her looking unhappy when they were together, lately anyway. But tonight there was something different about her sadness, something missing. "Suddenly," she said, "everyone starts thinking the only way you can solve a problem is with violence. Just because violence is easiest."

Pity. That was it. Her sadness had always been fueled by pity, ever since he had confessed his love, and fueled only by pity. Here in this bar, on this night, she wasn't fixing him with that sad gaze like she just wanted him to get over it, like if he stopped being so miserable everything in her life would be fine. She was hardly looking at him at all. She was not quite frowning, but her face hung on her head like she didn't have any use for it.

"Yeah," he said. "Yeah, you're right. Listen, I tried saying as much to Adam, but he was just so lost."

"At least you tried reasoning with him," she said. "The best thing Maynard could come up with was to beat the crap out of him."

"Oh, I don't think that was the idea." The words were out of his mouth before Howie had properly digested what they were responding to. She was complaining about Maynard. To Howie. "I mean," he said feebly, "I don't think Maynard and Jarvis *wanted* to beat the crap out of Adam." What was this? Not only was he defending Maynard; he was diffusing the blame. Why even mention Jarvis? He should be milking this.

"Who knows what they wanted," Adrienne said softly, looking down at her glass. Her drink was gone.

"I guess," Howie said. It was the best establishment of consent he could come up with. "You want me to get another round?"

Adrienne answered with a faint nod. He took her glass and walked to the bar, finishing his drink as he went. He ordered her the same thing and took a glass of Glenlivet for himself. He wondered, as he was walking back, whether he should keep the conversation focused on Maynard, or if that would turn Adrienne's mood sour. When he sat down he didn't say anything. He just slid her the drink, and she took a big sip. They sat in silence for a moment, she looking still down at the table, and Howie studying her face, trying to still the thumping in his chest.

"I lived in a house in college," she said finally, "a really big house, with six rooms. People just came and went. One of my roommates was this Russian guy. I don't know how Russian he was; his accent would get thicker when he was trying to impress people. Anyway, there was this one night when we were hanging out, just him and me, and he was talking a lot about this old girlfriend of his, and there was a word he couldn't figure out how to say in English. Razbliuto, or something like that. I couldn't help him out. I don't know if we even have a word for it. It's the feeling you have for somebody you loved once, after the love has gone. The way he described it, it was sort of a bittersweet emotion— no hard feelings, just a sort of remorse, and a longing for the way you used to feel. *Razbliuto.*" She took a drink.

Howie didn't say anything. He couldn't think of anything to say.

"I guess we need a word for that," Adrienne said. She looked up at him finally. "Don't we?"

Her eyes were really beautiful. Of course, he had always known that. He knew her eyes were beautiful. But he had fallen in love so hard with *who* she was, inside, that sometimes he actually forgot how perfectly beautiful she was physically. She was the only woman that had ever been an issue with. Howie slowly nodded. Then he asked, "How are you doing, Adrienne?" It had been a while since he asked a question like that, not as an innocuous greeting, but with a sincere wish to hear her response.

"I'm okay," she said. She took a big drink. It was impressive. "I'm... I guess I'm confused. I don't know what I want anymore."

Howie sipped his whiskey. He tried not to imagine that she was talking about Maynard. What could she be talking about, though? What was with all that stuff about the Russian guy?

"I'm staying at my sister's right now."

He nodded. This couldn't mean what it sounded like. Even if he did, he could not allow any trace of joy to make its way onto his face. Adrienne needed a friend now, somebody who would listen to her with compassion and not judge her decisions one way or another.

"I just don't know about Maynard anymore." She drank. "I mean, Maynard and me. Nothing's changed with him, really, but I keep looking for flaws. I dwell on them. It's like I *want* to hate him, and even if I know that's shitty, I do it."

Howie didn't move. He could hear his heart.

"I'm sorry, Howie. You're the last person I should be talking to about this." She reached out and put her hand over his.

"Hey," the bartender called out to them. Adrienne pulled her hand back to her side of the table. Howie finished his Scotch. "I'm closing up early tonight. I've got to drive all the way to Lakewood, and they're saying the roads are awful."

Howie looked around the bar. They were the only two left.

"You two want one last drink?" the bartender asked. "It's on me."

Damn him. He was making the night end! It couldn't end like this!

"How about it, Howie?" Adrienne asked. She was watching him and smiling. Her drink was gone, too. Howie nodded and they left their table to sit at the bar. Howie looked at the bottles.

"This is going to be a big one," the bartender said. "Somebody told me it's supposed to be the biggest blizzard since, like, '80 or '82."

"You want to do a shot, Howie?" Adrienne asked. "How about some Tres Generations?"

Howie blinked.

"Hey," the bartender said. "Yeah. Tres Generations! Let's do it." He pulled out three glasses and set them down on the bar, then turned his back on them and reached up for the bottle. Howie looked at Adrienne and Adrienne looked at him. She smiled a smile he couldn't begin to fathom and put her hand on his knee for just one second. Then the bartender was back and pouring the shots. They were generous shots. Howie felt dizzy. "What are we drinking to, guys?" the bartender asked. He set the bottle down and picked up a glass. Adrienne picked up another and said, "To misery." That was what Howie heard, and he took his glass, and as he threw back the shot, the bartender said,

"To miserable weather!", like maybe Howie had heard wrong.

"Sorry to kick you guys out," the bartender said. "I just don't want to be driving in this if it gets worse."

"No problem," Adrienne said. "But, hey, how about another shot? We'll pay this time."

The bartender grinned. "Okay," he said. "Okay. But I'm sitting this one out." He poured their drinks and took Adrienne's money. Howie drank his without waiting for her to toast. She held her glass up anyway, and said, "To marriage." Then she drank. Howie wanted to be sick. He never should have had the well whiskey. That was just stupid.

"You two be safe out there," the bartender said as he took their glasses. Adrienne smiled. They walked outside. The snow was thick on the ground now, and there were no cars anywhere on Colfax. The street still wasn't plowed and the snow was as thick there as it was on the sidewalks. They crossed the street, Adrienne just ahead, leading the way, almost bounding forward, Howie trudging along behind with his fists shoved into his pockets, sniffling. Adrienne stopped when she got to the north side of the street and turned around, "What now, Howie? My car's at St. Joe's."

"Yeah," Howie said. "Let's go back to St. Joe's." They'd go back and get in her car and they'd have to drive back really slowly. They'd get a few more minutes together, but then she'd drop him off at Adam's, and that was going to be it. No more. He couldn't keep doing this to himself. He would let her go. They would see one another around the city, they were bound to, but never like this again.

"I love the snow," she told him. "To me it marks the beginning. Everybody thinks of spring as the time of rebirth, but you need the snow first to wipe everything else out. Erase it all. Then you can start over."

"That sounds appealing," Howie said. In front of them, the sidewalk was clean and white and new, like nobody had ever walked over it before them. When he had tried to get away from here on the night of Adrienne's engagement party, he had been too wrapped up in his current life. His decision to leave had been fueled by the very thing he wanted to escape. That couldn't work. Adrienne was right. You had to obliterate every trace of the old if you really wanted to make something new.

By the time they came to the parking garage, Howie's shoes were soaked through and his feet were all cold and wet. What he'd do when he got back to Adam's is turn on Adam's little gas fireplace, wrap a blanket around himself, and sit right in front of it and let it cook his feet. He'd get one of Adam's bottles of single malt and a glass and he'd end his night like that, end this whole phase of his life.

"Howie," Adrienne said. She stopped walking. Howie stopped, too, and he turned to face her. She put her arms around him and raised herself up onto the balls of her feet. Then, good God, she was kissing him. He reacted even before he really understood what was happening, kissing her back, a long slow kiss turning into a seemingly endless series of small, perky ones. Her lips felt like they had been engineered to fit into his, and he could smell the snow in her hair. Also, he could smell tequila. He tried to remember how many drinks they had drunk. She had told him she was done with Maynard, hadn't she? Jesus! How had he not recognized that?

"Howie," she said when they had pulled their faces apart. They were still holding one another. It felt great to be held now in this cold March air, with the snow whipping around just a few yards away, beyond the cover of the garage. "I don't want to go back to my sister's place."

"We could go to Adam's," he offered. He immediately felt awful about it, picturing Adam unconscious in the room above them with tubes stuffed into his body. He should go see Adam, even if Adam couldn't know he was there. "Or, maybe that's not... maybe not Adam's."

"I'm not so sure I should drive, anyway" Adrienne confessed. "And you? You can't drive, huh?"

He probably shouldn't, although he felt confident. The booze was what did it. She got drunk and feared driving; he got drunk and he was Superman. Well, Superman wouldn't drive, but it was just how he felt. And she was kissing him again.

"We can sleep in the car," she said. "I'll turn the heater on. We'll stay here until the snow blows over."

Howie was pretty certain that the snow wasn't going to blow over, not for another few days. The prospect of being in the car with Adrienne for days hit his brain like another shot of Tres Generaciones and he squeezed her close and kissed her.

She pushed herself away, smiling, and she turned and unlocked the door. They had stopped right next to her car and Howie hadn't even noticed. It was a small thing, just two doors, and looking past her into the back seat he was struck by how small it was. His heart rate quickened. Adrienne started the car and turned the heat on, then stepped out again and put the driver's seat all the way forward. They crawled into the back and they were kissing again. For Howie it felt like being in high school again, kissing for the first time, focused so intently on the kissing that the universe shrunk and all he was aware of were their faces. Then he was aware of her hand pulling at the buttons of his pea coat. He remembered that underneath the coat he was wearing his ketchup-stained white work shirt, and remembering that was almost enough to make him pull away. Fortunately, it was pretty dark in here. Did he still smell like grease? God, he hoped he didn't. Adrienne was untucking his shirt, and then her fingers were brushing against the hair of his belly, at his waist, just above his pubis. His body jerked involuntarily.

"Sorry," Adrienne said. "My hands are cold."

"It's fine," Howie muttered. He started kissing her again, kissing her slender neck now. They were on their sides facing one another, their legs folded up against the backs of the front seats and their hips pushed in against the edge of the back seat. It was not the most comfortable position Howie could imagine but he tried not to let that bother him. He was going to be quitting Johnny Rockets soon and he'd get another office job. Since he hadn't been paying rent in so long, he was managing to save up money again. He'd be able to pay the deposit on a new apartment soon and he'd get a bed first thing. Adrienne probably wouldn't want to move in together anytime soon, and that was okay with him. He wasn't going to force anything. Maybe she'd stay with her sister for a while longer, or maybe she'd get her own place. Either way, they'd have beds, they'd be doing what they were doing now on a bed, in a private place. One day they'd look back at this moment of pure lust and the irritation they were willing to endure to consummate it—they'd look back at it soon, in bed together inside with the heat on and the blinds closed and embracing each other buried beneath a huge down comforter, and they'd laugh about it, laugh at how they had acted like a pair of horny teenagers because sometimes you just couldn't contain yourself, not with feelings like this inside you.

She had unzipped his pants and she had his penis in her hands. Now the iciness of her hands was almost pleasant. He unbuttoned her pants and started to pull them down. She rolled away from him, arched her back and thrust her pelvis into the air to wriggle out of her clothes. Howie moved to kiss her belly, but it was hard to maneuver in this tiny space, and she was trying to get back over to him, so her hip banged into his nose. She pushed him back and lifted her leg over him. He had no back support now, and his neck was bent at a horrible angle, with the back of his head pressed against the fold of the seat and his tailbone into its edge. His knees were pressed together with the console between the front seats digging into his shins and his feet pigeon-toed on the floor space in the back. But Adrienne was straddling him, and then he was inside her. That fact alone was enough to keep him hard, even with every other circumstance working against him. Adrienne tried to sit straight up, but her head hit the roof, so she bent at the waist and put her arms against the seat on either side of him. Howie couldn't really move, although he tried to thrust upward occasionally. Mostly, though, this was her thing, which was fine. It was great. This was what had motivated his every act for the past year, maybe not down to the exact detail, but in spirit.

There was no noise, no outbursts leading up to the moment when she collapsed on top of him and it was all over. He hadn't had an orgasm, but having an orgasm didn't really seem necessary right now, or even desirable, with the mess it would cause. Already he was losing his erection. Adrienne pulled herself off of him and rolled over to his left side. He put his penis away and zipped up his pants. Adrienne pulled her clothes on, then leaned forward and turned off the ignition. It was hot inside the car now and the windows were all fogged up. Howie tried to get comfortable. Adrienne put her head on his chest and for a little while they slept, curled into knots on her back seat. If Howie was not perfectly content at that moment, he was at least sure then that contentedness was not lost to him forever.

He slept in fits, constantly having to readjust his position to accommodate a limb whose blood supply was being cut off, and at one point being woken up by the cold, with Adrienne shivering on top of him. He managed to pull himself out of his coat and he did his best to wrap it around the two of them. Adrienne stirred and tilted her head up toward him. Without opening her eyes she said, "I'm sorry, Howie."

Howie kissed her forehead and told her it was okay and that she didn't have to apologize. When next he awoke, Adrienne was sitting up in the seat watching him with an expressionless face. He blinked and looked out the windows. Outside the garage, by the light of the street lamps, he could see snow falling still. "What time is it?" he asked in a froggy voice.

"About three, I think," Adrienne said. Her voice was clear and steady. He wondered how long she had been up. "I think I should head home. It's going to get worse before it gets better."

Howie nodded. He sat up and pressed the heels of his hands into his eyes.

"Do you want a ride to Adam's place?"

Before he responded, a flicker in his memory made him hesitate.

Often in dreams Howie would remember things that had happened earlier in the dream. There would be a moment of dissonance, followed by the realization that what he was trying to remember hadn't been dreamed yet, or hadn't happened exactly as he dreamed it. Since it was all happening inside his mind at an instant, the memory would form right there, in tandem with the rest of the dream.

What happened next in the car with Adrienne was a lot like that sensation. He saw himself a few hours earlier, pawing at Adrienne, kissing her, and then being pushed away, or held back briefly. "Howie," she said, "if we do this, it's only going to be this once. I need to know you understand that. After this... This is it. It's over. We cannot be."

Howie nodded. He told her, "Yes," and then he was back in the present. The bliss was gone and there was just a hollow feeling in his chest.

How had he agreed to that? What had been going through his mind?

"Howie," she said, now, in the car, in the early morning, with the snow outside and the memory of coitus nothing more than a shared misery.

"Um," Howie said, reaching as he spoke past the passenger's seat for the door handle. "I think I'm going to stay. Here. So, you don't need to give me a ride. I'm going to go see Adam. I don't have to work today. I guess I'll just hang out here. I don't want to be... at his place," and in the ellipsis was the word that had been haunting him: *I don't want to be* alone *at his place*, he meant, but he could not say that to Adrienne now, did not want to give her any cause to feel more guilt than her limpid eyes suggested she already did. He fumbled at the side of the door. When he found the handle and pulled on it, nothing happened. He looked at it, saw that it was locked, and unlocked it before looking back at Adrienne. Her pants were still unbuttoned and he could see her panties. His heart lurched. "I'll—" What? He didn't know what to say. *I'll see you?* No. Seeing her again was not a good idea. He could not survive seeing her again. *I'll talk to you later?* But she wouldn't want him to talk to her, either. He opened the door and offered her the best smile he could. "So long, Adrienne," he said, and he walked away.

40. Everything is all right forever and forever and forever

When Adam awoke and saw Howie sitting in the corner of the room he mistook Howie for another ghost. Howie was asleep and the sky beyond the window behind him was white, white swirling with white. He tried to say Howie's name but realized that his mouth had something in it, in it and holding it open. He would have to remove that before he could say anything. He lifted his hands to his mouth and over the index finger of his right hand he saw clamped a big white piece of plastic shaped like the mouth of an alligator, maybe slightly bigger than a thumb. The removal of whatever held his mouth open would require a degree of motor skills unachievable while the thing was biting down on his finger. With his left hand he pulled the clip off, then set to work on his mouth. There was tape near his lips, but a mild, ineffectual tape that took no finesse to pull away. After that it was a simple matter of pulling the object out of his mouth, which now that he was shaking away his sleep he noticed was part of a longer thing, a tube that went down across his chest and off the edge of the bed, and then there were people in the room hovering around his bed, looking at him with worried faces. He was aware now of a steady, shrill beep. Could it be called a beep, he wondered, if it never ended? Was it then just a *beeeeeeeeeeeeeeeeeeeeeeeee*—

One of the women clamped the plastic piece over his finger again. The beep ended and was replaced by a series of smaller, staccato sounds. "What did you do?" the woman asked. If her voice evinced a tiny bit of censure, her eyes were gentle and she was smiling. She looked at the machines near his head and made adjustments. She was the only one left in the room now, she and Howie. Howie had come up behind her and was watching him sleepily.

"Howie," he tried again, but even with the tube out of his mouth the word was too much. It came out as a feeble croak. Howie didn't blink. The nurse rubbed Adam's forehead and told him not to get himself worked up. The doctor would be happy to know he was awake, she said, but for now he should just lie back and take it easy. He had been through a lot.

"Hey, Adam," Howie said shuffling up to the side of the bed. "How're you feeling?" He shook his head fiercely. "Sorry—stupid. That's a stupid question. I'm sorry."

Adam's voice was beyond him. He lifted his hand and Howie took it and squeezed. He tried to pull it away but Howie was holding on tightly and he was weak still.

"They brought you here—" Howie hesitated. "Listen, how much do you remember?"

He looked into Howie's eyes. He said nothing.

"Jarvis and Maynard..." Howie's face blanched. He licked his lips. "I guess maybe this can wait, huh?"

Adam sighed and lowered his eyes. It would have to wait. Before long the doctor came in and asked him a slew of questions he could nod *yes* or shake his head *no* to, and after he had answered them the doctor talked to him about all they had done to his body, interjecting every once in a while to tell him how lucky he was. Then there was talk he couldn't understand or didn't care to. Howie retreated to the background again. All told Adam was kept busy for the next few hours. They were hopeful. He seemed to be in great shape, even if he wasn't much to look at. Of course, he'd want to check in regularly with his primary care physician, but as far as the doctor could tell he'd be okay to leave tomorrow. Or he would be if the roads were opened. It was looking bleak out there. They hardly ever closed the roads in Denver anymore, not with the modern equipment at their disposal, but today it was snowing so hard that as soon as the snow plows finished their routes four inches of snow had fallen in place of what they had just removed. The fleet wasn't big enough to take care of all that snow. Businesses were closing. Everyone was staying home.

Anyone living in the Denver metro area in March of 2003 will remember that storm. They will be able to tell you exactly where they were when it happened. I was stranded in the house on High Street with my roommates and a poorly stocked kitchen. The night before I had watched the snow fall from our glassed-in front porch and saw a man on skis glide past me on the sidewalk. In the back yard the awning above my window got so weighted down with snow that it collapsed. One of its arms punched a hole through my window. We managed to pull it out and cover the hole with plastic, but I spent the next few nights on the couch. There were six of us in that little house, and we were all we had until the snow stopped falling and the plows could make it back out.

For Adam and Howie, and for the staff of St. Joseph's who had to stay late and work thirty-six-hour shifts, the situation must have felt desperate. Or maybe, like the rest of us, they got caught up in the novelty of it and it fostered a sense of connection, ephemeral as it might have been.

Howie told Adam he had called Danelle, but she couldn't get out of the house. Adam's uncle was in town but stranded in his hotel. For the next few hours, Howie said, it looked like they would have to stay where they were. Howie couldn't have known that "the next few hours" was a generous estimate, that they would have to spend another night there and several hours into the next day. Adam didn't know it either, not exactly, but he knew they would have time enough.

"Howie," he said when they were finally alone, or alone as they could be. He was still on a saline drip and he had to push the IV stand along with him, but he could walk in spurts. By the time they reached the end of the wing he needed rest. A small circle of chairs faced a window looking out at the skyline, and behind the skyline, the mountains, semi-obscured by whorls of snow. In the corner of the room, a few feet away, a man in a wheelchair sat watching the same snow. Adam took a deep breath, leaned toward Howie, then hesitated. He turned and looked again at the man in the wheelchair.

"I need to rest," he said. Howie nodded. They sat down in two chairs in the corner furthest from the other patient.

Howie sat watching him with a frown that made his lips jut out. His eyes were red and listless. "Is that it?" Howie asked. "For the whole..."

"That's it," Adam said.

"We're not going out on the streets again?"

"No," Adam said.

But that didn't mean they were done fighting. They had to move past their hurt, and that could only happen with time. Outside the window the ghosts of Adam's parents hung drifting in the wind. His sorrow was drifting too. Soon even that sorrow and the ache it caused would wane, as the love he had felt waned. The loss of that love would lead to a new grief, a grief which itself would lead to healing.

The ghosts disappeared in the snow. Howie lowered his eyes. Adam looked to his right and saw that the young man in the wheelchair had gradually been making his way toward them. He nodded to Adam. Something about the man's face struck him. He wondered briefly if they knew each other, but a glance downward deflected his suspicion. The legs below his knees were gone. Adam was certain he had never met a young man with no feet. He smiled and nodded back. The only sound was the sound of the wind buffeting the glass.

The other patient stopped with his wheelchair at a perfect forty-five degree angle to Adam's. He looked young, maybe in his early twenties, but his face was haggard, etched with deep creases that seemed almost artificial, as blatantly premature as they were. His eyes, though, glowed with a kind of mirth. When he noticed Adam looking at him his smile widened and he turned his gaze to Howie. Neither spoke, but the contortions melted from Howie's face. Outside all was white. A giant piece of butcher paper could have been taped to the window, for all the view it afforded, but they kept watching.

Adam stopped struggling with his thoughts. It was enough that they were here now. There would be time to make sense of all this later. They had the will. All they needed was devotion. Devoted, working toward some measurable goal, they would finally transcend their misery. They would change the world. Until then, it was fine to sit as they sat now, in silence.